M000159138

SIGNAL

(FROM BEYOND, BOOK 2)

JASPER T. SCOTT
NATHAN HYSTAD

Cover Art by Jake Caleb

https://www.jcalebdesign.com/

Edited by: Scarlett R. Algee

& Christen Hystad

ONE

Lennon

Rural Kentucky

"Did you hear that?" Dark Twenty lifted his chin.

Lennon cut the feed, straining her ears. "I'm not picking up anything but snoring cattle."

Someone laughed, and Lennon was unsure which Dark Team member it was. Surely not Rutger.

Dark One walked ahead of them, his alien armor all black, blending him with the night. Lennon peered through her modified visor, finding traces of IR radiation emanating off Rutger. The technology hid their presence from alien and human sensors.

There was a crack, perhaps a branch under a heavy footstep, and Lennon swung her rifle in that direction. Subtle markings glowed in preparation, but she refrained from firing.

Rutger's voice was restrained. "Twenty. Check it out."

The big man, whose actual name was unclear, crouched low, weapon raised as he silently entered the tree line. They were within a farmer's field, close to an hour from any established civilization. Lennon appreciated these people's desire to live a simpler life, but the solitude would eventually drive her crazy.

Lennon braced herself for the inevitable. They were hunting the damned Stalkers, after all, and the aliens had become their prey.

"Nothing here," Twenty said, and they all followed. After a few steps, they found a broken twig on the ground in a flattened patch of grass.

Lennon bent to pick it up with her gloved hand. A dollop of slime seeped from the end. "I was hoping I'd never see this again."

"Which direction?" Dark Thirty-Four asked. She was obviously a newbie, greener than the Midwest's summer grass, and it showed with each hesitant step she took.

The woman's eyes darted behind the gentle glow of the visor. They'd only recently met, and already Lennon felt responsible for the crew. Rutger could take care of himself.

"East. That's where the pod crashed," Rutger whispered.

They kept moving, Lennon catching the occasional glimpse of a harvest moon through the bare trees.

The walk was easy enough, and soon she caught the scent of manure on the breeze. The farmland lay to their left, the pod supposedly straight ahead. Their actual locations were sporadic. According to Rutger's information, only forty-nine of them had settled on ground. Another twenty-seven had been dropped into bodies of water. Lennon couldn't fight under the ocean, but she could sure as hell battle the beasts up here. This was their territory, not the Stalkers'.

"I never liked farms," Twenty said. "Too many tools. And early mornings. Pigs. Yuck."

"Would you shut up?" Lennon hissed.

She saw the glint of moonlight off the alien hull and lifted a hand. The farmhouse was a couple of miles from this position, most of the land unused and forested. It was by simple chance that the pod had remained undiscovered. The ones that had arrived in the States were quickly being disposed of by teams like hers, and as it stood, the population was none the wiser. But it had only been a day.

The secret wouldn't be buried for long.

They observed the pod for a while, Lennon noticing that the shape was similar to the *Interloper*—lengthy and lean, but with no distinguishing black spikes or pulsing green lights. It resembled a tin can, with the sole purpose of dropping the four-legged Stalkers to the surface.

"They're gone," Rutger murmured, taking the lead.

Lennon let him. If he wanted to be first in line to get shot by an alien, so be it. Lennon had already faced a few of them herself, and had lived to tell it. And that was before Dark

Leader had given her all this alien tech. The armor wasn't invasive, almost like a second skin. It was impenetrable, and after a display from a brave Dark Team member, it had been proven to be alien pulse *resistant*. Which wasn't the same thing as pulse *proof,* but still better than conventional armor.

They approached the object, which was buried several feet into the soil. A tree had been crushed in the collision, and Lennon searched for a doorway. "What will you do if we find an opening?" Twenty asked. His big brown eyes scanned the tree line.

"Make you go in first," Lennon answered.

"Over here," Rutger said, slinging his gun over his shoulder. The door was ajar, and he pried on it, the metal scraping as he yanked on the dented panel.

A horrible stench caught in Lennon's throat, and she raised a hand over her mouth.

Rutger flicked the gun's light on, and the cavity brightened. Lennon gasped when she saw the colossal Stalker, and swung her weapon up.

"Wait." Rutger set a finger on the barrel. "It's dead."

She poked the body, and it didn't move. But it sure as hell reeked like a rotting fish in the sun.

"That's what we're fighting?" Twenty asked. "It's huge."

"Bigger than you, even," Thirty-Four joked. Good. They were getting comfortable.

Lennon ensured her camera was recording as she entered the alien escape pod. The interior was rounded, and since it was sideways, her steps were uneven. "I don't see any screens."

"There." Dark Thirty-Four indicated a spot above her on the wall. "Looks damaged."

The room was barely big enough for four or five of the Stalkers, but she couldn't quite reach the controls. Lennon gestured to the dead alien. "Can you bring him over?"

"Like... touch it?" Twenty asked.

"Stop being a baby," Rutger said. "Why did I let Dark Leader talk me into this?"

Rutger grabbed the alien under the arm, and Twenty repeatedly swore as he took the other arm. Together they dragged the corpse so Lennon could climb on top of its chest. The exoskeleton was as hard as a rock.

She tapped the cracked screen, but nothing happened. Lennon clawed at the edges, pulling it free from the wall. Small detonation marks were burned on the rear. "Think they blasted it. Or the console is set to self-destruct on impact."

"Smart. They planned to abandon the pods, so why leave any intel behind?" Rutger rubbed his chin, doing a last survey of the interior. He went into a bag strapped to his thigh and retrieved a blinking device. "The department can deal with the mess. We keep going." Rutger slapped the compact piece of electronics onto the door on the way out, and Lennon followed him.

The fresher air was invigorating, and she inhaled deeply as they continued. "If I were a nine-foot alien on vacation, where would I go?"

"You said they were in cryo, right?" Thirty-Four asked.

"Yep."

"Then they must be starving," Twenty added.

"Exactly." Thirty-Four was young, maybe a year or so older than Lennon had been at the start.

"What are you thinking?" Lennon asked her.

"The cattle. They'd be a convenient snack."

"Come on. Aliens eating cows?" Twenty joked.

"I'd guess you've consumed a few yourself," Lennon quipped, and he actually smiled.

"Can't a guy have a steak on a Saturday night?"

"Enough." Rutger stared at the barn. "If they intended to eat, they might still be nearby."

They hurried, not as concerned with noise now. The cleanup crew would be coming for the pod within the hour, and that meant they needed to hunt down the remaining Stalkers and prepare them for extraction.

Once they were within the grazing fields, there was nothing to impede their passage. The four of them ran, with Twenty lagging behind. He might be a strong man, but in certain situations he'd be a detriment. *Play to their strengths. They each have something to offer.*

Lennon grimaced as her old training came naturally. She'd been out of the game for years, but this was like riding a bike. The barn was old, the red paint chipped and faded to a tarnished orange from decades in the elements. On top was

4

a rusted rooster, telling them the wind was coming from the north.

They pressed their backs to the structure, with Lennon at the forefront. She crept toward the doors. If one was dead, that left three or four alive. They wouldn't have gone far, not in a short span, but she wasn't sold on the idea they'd evacuated the area. There wasn't enough intel on their patterns yet. The news channels were clear of reports of alien sightings, as the Stalkers were trying to keep their presence a secret. But until when? And why?

Dark Leader swore they were after something. A *signal*. Whatever that meant.

The door wasn't locked, and she saw a smear of blood as soon as she approached it.

A rifle rested on the hay, and Lennon spotted the wife first. She was old, maybe eighty, wearing a dress, boots, and a heavy jacket. Her head was facing the wrong direction.

The husband, a rotund man with white, wispy hair, had on coveralls, and his heart had been torn from his chest. She stared at the empty cavity, then peered inside the barn to find a trail of blood. This had happened recently.

A light bulb was on, dangling from a cable, and it swayed gently, casting shadows across the loft.

Three of the Stalkers were thirty feet away, feeding noisily on a cow. Lennon had endured countless horrors, but the sight of them devouring that animal's guts set her stomach into spasms. "They're here," she whispered.

"Stand clear. We're going to torch it," Rutger's voice said in her ear.

Would fire even kill the Stalkers? Lennon suddenly couldn't remember Dark Leader's words.

"I think we should..." Lennon backed up, kicking an empty aluminum pail. It clattered to the ground, and all three Stalkers simultaneously gawked in her direction.

Lennon saw another bucket near the workbench. It was full of bolts, probably saved from a lifetime of farm equipment repairs. She picked it up, daring to dispense the contents as far as she could. The metal pieces rolled and scattered across the barn's floor, sending the Stalkers into a frenzy. They were covered in animal blood, and the moment they diverted their attention, she aimed for the closest one.

The weapon hummed and kicked on, jarring her shoulder. The plasma blast shot forward, striking the Stalker in the head. One second it was there; the next she was staring at the other alien behind it where the first's cranium used to be.

"Cool," she muttered as the doors kicked open.

Dark Twenty rushed in, guns blazing. He had two smaller versions of the pulse rifle, and he shot plasma bolts in tandem, hitting all three torsos. The leader finally crumpled to the floor, but the Stalkers found their own defenses, and began to return fire. Lennon ducked behind the workbench, flipping it over like a barricade.

When she peered around it, there was one less Stalker. A fat drop of blood fell from above, landing on her arm, and Lennon spun onto her back to retaliate. The plasma sped from the barrel, missing the target. She tried again, forgetting a weapon of this much power required a slight recharge period.

The alien dropped from the rafters, standing a few feet from her. Lennon had rushed in on adrenaline and anger, but the moment she faced one of the Stalkers, her own blood turned to ice. Its nose, in the middle of a dark forehead, moved, the thin legs bending and straightening as if taking a moment to assess the danger.

Lennon tried to stay calm while reaching behind her to pull an explosive from the satchel on her hip. With the flick of the manual override, she activated the bomb, and she reversed the modified shell of the sphere. Tiny razor-sharp spikes protruded, and she threw it with all her might at the Stalker.

It paused, as if trying to figure out what had just stuck to its chest, and she ran for the exit. Outside, the rest of her team had the remaining Stalker cornered against the barn. They surrounded it, and Lennon saw that it wasn't armed.

The bomb detonated with a deafening bang. Lennon leaned around the entrance to ensure the Stalker was no longer a threat. Pieces of it clung to the walls, and char-blackened bits rained to the hay-strewn floor.

She marched up to Rutger, taking the high-caliber gun from his holster.

"Dark Leader wants a hostage," Rutger said.

Lennon stared at the monstrosity, rage filling her. She stepped around Dark One and took aim. She fired directly into one of its eyes. It barely made a noise, and she respected that. "We'll say it had other ideas. Come on, team. There are more escape pods to find."

Lennon shoved the gun into her own satchel, and walked into the dark, knowing someone else would come and clean up the mess.

TWO

David

Unmarked Building, Long Island, NY

David Bryce paced the cafeteria floor. He checked his smart watch for the umpteenth time, and the display lit up—9:37PM. He'd waited all day for his family, and he'd already been here for almost forty-eight hours, wearing down Booth and the other officers in charge. Eventually he'd convinced them that if he couldn't go see Kate and the kids in Missouri, then they needed to be brought to him.

Booth had warned him about the disruption to their lives. That they could no longer return home. Cover stories would be spun to explain their absence. But David had insisted that none of that mattered. He knew Kate, and recalled what had been aboard the *Interloper*. It might not be public knowledge yet, but those things were on the loose: the spiders, the four-legged pods, and the Stalkers. With the three different species on the loose, shit would eventually hit the fan, and he didn't want to be thousands of miles away from his family when it did.

"You're going to wear a hole in the floor," Carter quipped from where he sat devouring a burger and fries at the table beside him.

David stopped to glare at Carter, then continued pacing. They were the only ones around. Even the kitchen staff was gone, but that hadn't kept Carter from having a late-night snack. He'd offered to make a burger for David, but he was too anxious to eat. His stomach was tied up in knots. There'd been a time—no, several occasions—during the past few weeks when he was convinced that he'd never see them again.

8

"At least take a seat. You're giving me indigestion."

David relented and sat opposite Carter. "When are you leaving?"

Carter put down his burger and snatched a paper napkin from the table. "Soon. That's why I'm here. I can't stand airplane food."

David grunted at that. "Beats ORB's MREs."

Carter grimaced. "Not by much."

"They still haven't told you where you're being assigned?" David tried.

Carter shook his head. "A different black site. Another bunker disguised as a warehouse." He waved his hand to indicate their sparse surroundings. Bare concrete walls and floor. Exposed conduits and ducts in the ceiling. "Seems like Dark Team could use an introduction to Décor Team. What was it they called their outfit...? The Association," Carter said, and bit into his burger before David could reply. Carter leveled a greasy finger at David's chest. "I don't trust them."

"Lennon's one of them."

"My point exactly. She tried to blow us up!"

David winced. "In hindsight, it might have been for the best if she had. Now look at what we're dealing with."

Carter dipped his burger in a puddle of ketchup, leaving his fries largely untouched. He appeared to consider the matter while munching on his burger. "What do you think they're after?"

David shrugged. "Maybe nothing. They crash-landed, remember?"

"Yeah, but they were headed for Earth before you incapacitated their ship, so they chose Earth for a reason. You think it has to do with that Signal he mentioned?"

David sighed and crossed his arms. "Honestly, I have no clue. And right now, I don't care." David's gaze wandered, fixing on the doors of the cafeteria once more. He absently patted his thigh for his Holo, thinking of sending Kate a message. Then he remembered it wasn't there. He'd lost it in the crash, and no one had offered a replacement for him.

"I might learn what's transpiring," Carter said, wagging a ketchup-covered fry at him. "They want my help translating something. Translating what? I'd bet my left nut it's an alien comm that they intercepted from the *Interloper.*"

David observed Carter. "How would you even begin to translate that?"

Carter shrugged. "Look for patterns."

"Sounds like a crapshoot to me."

"Maybe, but it'll keep me busy. What are you going to do? Binge watch old TV shows until your eyes turn to jelly?"

"No. I think we're supposed to be joining you after Kate and the kids come."

Carter's eyebrows shot up. "Really?"

"So I'm told. I guess it makes it easier to keep an eye on us so we don't leak anything to the press."

"Why would we?" Carter asked. "That would just incite panic."

"Or give people a chance to prepare. For all we know, Boston is crawling with alien spiders. No one has had any warning. If those things survived, and you can bet they did, there *will* be casualties," David said.

"Same is true if we tell the world that aliens have invaded. Can you imagine the chaos? Looting. Riots. Sycophantic fan groups..."

"It might not play out that way," David replied. Carter stared at him until he relented. "Okay, you're right. I hate knowing that they're out there and we can't do anything about it. They have us hiding in a glorified basement, for Pete's sake!" David kicked a chair, and it went flying into the adjacent table.

"What did Pete ever do to you..." Carter muttered.

The doors of the cafeteria burst wide, and David shot from his chair with his heart pounding and hands sweating. Two soldiers held the entrance open, and he watched as a familiar group of three people came striding through, wide-eyed and confused.

"Kate!" David cried.

"David?" she asked.

"Daddy!" Rachel added.

The four of them crashed into each other in the middle of the room. Kate kissed him, and he pulled her into a fierce embrace. The kids were clinging to his legs, both shouting for his attention. He dropped to his haunches and hauled them into a hug.

"You're back!" Rachel said, grinning wildly at him.

"I am."

Mark frowned. He was ten—only eighteen months older than his sister—but he was much harder to fool. "I thought you weren't coming home until next year?"

David cracked a tight smile. "It's a long story, buddy." He straightened as one of the soldiers entered the room and stood at parade rest.

"Mr. Bryce." The soldier gestured at the exit. "Your quarters are ready."

David frowned at that. "They already assigned me a room."

"Not with enough space for the four of you. Dark Leader has graciously offered his room for you tonight."

"Dark Leader?" Kate asked, her green eyes widening with the code name.

"This way, please," the soldier insisted.

Someone cleared their throat, and David turned to see Carter standing behind him.

"You were going to leave without saying goodbye?" He put on a wounded expression, and David stuck out a hand. Carter eyed it with one eyebrow raised, then stepped forward and gave David a back-slapping hug.

"See you soon, Carter," David said.

He wasn't so easily dismissed. His gaze found Kate and a crooked smile touched his lips. "This beauty must be Mrs. Bryce. I'm Carter Robinson."

Kate nodded slowly with the introduction. "It's nice to put a face to the name."

"Oh?"

"David told me about you."

Carter grinned. "My reputation precedes me."

"Actually, it was more of a warning," Kate said.

Carter pretended not to hear, his attention on Rachel and Mark. "Hey, kids. Want to see a magic trick?"

Mark perked up at that, but the soldier waiting for them made an irritated sound. "We have to leave, Commander. And so do you, Mr. Robinson. You were supposed to be ready to leave an hour ago."

11

"Wet blankets—all of you!" Carter erupted. "See you soon, Commander—hopefully you as well, Mrs. Bryce," he added with a wink, and then breezed out of the room.

"Is he always like that?" Kate whispered as they followed the soldiers from the cafeteria.

"Yes," David replied, smiling despite himself. His hands slid into Kate's, and suddenly his nagging concerns disappeared. Whatever chaos threatened to be unleashed, his own world was falling into place.

***

Sergeant Martinez

His legs ached with every step. Another annoying characteristic of the human body. He'd managed to catch a lift south. Apparently donning a soldier's uniform was enough to curry the favor of the American people. Martinez glanced at his fatigues, finding them dirty and stained with sweat.

None of that mattered. He'd almost completed his task.

Martinez inhaled the night air, enjoying the scent of the park. A fountain ran continuously a short distance away, and he sat on a bench, just beyond the yellow glow of a streetlight. His stomach protruded, his shirt untucked as a result.

It had been four days since he'd first taken over this body, and he understood Earth's inhabitants more than he desired to. Something churned in his gut, and he set a hand on it. "Soon," he whispered.

The sensation was constant. He felt the others reverberating through his body, into his mind. Their orders echoing vibrations in his guest's carapace. The thing on his neck had lowered, hiding beneath Martinez's shirt. A lone spike jutted out from the collar, and he pushed it under.

All around the world, similar hosts would be doing their jobs, setting up for invasion. Martinez was thrilled to be a part of it. Something moved behind him, and he jumped, startled at the sound. The creature was masked, its tail ringed with black circles. *Raccoon*. He pulled the reference from deep inside Martinez's brain.

It rose on two legs, and hissed before scurrying away.

He was tempted to chase after and eat it, but refrained. He was almost done, and preferred not to draw any unwanted attention. Specifically, not here.

Martinez glanced to his right, catching the lights from the White House yard. To his left, the Washington Monument stood tall and proud.

He coughed, and his stomach roiled. The incubation chamber was prepared.

The organism inhabiting his neck released, and he watched as it jumped to the ground, glancing at him before burrowing into the soil, leaving a pile of dirt in its wake.

He suddenly felt empty, his mind a blank. He gazed at his surroundings, wondering what he was doing in DC. His throat constricted, and he gagged as something emerged from his lips. He tried to close his mouth, but they persisted. Each the size of a quarter, the creatures poured out of him, tearing him apart from the inside.

Martinez screamed as they funneled off the park bench, heading for the big white building in the distance.

He took a last breath, trying to warn someone of what he'd seen. But no sound escaped.

THREE

Atlas

Unmarked Building, Long Island, NY

The area was quiet. Atlas questioned why Booth chose this location as his primary base. The entire region was made up of giant warehouses, each larger than the next. During the day, he heard forklifts and the beeping of a truck in reverse, but now, in the dark of night, there was nothing but his own breathing to keep him company.

Atlas peered to the sky, recalling how he'd ended up in this predicament. Would he be better off to have no idea their world was being invaded?

He'd seen countless feeds on his Holo of people posting images from the night of the supposed meteor shower, but amazingly, they were retracted seconds after they landed on the social media sites. That sparked a flurry of home sleuths and conspiracy theorists to pry into the events of the alien ship crash, but while speculation was rampant, none of the theories came even close to what had really transpired.

A gigantic alien vessel had crashed off the coast, near Boston, and the entire crew, including thousands of palm-sized crawling creatures, had vacated into the ocean. The whole situation had his nerves on edge—and he was expected to help somehow.

He noticed one star twinkling, and realized it was just a satellite in orbit.

"The view isn't great, but it's as good a spot for a smoke as any." The gruff voice belonged to the man responsible for keeping him here, and Atlas turned, acknowledging Dark Leader with a nod.

Atlas leaned his elbows on the metal railing at the back of the docking bay and accepted the cigarette. When Booth offered him a light, he shook his head. "Nah. I haven't had one in years."

"Suit yourself." The match ignited; the tip of the cigarette glowing bright orange. "I quit when I was out of basic training. More years ago than I'd care to admit."

"I expected someone like you went straight to West Point," Atlas told him.

"My father wanted me to. He was a military man himself. Always an officer. Never a gentleman. My dad was a grade A asshole, and I chose to carve my own path." Booth exhaled a gray plume of smoke, and it dissipated a few yards away.

"Looks like you did well for yourself," Atlas murmured.

Booth gazed in his direction, making eye contact. "If you were in my shoes, you'd think otherwise."

Atlas jabbed a thumb at the doors. "They're scared of you."

"The Dark Teams?"

"Yeah. It's written all over their faces."

"I haven't made the world's deadliest force by coddling them, Mr. Donovan. They require discipline. Order. Rules. That's what the military thrives on."

"But you're not military," Atlas said.

"Not in the public sense. But our motives align." Dark Leader took a pull from his cigarette and tossed the butt onto the parking lot below.

"If you quit, why start smoking again?"

"Because there's no telling how long any of us have. May as well enjoy what time is left." Booth turned on a heel and stalked toward the entrance. "Come with me, Mr. Donovan."

Atlas followed the other man into the building, tucking the cigarette behind his ear.

A pair of armed soldiers greeted them, stepping aside to allow them passage through the hallway. The lights were low. He glanced down the corridor, spotting the area where Commander Bryce and his family were staying. From what he was told, they were leaving at dawn. Atlas was eager to depart as well, but so far, Dark Leader was evading questions about his next moves.

Atlas didn't feel like a prisoner, but he knew that this man wasn't going to let him off the hook so easily. Certainly not after sharing so much of their operation.

They strode into an elevator, returning to the lower level of the facility.

More of the Dark Teams were inside, but this time their faces were unfamiliar. "Staff changes? Where's Rutger... and Lennon?"

"They're busy. My teams are in the field, defending Earth," Dark Leader said. "These are their replacements."

"How's that going?" Atlas tried to picture the soldiers battling these giant aliens, and struggled to imagine any of them surviving against the behemoths.

"Better than anticipated. Having their technology has proven advantageous. We've only lost twelve percent of our operatives."

"Twelve percent!" Atlas exclaimed. He caught himself, lowering his voice. "How many citizens have been killed?"

"Not as many as you'd expect, but the logistics of the cleanup are growing tiresome. It'll become more difficult to keep this a secret, Mr. Donovan. With every sunset, the chances of the world remaining ignorant decrease. We need you to move," Booth said.

Atlas noted how callously he spoke about the dead, as if the supply chain issues were more gut-wrenching than his soldiers' lives. He stared at the displays on the wall, the dozens of screens showing footage of the Dark Teams combat. "Where am I going?"

Atlas slowed when he saw Rutger on film, crouching low and rushing forward with a giant alien weapon in his hands. One of the creatures dropped from a tree, knocking Rutger to the ground. The person with the camera strapped to them blasted a hole in the Stalker's chest. It started to tip over, and he felt the urge to shout: *Timber.*

He recognized Lennon as the feed cut to another soldier's angle, and she kicked the alien in the leg while grabbing Rutger and dragging him from the falling alien. It crashed to the grass, and she fired another shot at its head, pulverizing it.

"Impressive, isn't she?" Dark Leader asked.

Atlas stared at Lennon, her black uniform covered in blood and slime. She grimaced, and the screen went blank. "Yes. Very." He hoped she returned from the mission unscathed. He couldn't recall the last time a woman had drawn his attention like she did. He'd hardly had a chance to speak to her, but he'd heard the stories of her time on the *Interloper*.

She'd tried blowing the alien craft up with her own crew on board. Given what was happening now, it was a pity she hadn't succeeded.

"This way." Dark Leader brought him to the edge of the room and pressed a palm to an invisible screen. Atlas hadn't even known of another door. The frame illuminated, and the slab slid open, granting them access.

While the other space was incredibly organized, with endless rows of weapons, armor, monitors, and information, this was chaotic by comparison.

The wall had a projected image over it, with a map of the world, and various places highlighted with glowing indicators. Most of them were blue, but a handful stood out with bright red dots. He noticed small numbers near the symbols, and guessed they were placed in order. But of what?

Atlas walked to it, counting ten or more in Asia. The Philippines, Vietnam, Thailand, Malaysia. He'd been to several of those while pursuing the alien vessel, and clearly Dark Leader had taken the same tour as he.

"What are you thinking?" Atlas scanned the space, seeing a single desk across from the projection, the chair facing it. A few displays rotated through the Dark Team footage nearby, and Atlas watched as a soldier lost an arm in battle with an alien. He squinted to read the location on the bottom right corner. *Northern Siberia.* He flinched and returned his attention to Booth.

"The Signal is out there. We're trying to learn why it was taken in the first place, and I'm counting on Carter Robinson to assist with that."

"The astronaut?"

"He's a linguistics expert. I tried to bring him in before his mission launched, but ORB wasn't willing to part with him, and I couldn't very well explain to the conglomerate why I

17

required one of the only crew capable of making the Mars run with Commander Bryce, now could I?"

Atlas suspected this man could convince anyone of anything, but didn't say that out loud. "You want him to speak with an alien?"

"Not just any alien. A pilot like the being you found. The bipeds. We call them Grazers because they're herbivores, and as near as we can tell, they were running from the Stalkers when they crashed on Earth. I believe the *Interloper* followed them here, perhaps in connection with the Signal, but that's pure supposition at this point."

"You have one of them? Alive?" Atlas blinked in shock.

Booth smiled. "We do."

"And you expect Carter to... communicate with it?"

"I have some ideas about what they've been alluding to, but our attempts at communication have been... lackluster, to say the least. The drawing of the Signal was the only thing he was willing to share with me."

"What's your guess? That these second aliens have something that the Stalkers desire? This Signal? Is it a weapon?" Atlas stared at the map, noticing a lot of red dots in a single region.

"It might be a weapon, but I fear it's much worse," Booth said.

"Worse?"

"A beacon," he whispered. "Intended to draw more vessels like the *Interloper* to Earth."

Atlas shuddered at the image in his mind. Thousands of alien ships drawing closer to their home. They'd be unstoppable. His gaze drifted to the screens, and he saw another two had gone dark. The Stalkers weren't going down without a fight. "How can we stop this?"

"We locate the Signal. It's on our planet. We need to find it before the Stalkers," Booth told him.

"So that's why they're here. To acquire the Signal." Atlas let out a deep breath. "How can I possibly beat them to it?"

"You won't be going alone," Booth promised.

"I don't even know where to begin."

"Look at the map. What do you see?"

"The Amazon. That's your guess?" Atlas observed the cluster of red dots within the vast jungle.

"I assume in the course of your artifact hunting, you were directed there as well?" Booth crossed his arms.

"As a matter of fact, I was." Atlas had a folder full of evidence detailing sightings in Brazil from around the same time as Vietnam.

"Then why didn't you investigate them?" Booth asked.

"Because I was one man on a mission without consequence. I had no funding. Only speculation and half-whispered leads. I knew my father had found a piece in Malaysia, so that's where I focused. Not to mention the fact it's almost impossible to traverse that jungle. Even the locals won't travel to certain regions of it," Atlas explained.

"That's why I believe the Signal has remained undiscovered. It won't be easy, but nothing worthwhile is."

"Me?" Atlas pointed to his own chest. "You think I'll be able to enter the Amazon jungle, and walk up to this Grazer's ship? I'm not a hero, Booth. And I'm sure as hell not a soldier."

"You managed to stay ahead of me and the Team. Even escaped one of my better agents. I have faith in you, Mr. Donovan." He walked over, placing a device into Atlas' palm. "When you locate the Signal, do not activate it. You push this button, and we'll come for you with everything we have."

"I... I have to see my brother first."

Dark Leader glowered at him. "What does your brother have to do with anything?"

"He..." Atlas tried to be quick on his toes. "Hayden has access to my files. I left all my notes at our father's cabin in Vermont. He has the keys."

"Don't breathe a word to him about any of this. Get whatever you think will help with the mission, but I want you landed in Rio in two days' time. Do you understand?" When Dark Leader gave the order, Atlas tensed up, and realized why the soldiers obeyed him. He was a presence you couldn't deny.

"Yes, sir."

"As I stated, you won't be traveling alone." The door opened, and in walked James Wan. He wore a full black uniform and was armed to the teeth. "Dark Seven is as capable as they come."

19

"If he's coming to my brother's, can he at least change? It might be hard to explain who he is otherwise," Atlas said.

"I'm sure you'll think of something," Booth said.

"I've sent all the details of my leads for the Amazon to your Holo." Booth set his big hands on Atlas' shoulders. "Don't fail us, Mr. Donovan. The world is relying on you."

Atlas swallowed and pulled the cigarette from his ear.

"Got a light?"

FOUR

David

In the Air, Over Alaska

David sat with his back against the side of the C-17, his wife's head resting on his shoulder, and his daughter next to her. He stared at the wall of cargo crates secured in the center of the aircraft, listening to the steady roar of the massive turbines, feeling the vibrations shudder through him. He carefully checked his Holo watch, and the display snapped on, telling him it was after one PM.

Almost there. They'd departed before six AM on a direct flight from Long Island to Anchorage, Alaska. It was supposed to be an eight-hour trip, but it felt more like twelve.

Riding in the rear of a military transport wasn't anything like a commercial flight. No windows. No in-flight entertainment, and no air hostesses offering drinks and snacks. Before take-off an Army private had passed out bottles of water and a handful of dry snacks, but that was the extent of the hospitality on this flight.

At least Kate and Rachel were asleep now. That would make the time pass faster for them. David leaned forward to catch his son Mark's eye. He was scowling, looking tired and grumpy. Soldiers had confiscated his Holo just before he'd arrived in Long Island, and he'd been bored and miserable ever since.

"Almost there," David whispered.

Mark's scowl turned to a frown, and he sighed heavily, not responding.

21

David followed suit and allowed his eyelids to slide shut. Soon the steady thrumming of the turbines lulled him into an uneasy sleep.

A shadowy creature crawled through his subconscious, reaching for him with snaking black limbs. A mouth full of translucent teeth yawned wide, and it let out a piercing shriek—

David's eyes sprang wide, his heart hammering with adrenaline.

"Commander Bryce." The Army private strode toward them. Peach fuzz-short black hair. Medium height, with a mottled skin tone that suggested he'd spent far too much time in the sun.

He stopped in front of them, and David took a moment to read the name on his uniform. *Reed.*

"We're beginning our final descent." the private explained.

Kate stirred at the sound of the man's voice.

"If any of you have to use the head, now would be a good time."

"The what?" Kate asked.

"The restroom," Reed said.

"Oh. Yes, thank you." She fumbled with her seat buckle, then stood up and asked the kids if they had to go. Both of them said that they did, leaving David alone.

Private Reed turned to leave, but David stopped him. "Is our destination close?" he asked.

"Close enough," Private Reed confirmed. "But we have another flight to catch."

David groaned. "Where are you taking us—the North Pole?"

"That's classified, sir."

"Of course it is."

He was growing tired of all the secrecy. Not only were they not allowed to have any contact with the outside world, but they were being flown to a government facility in the middle of nowhere with no indication of when, or *if*, they would be allowed to leave.

But we'll be safe, David supposed.

***

"Everybody up! Come on, let's move! I don't have all day," a man with short silver hair and a lieutenant's insignia snapped at them. David stood with his family, and Private Reed emerged from between the secured crates centering the massive aircraft.

"This way, Commander," Reed said.

The residual whine of the C-17's turbines faded into silence as David trailed after Private Reed, leading his family past the cargo.

Halfway down the length of the aircraft, Reed stopped to open one of the crates and retrieve their bags, four carry-on bags that David recognized from the matched sets of luggage he'd bought with Kate for the handful of family vacations that they'd taken. Reed withdrew a heavy military duffle bag for himself and slung it over his shoulders before continuing.

A loud *thunk* sounded from the rear of the aircraft, and then a bright swath of sunlight poured in from the tail of the vessel, followed with a blast of cold air and flurries of snow. It was the beginning of November, and Anchorage had plenty of precipitation. They'd been provided with appropriate clothing before leaving Long Island, but none of them were wearing their gloves or headgear yet. They'd packed those items into their luggage.

"I'm cold!" Rachel cried as they accompanied Reed down the ramp.

"Stick your hands in your pockets. Or under your arms," Reed suggested, flashing a smile at her as he released his rifle to illustrate the posture.

Rachel mimicked him, but a cutting wind blew across the airstrip, and she said, "It's not working!"

Kate paused at the bottom of the ramp to search for matching pairs of black gloves and beanie hats.

"Keep moving," Private Reed said. "You'll be warmer inside the convoy."

"Give us a minute!" Kate snapped at him.

23

Reed looked to David for support, but he gave the private a helpless shrug. A mother caring for her children is an implacable force.

Reed frowned as he studied their surroundings. David joined him. Air strips crisscrossed every which way. A gray, overcast sky draped the scenery, while hazy clouds of blowing snow cut visibility to just a few hundred yards. It wasn't exactly flying weather, leaving David to wonder if they'd be able to catch that other plane today. But these weren't exactly commercial flights, so maybe they'd risk it.

A bustle of activity erupted behind them as a group of soldiers cried out, "Hooah!" descending the ramp in a tight formation, their rifles at the ready.

"That's my squad. We need to go," Reed insisted, restlessly flexing gloved hands on his weapon.

Kate thrust a pair of gloves and a hat at David. "Here."

"Thanks," he said, sliding them on while she zipped up the bag.

"On me," Reed said, watching as his squad double-timed to a group of transports with their headlights shining amidst the gloomy swirls of snow. "Let's go!"

David scooped Rachel up and held her up with one arm while he grabbed the handles of two carry-on bags with his other hand. Kate and Mark each took a piece of luggage, and together they hurried after the private.

The harsh wind quickly froze David's ears and nose. Rachel buried her face into his neck to stay warm. Within a minute they'd reached the waiting convoy: three old JLTVs painted in white and black camo patterns. They rumbled noisily with outdated internal combustion engines, broad chassis, and thick armor.

Reed stayed next to the foremost vehicle with the rear door wide. Kate ushered Mark in ahead of her, and then climbed in after him. David set Rachel beside her mother, then helped Reed stow their luggage. As soon as they were done, David crowded in with his family and slammed the door, shutting out the searing cold.

Kate helped the kids put on their seat belts, and David clasped his own. He noticed that the driver's seat was already occupied by another soldier. This one had a staff sergeant's stripes on his uniform.

Reed hopped into the front passenger's seat. They roared down the tarmac, with the sergeant speaking into his comms. "Bravo Leader rolling out. Keep it tight back there."

"Copy that. Bravo Two is Oscar Mike."

"Three, right on your tail, sir."

Reed glanced at them with a crooked smile. "We all good?"

David scanned his family's weary faces. Kate looked stressed. Mark still seemed bored by it all, and Rachel had sunken into the collar of her oversized jacket, appearing tiny and cold. Her button nose was red and her cheeks flushed.

"When will we get there?" Mark asked.

"Soon," Reed answered.

"Where are we going?" Kate asked.

"Can't say," the sergeant replied.

David watched Private Reed. "I thought you said we have another flight to catch? Isn't it at this airstrip?" he added, gazing through his window into a blank wall of swirling snow. It was becoming a blizzard.

"This isn't an airstrip," the sergeant said. "It's Elmendorf AFB. And unfortunately, it's not that simple anymore. Look outside. We were going to take a helo, but this ain't flyin' weather anymore, so we're driving."

"How long will that take?" Kate asked.

"Can't say," the sergeant replied.

"What *can* you say?" Kate muttered.

A dark shadow swooped right in front of them, and the sergeant swerved, cursing viciously. "What the hell is a deer doing on the airfield?"

A bang sounded from the roof of the vehicle, drawing David's eyes up.

And then the comms came alive with screaming voices: "Contact! Contact! Bravo One, you have a bogey on your back!"

Skinny black limbs slapped the windshield with three-fingered hands. Claws screeched on the glass, and a ghastly face surfaced. Four eyes, and a vertical opening for a mouth. It gaped wide to reveal a horror of translucent teeth strung with sticky strands of drool. David blinked to clear away the apparition, thinking he must be imagining it.

But the Stalker didn't disappear. It unleashed a piercing shriek.

"Sarge!" Reed cried.

"I see it!" The sergeant slammed on the brakes, and the creature flew off the roof. It quickly recovered, picking itself up and rising on four skinny legs attached at two hip joints. A pair of equally lengthy arms reached around behind it and produced a giant black rifle. The barrel swung into line with their vehicle.

"Duck!" Reed cried as the weapon flared with a burst of light. The sergeant slumped over the wheel, and the engine roared as his lifeless leg fell and jolted the accelerator.

"Watch out!" Kate screamed as the solid gray wall of a hangar emerged ahead of them.

Private Reed grabbed the wheel and cranked it. Tires skidded and spun through the snow, sending them sliding sideways toward the hangar bay. "Brace!" he cried.

David curled his body around Rachel in a protective shield before the JLTV crashed into solid concrete.

FIVE

Carter

Somewhere in Northern Alaska

"Wake up."

Carter blinked his eyes open to see a grumpy-looking soldier standing over him. "What..." He sat up, rubbed his eyes and covered a yawn. "What time is it?" He searched for his Holowatch and found it on an end table beside him.

"Fourteen-thirty hours," the soldier said before Carter could check it.

"What is that in normal-people time?" Carter asked.

The soldier glared at him. "You were supposed to report to your task leader at oh-nine-hundred."

Carter swung his legs off the bunk. "I set an alarm on my watch. Guess I must have hit the snooze. For future reference, you might consider a different form of transport. Those cargo planes aren't exactly conducive to sleep."

"Get dressed. Doctor Nielson expects you in the lab."

"What about breakfast?"

"You slept through it," the man said as he exited the cramped quarters.

"And lunch?" Carter called after him.

The door swung shut with a groan of metal hinges. Carter frowned and glanced out the quarters' small circular window. A blank white canvas of snow shone brightly in the sun, but there were no signs of vegetation, or of the towering mountains that he'd seen early that morning on the helicopter flight from Anchorage. They were somewhere in Alaska, but the precise location was a mystery.

27

Carter shivered as he stood up, his bare feet touching the ice-cold concrete floor. Wherever they were, apparently creature comforts like heated floors hadn't been a consideration. He zipped his luggage open and hurried to pull on blue jeans, a plain white t-shirt, and a knitted gray sweater that had all evidently been taken straight from his closet in Norfolk.

With an urgent need to use the facilities, he stepped to the toilet and relieved himself before washing his hands and face at the sink. The fixtures were right beside the bed, but there wasn't any sign of a shower. Carter made a face at that, realizing he'd be sharing those facilities with everyone else. It was still better than being cooped up aboard *Beyond III* for months. He studied his reflection in the mirror. Stubble darkened his cheeks. Most of it stayed brown, unlike the thinning gray hair atop his head.

"You handsome devil, you," he said to himself with a lopsided grin and a wink before exiting the room.

The soldier waited there for him.

"Oh, *you* again," Carter said, as if surprised to see him.

"Let's go."

"Do you have a name?" Carter asked as he followed the guy into a bare concrete corridor. The man was tall and broad across the shoulders, with military-short black hair.

"Dark Sixty-Two," he replied.

"Helluva name," Carter said. "Kids must have clobbered you at school."

The man refused to take the bait. *Not much for conversation,* Carter decided.

They came to another heavy metal door, but unlike the one to Carter's room, which could be locked and unlocked by peering up into a camera, this required the soldier to place his palm against a control panel. It glowed blue while he simultaneously stared into a retinal scanner.

The door *whooshed* aside, and they stepped onto a landing at the top of a metal staircase leading into a vast, windowless laboratory. Carter gaped at the view, grabbing the railing as he leaned toward the bustle of activity below.

The floor was crawling with people in white lab coats. Workstations were arrayed in broken circles around a massive glass cube in the center of the space. Within those transparent walls was an open space decorated sparsely with furniture. Some type of living arrangements. A solitary figure sat on a couch, gazing at a glowing azure hologram.

"This way," Dark Sixty-Two said, leading him down the steps.

Carter kept his eyes on the figure in the glass cube as he descended into the room.

His heart rate kicked up a notch as the soldier took him straight across the laboratory floor to the nearest wall of the chamber. "What is this?"

"What does it look like?" the soldier replied.

"A holding cell," Carter said, answering his own question as they reached a glass barrier connected to the transparent chamber. There was a second entrance on the opposite end, creating an airlock. Grated floor panels inside suggested that it had been designed to comply with decontamination protocols.

"I need an analysis of this!" a woman shouted as the dark figure sitting on an oversized couch in the center of the cell drew in the air, adding structures to the hologram in front of it. Carter identified a shiny black head, *three*-fingered hands, and long, skinny black arms. A shiver coursed down his spine as he realized what it was.

A Stalker.

"Working on it!" someone replied.

"You must be Dr. Robinson," the woman's voice returned.

Carter jumped at the sound and spun around to see an attractive woman, five-foot short and petite, with piercing blue eyes and her long dark hair tied up in a bun.

"I've been following your work," the woman added.

"You... *my* work?" Carter placed a finger on his chest, his mouth suddenly dry. He didn't know who this woman was, but he had an inkling she was important. He couldn't help feeling flattered, but he quickly covered it with a smug grin. "Well, it's always nice to meet a fan." He stuck out his hand. "Carter Robinson. A pleasure to meet you, Miss..."

"*Doctor* Nielson," she replied without shaking it. "And you can cut the bravado." Her mesmerizing eyes drifted from him to the holding cell, and she jerked her chin to the occupant.

"We could use your help with this one. Project Babble has been in the weeds for nearly a century. But the tech has been getting progressively better, so we're hopeful that we'll have a breakthrough soon. Especially now that you're here. I'm told that your AI learning algorithms are the best."

"I'm sorry, did you say a *century?* How old *is* that thing?" Carter muttered.

"Ancient. As far as we can tell, their species never dies of natural causes. Perfect for a spacefaring race."

"I don't understand," Carter said slowly. "If you—or people like you—have been trying to crack their language for a century, you must have made a ton of progress by now."

"Hardly any, actually. But to be fair, we had to figure out how to wake it from cryo before the conversation could even begin, and that didn't happen until eleven years ago."

"If they don't die, why do they need cryo?" Carter asked.

Dr. Neilson raised her eyebrows. "You've been in space. Would you want to stare at the wall for a hundred years while crossing galaxies?"

"Good point."

Dr. Nielson gave Carter a glittering smile. "Care for an introduction?"

"That depends. Do I have to go in there?"

"No." Dr. Nielson reached for a control panel beside the airlock entrance. "Chris, come here, please. There is someone I would like you to meet."

To Carter's horror, the creature sitting with its back to him rose from the couch to an impressive height before facing him. Two sets of black eyes blinked to either side of a vertical mouth that parted like a Venus fly trap, revealing dull sets of translucent teeth. A muffled snort came through the speaker grille above the control panel that Dr. Nielson had touched.

And then it stalked closer to them on skinny black legs.

Two legs. Carter blinked and stared at the being to be sure. This wasn't a Stalker. At least, not like the ones they'd run into aboard the *Interloper.*

"You look surprised," Dr. Nielson said.

"I've never seen this type."

"No," she replied. "This is a Grazer, not a Stalker. The species are related, but they diverged millions of years ago.

One evolved to hunt, the other to graze—hence why we call them Stalkers and Grazers. Predators and prey."

The Grazer reached the glass barrier, towering above Carter. He peered up into its blinking black eyes. "His name is Chris?"

"Christopher, actually."

"Cute," Carter muttered. "He came when you called him. Does he understand our language?"

"We're not sure. Sometimes he does, and sometimes he doesn't. But he knows his name."

"May I?" Carter asked, gesturing to the control panel below the speakers.

"Of course." Dr. Nielson retreated from the controls, hands clasped in front of her. "It's already set to transmit on both sides."

"Hey there, Chris. I'm Carter Robinson."

The alien slowly lowered itself into a crouch, its legs bending at two separate knee joints until they'd folded up to half their length, bringing it to eye level with him. Its mouth parted in a gaping slit, revealing blunt, crystalline teeth connected by strings of drool. Thin black lips curved into a shape like a crescent moon.

"What's he doing?" Carter asked, looking to Dr. Nielson.

"He's smiling, or trying to. He's become quite the mimic."

As if to confirm that fact, a deep rumbling growl issued from the cell: "Hey there, Chris. I'm Carter Robinson."

He leapt back from the cell as if he'd just been electrocuted. "It's capable of vocalizing our language?"

"Yes," Nielson replied.

"Well..." Carter trailed off, trying to decide what that meant. "Then how have you not taught it more of our language in all this time?"

"They don't appear to process language the same way we do. They're better at visual communication. And vibrations."

"Vibrations?"

"Place your hand against the glass," Nielson suggested.

Carter hesitated before doing as he was told, planting his palm against the cold surface, fingers splayed.

Chris did the same thing, matching three fingers to his five. A moment later the partition began to shiver. It reminded him of a cat's purring, but the way it kept changing in pitch and frequency, filling the air with ominous humming sounds—was as alien as anything Carter could have imagined.

"Amazing," he whispered.

"Are you ready to get to work?" Nielson asked.

Carter waited for the vibrations to stop before withdrawing from the glass. "I was born ready, sweetheart."

"Don't be stupid. Now that the Stalkers have arrived, the fate of the human race could very well rest on the outcome of our efforts. So keep your head in the game. This job is the most important thing you will ever do with your life."

"Yes, ma'am," Carter said, forcing himself to be serious.

"Come. I'll show you to your station."

***

David

Elmendorf AFB

David's seat belt cut into his lap and shoulder like a knife, and his whole body surged into Kate and Rachel. Everyone screamed. Ballistic glass shattered, and the armored chassis crumpled. Cottony silence rang in the wake of it, but the muffled roar of rifle fire interjected—

Punctuated by the agonized screams of soldiers.

David peeled himself from Rachel to check on her. She was as pale as the driven snow, but otherwise unharmed. Kate and Mark were also fine, but that was more than he could say for the sergeant in the driver's seat. He had a smoking hole in his chest. Private Reed unbuckled, popped his door open, and twisted around in his seat to stick his rifle out backwards. He flipped down a screen from his helmet that covered his right eye, and appeared to be using it to aim the weapon.

"How many?" David asked, but he barely heard his own voice through the ringing in his ears.

"I have eyes on one tango," Reed replied.

Staccato bursts of rifle fire continued, only to cut off sharply with the dying cries of the soldiers.

"It's tearing them apart!" Reed hissed.

"They're bulletproof," David said.

"They?" Kate asked. "What *was* that thing?"

"Bulletproof, huh? Well that's a shit surprise," Reed replied. "We have to scram."

"Where?" Kate asked. David peered through his window, seeing nothing but swirling snow and bright muzzle flashes.

Somewhere in the distance a .50 caliber turret machine gun began thumping out death and destruction. It stopped abruptly, and then all was silent but for the whistling wind.

"That's *it?*" David asked. "I thought this was an Air Force base?"

"It was evacuated before our arrival," Reed explained. "We couldn't have just anyone seeing you sauntering around when you're supposed to be on your way to Mars."

Reed flipped up his targeting optics and unbuckled the sergeant. "We seem to be clear for the moment. Commander, I'm gonna require your help to move the sergeant."

"You're joking, right? The Stalker is still out there!"

"We're not driving anywhere with a corpse behind the wheel. Either he goes, or we exit and run for it."

"We'd better be quick. It could be circling back to check on us as we speak."

David stepped into the storm, and with Reed's assistance they pulled the dead sergeant from the vehicle.

The body flopped onto the tarmac, and then Private Reed dove in and clambered past the equipment between the two front seats. David jumped into the passenger's seat behind him, and the private removed his rifle and handed it over. "Take it."

"What for?" David asked. "Guns are useless against their armor." But then he recalled a lucky shot from Lennon, striking one of them in the eye.

"They have to have a weakness."

"The eyes," David confirmed. "But that's a hell of a shot to make."

"I have faith in you, Commander." Reed grabbed the wheel and exhaled a shaky breath. David gripped the rifle uneasily, being careful to mind the trigger and keep the barrel pointed away from people.

Reed feathered the accelerator. The tires spun, and metal screeched against the concrete of the hangar.

"We must be wedged on something. Come on, baby..." Reed muttered, steering back and forth, but all four tires spun uselessly.

David stared at his side mirror, watching for signs of trouble. There were only fat, scurrying flakes of snow pinwheeling from the sky.

"David," Kate whispered.

"Come on!" Reed cried, slapping the wheel in frustration.

"David, what's happening?" Kate pressed.

"It's..." David trailed off, wondering how to explain about the *Interloper* and the Stalkers.

A pair of headlights from one of the other trucks swerved their way.

"Hey, I think some of the soldiers made it," David said.

Reed eased up on the gas and frowned. The bright beams swept into line with the side of their truck, approaching fast. David listened to the rising roar as the driver gunned the engine.

"What's he doing?" Kate asked as the beams grew close enough to blind them.

"He's going to ram us!" Reed cried. He stomped on the accelerator again, and the engine revved high with a throaty roar.

"David!" Kate shouted, her voice rising in alarm.

A piece of metal snapped with a loud *ping*, and they shot from the hangar, flying down the runway.

The approaching vehicle swerved, and a dark shadow leapt clear just before it slammed into the concrete with a thunderous *boom*.

David grimaced when he realized what that shadow was. It was the Stalker. It had figured out how to use their vehicles.

David watched the fiery ruin of the JLTV disappear behind veils of snow.

"Where are we heading?" Kate asked.

Private Reed spun the wheel, turning sharply to avoid burying the JLTV in a snowdrift beside the runway. "I don't know!"

"What do you mean you don't *know?*" David demanded.

"I wasn't told where we were taking you. Only Sergeant Recks had that information, and maybe not even him. This mission was highly classified. You're not even supposed to be here!"

David caught a glimpse of a galloping black blur in his mirror. "Reed, we have incoming!" Somehow it was using all four legs and both arms to run. With six limbs churning, the Stalker was actually gaining on them.

Private Reed peered at David's mirror. "Holy crap, that thing is fast!"

Faster than any biological creature had a right to be.

Reed braked roughly before reaching the end of the runway, then skidded through another turn. The Stalker took full advantage of the opportunity and closed to within a few feet of them, then launched off the tarmac and landed on their roof with a heavy *thud.*

Reed slammed on the brakes, but this time it didn't fly off.

A sharp crack of energy discharged from the roof, accompanied by a flash of light and heat. The display in the center of the dash exploded.

Reed yelped with shock.

David jumped from the vehicle, snapping the rifle up, and backed away steadily. He took aim and fired one-handed at the shadowy black mass clinging to the roof. Recoil hammered David's shoulder, and most of the shots went wide, but it got the Stalker's attention. It looked up with a shriek. David flicked the rifle to single-fire mode and aimed for the eyes, pulling the trigger repeatedly.

Two bullets plinked off its skull before a third crunched into an eye socket. The Stalker screamed and fell off the roof.

But it wasn't dead yet. It gave a wheezing cry that sounded almost like a dog's bark, and then David saw it roll over and make for the open door of the vehicle.

A jolt of adrenaline coursed through David's veins as he imagined it crawling inside and tearing his family apart. He sprinted toward the Stalker, squeezing off hasty shots, but none of them succeeded. Private Reed drew his sidearm and fired at its head from the driver's seat. The Stalker shrieked in time to each bullet, but they shattered on its impenetrable exoskeleton.

David reached the alien and dropped his rifle to grab one of its legs. He heaved with every ounce of strength he had, tearing it away from the door. The Stalker shrieked again and writhed in his grip, rounding on him with snapping jaws. Reed lunged from his seat, encircling the Stalker's iron throat with both arms. It rose on wobbling legs to its full nine-foot height, dragging him with it. Reed pumped a few rounds into the side of its head at point-blank, to no effect.

The Stalker bucked and scratched at Reed, trying to throw him off. David spun around to find the rifle he'd dropped, and he lunged for it, falling hard on the snow-covered pavement. He rolled onto his back and set the rifle to full automatic before aiming at the Stalker's torso and strafing it with a rattling burst. Shrapnel flew as the bullets exploded harmlessly on the being's armor and plinked off the JLTV.

The Stalker planted its feet wide and released a piercing cry, as if calling for reinforcements.

Reed stuck his weapon straight down its throat and tapped the trigger. Muffled shots rang out. The Stalker shuddered and sank to its knees. Reed leaped away, and the alien planted its face on the ground.

David and Reed gasped and stared mutely at their kill, waiting for it to twitch. A blinking green light on the Stalker's hip caught David's eye. It was close to the same size as a Holo reader. David withdrew the flat black rectangle secured to the creature's hip.

"Careful," Reed warned.

When he rotated it, a bright image glowed as it floated above the device. It was a hologram of the airfield, in miniature, from a top-down aerial view, as if this were a live recording from an active drone. David could see the hangar, the crashed JLTV pumping out a column of greasy black smoke, their own vehicle, the dead Stalker—shaded green, but quickly fading to blue—and each of them shaded yellow. The scanner picked up his wife and kids through the armored doors of the truck, and had shaded them yellow, too.

"What the hell is that?" Reed asked, crowding in for a better look.

David shook his head, words failing him. It was better than drone footage, because it wasn't obscured by the storm. Somehow the tech saw through all of that, giving a clear picture of lifeforms in the area.

And right now, there were four green markers bounding in at the edges of the airfield.

"Are those what I think they are?" Reed whispered, pointing to the hologram.

"We have to leave," David said. "Now!"

Reed tore around the truck and returned to the driver's seat. David was about to follow suit when he remembered the rifle the Stalker had been using. David stepped up onto the running boards, dropped Private Reed's rifle into the truck, and leaned over the roof to grab the alien weapon.

It was heavy—at least twenty pounds—and quite a lot larger than Reed's army carbine. David sat down, taking a moment to accommodate the two weapons between his legs and the alien scanner in his lap. The green-shaded Stalkers were moving fast, converging on their location.

Reed gunned the engine, roaring away. "Can you see them yet?" he asked.

"There are more of those things running around?" Kate cried.

"No visual yet," David said to Reed.

They came upon a chain-link fence and a gate, but Reed made no attempt to slow. "Hang on!" he said.

The kids both screamed, and Kate cussed the private as they crashed through the fence and onto the open road, dragging pieces of chain-link and kicking up a wall of sparks before leaving the airfield behind. David studied the alien scanner as the green-shaded Stalkers reached the shattered barrier. They slowed, then stopped. David caught a glimpse of three tall black shadows, faded white by the blowing snow, watching them leave.

"Will someone tell me what the hell is going on?" Kate insisted.

David hesitated, wondering how much of what had happened he was actually allowed to tell his wife. But with real,

37

live aliens loose on Earth, it hardly seemed to matter anymore. He drew in a deep breath, finally revealing where he'd really been for the last three months, and what he'd discovered aboard the *Interloper*.

SIX

Lennon

Prairie City, Oregon

Lennon shoved the corpse's leg with her boot. The skinny appendage twitched, and Rutger fired again, blowing the monster's foot off.

She sat, panting from the exertion. "How many is that?"

"Fourteen," he said, plopping to the earth with her.

Dark Twenty and Thirty-Four were below them, chasing the last Stalker past the old railroad station. Rusted-out cars sat parked on the tracks, likely there for the better part of a half-century.

The sun began its descent beyond Strawberry Mountain, sending a chill through the air.

Sounds of the battle below echoed to their position, and Lennon struggled to her feet. Everything ached. She swiveled her shoulder, knowing it was bruised, but hurried to the aid of the other two.

Before they arrived, she heard the rotors as their extraction team approached.

"They're early," Rutger said.

"Better than late." This got a gruff nod from the German, and Lennon lingered on the tracks, trying to listen for signs of the skirmish.

Dark Twenty was running, which in itself was a sight. The Stalker fired after him, and the big man ducked and rolled, landing on the opposite edge of the train car. One blast and the walls melted, revealing an opening between Twenty and the Stalker.

"I despise these things," Lennon said, running around the pair of them.

She aimed her weapon, pulling the trigger. But the charge was out, or the battery was fried. Dark Leader had manufactured the weaponry in haste, and they'd barely been field tested. Lennon supposed that's what they were doing now.

Lennon tossed it to the tracks, the metal clanking loudly, and the Stalker shrieked, flipping toward her.

Rutger sneaked behind it, his footsteps oddly silent on the gravel.

"You want to do this?" she bellowed at the Stalker, noticing Brighton approaching from the tree line. They had it cornered.

"Lennon. He requested more samples," Rutger reminded her.

"Dammit." Lennon aimed her handgun at its face, aware she could kill it with a shot to the eyes.

Brighton heaved a ball overhead, and a net deployed, the corners landing and exploding into the ground, securing the target. The Stalker thrashed within the net, trying to raise his gun, but the pressure was too much.

Lennon walked right to it, staring up three and a half feet at its hideous maw. "I hate you," she whispered.

It was only a foot away, and she could smell it. Rank as a fish market.

"Dark Three, you have a death wish?" Dark Twenty asked.

"Not anymore."

The helicopter landed, and she stepped back. "I saw a motel in town. Let's leave in the morning. We need the rest."

Rutger barked orders at the other two as their support crew came, ready to clean the mess they'd left scattered throughout the valley.

***

"You sure it's a good idea to be here?" Lennon asked Rutger as they entered the motel bar.

Rutger motioned for Dark Twenty to grab drinks, and they found an empty booth across the room. Slow country music played from a crackling speaker, and Lennon checked around, finding the place about a third full.

Mostly men, faces turned down into their mugs. A few younger people played a game of pool, talking loudly. One of them looked her up and down, then quickly averted his eyes when she caught him staring. She almost dared the kid to make his move. After a few days of fighting Stalkers, these people didn't seem like a threat.

"Where we off to next?" Brighton asked. Lennon was so used to calling them by their Dark codenames, she almost forgot her true name.

"Louisiana," Rutger said. "One of the pods landed near the bayou."

"Why are they all in remote areas?" Brighton asked.

"I have a theory," Lennon said.

Rutger's eyebrows lifted. "And that is?"

"They're searching for this... Signal, right? There aren't that many of them. A thousand at best. They want to stay hidden, waiting for reinforcements," Lennon suggested.

"I don't like the sound of that," Brighton murmured.

"Can we drop the work chatter for a few minutes?" Rutger slid over, making room for Hank.

Hank carried four bottles of beer, and slipped into the booth with them, barely fitting in his seat.

"You don't strike me as a Hank," Lennon told him, grabbing one of the drinks. Foam spilled down the neck.

"No? What would suit me better?" He swallowed from the bottle, drinking half the contents in seconds.

"Tank?" Brighton offered, and they all laughed.

Lennon closed her eyes, and images of the last few days burst into her mind. Blood. Death. Stalkers. She took a long sip, and opened them, trying to push the memories aside. There would be plenty more where that came from. But the Dark Teams were doing a good job containing the roaming Stalkers.

She glanced at the TV, which showed images of the flashing lights over Boston from the other night. Crashing debris, not meteors, but they appeared the same. Instead of trying to read it, she ignored the scrolling banner. That wasn't her problem. Lennon had enough to deal with.

"I still can't believe we're on your Team, Dark Three," Hank proclaimed.

"Can you keep it down?" Rutger ordered. "We're just four people passing through."

"Sorry," he said, finishing the beer. He lifted an arm, waving the middle-aged waitress over. "Another round."

She furrowed her brow at them, maybe sensing a tip, and finally smiled. "Sure thing, honey." She continued to the next patrons' table.

"Lennon Baxter," Brighton said. "You're a legend."

"I am?" Lennon asked.

"As if you don't know. There are at least five maneuvers named after Dark Three. Dark One used them all in our combat training," she said.

Lennon watched Rutger. They still hadn't spoken privately. All these years, he'd let her think he was dead. *Asshole.* "Is that so?"

"What, you want a royalty payment or something? You were good at your job," Rutger said.

"I *am* good at my job," she corrected.

"I can't deny that," Rutger admitted.

"Where are we again?" Lennon asked them. She couldn't remember the town's name. It was a hole in the wall, tucked between two mid-sized mountain ranges. The only reason it existed would be proximity to a railroad line from the late 1800s. Half of America was built for a different time, but these places hadn't got the memo to offer more than a motel bar, a post office, and a gas station.

"Prairie City," Brighton answered.

"Is it meant to be ironic?"

Hank stared at the pool table, and when the pair playing it left, he stood up, dragging Brighton with him. Lennon watched him tap the side of it with his Holo for payment, and the balls fell.

Rutger sat across from her. "You want to hash this out?"

"No."

"Come on, Lennon. We have to do this at some point."

42

"Why? I find it easier to kill the Stalkers when I picture your face on their hideous bodies." Lennon finished her beer and slid the empty to the end of the table.

"It wasn't my fault."

"Sure. It was Dark Leader's. I know the story. But it was *us*, Rutger. I thought we had something."

"We did."

"Then why not send me a message? Let me know you were alive."

"He..."

"Ordered you not to. I heard you before."

Rutger leaned closer; his jaw clenched. "You think it didn't hurt me? I thought about you every day."

Lennon sniffed and sat back on the bench. "Let's drop it." She heard someone sitting behind her and caught Rutger peering over her shoulder.

"Here you go. Anything else I can get you? We make a mean burger," the waitress said, stopping by with another round of beers.

Lennon looked around, seeing how dirty the place was, and doubted that.

"Hank, you want to eat?" Rutger hollered while Hank was lining up a shot. He missed and raised his big arms in exasperation.

"Always!" Hank replied.

"Four burgers. Fries." Rutger smiled at the waitress, the expression almost as alien as the Stalker's.

"Coming right up." The woman sauntered off.

"We can't stay out too late," Lennon muttered. "I have the distinct feeling that Hank is quite the wild partier, and I prefer to keep him half sober."

Rutger lifted a finger, and she knew to stop speaking. He spun it around and tapped his ear, indicating the guy behind her was listening. She started to reach for her handgun, but he shook his head.

Lennon dropped a napkin on the floor and went for it, using it as an excuse to check behind her. The man wasn't doing a good job of hiding the fact he was eavesdropping. Sitting alone at his table. One ear turned to her so he could listen. Eyes staring blankly at the wall. She scanned the room, finding the bar emptier now.

Lennon sat up and noticed Brighton picking up on their cues. She nudged Hank while he made another shot. The seven-ball careened into the corner pocket.

Rutger was the first to stand, and Lennon let him go ahead. He sat across from the eavesdropper, and Lennon slid in beside him, blocking the man's exit. Her gun was drawn under the table, aimed at the guy's guts. "Any particular reason you're listening to our private conversation?"

She finally got a good look at the man. He was skinny, his skin pallid and sweaty. Eyes red and darting around in deep sockets. "I don't know what you're talking about."

Lennon glanced at Rutger. "Meth. Maybe one of the newer drugs. Holosynth or a street version."

"I don't do drugs," the man said, a drop of drool slipping from his lips.

"He's whacked. Nothing to see here." Rutger left the table, and Lennon concealed her gun before leaving.

"Get the hell out," she told the man, and he nodded absently.

"Everything good?" Hank asked, sizing up the stranger.

"Just fine. I have next game," Lennon told him while their food was brought over.

For a moment Lennon forgot her problems. She disregarded her life in the organization, or her time away from it in Three Points. Lennon blocked the three months spent on *Beyond*, and the subsequent days on the *Interloper*. She sure as hell didn't think about tomorrow. There was only the now. She drank a few more beers, ate a burger that was surprisingly great, and goofed around with her team.

Rutger laughed as he scratched on the eight ball, and Lennon checked her Holowatch, seeing it was far too late. "We'd better go." They paid their tab, and she gave a big tip, knowing it all might be over soon. Why not use Dark Leader's money to put a smile on someone's face while they still breathed?

"That was fun," Brighton said as they congregated outside. The night was pitch black, the stars and moon hidden behind a thick layer of clouds.

The motel had twenty units, all in a straight shot from the bar to the front office. Hers was in the center, smack dab between Brighton and Hank's. Lennon pulled her jacket tighter as they crossed the street. Rutger grabbed her arm, his footsteps slowing suddenly.

"Twelve o'clock," he said.

"I see it," Lennon whispered. The door to her room was open.

Her gun was in her hand before she exhaled, and she was off, jogging toward the entrance. Instead of alerting anyone to her presence, she entered quietly. The druggie was at her bedside, searching through her bag.

Rutger rushed past her, grabbing the guy by the collar. "You messed with the wrong people, my friend."

He threw the skinny man into the parking lot.

"You won't win."

"Win what?" Rutger asked, shoving a heel into his chest.

"Earth is ours," the man said, his lips chapped, his eyes redder now.

"What is this fool saying?" Hank went to lift him up, and the man recoiled, his body going stiff as an ironing board. He screamed, and somebody watched from their room.

"It's okay. He's having a seizure. We're doctors!" Lennon called, but the woman seemed unconvinced. She closed her door, but Lennon saw her peeking through the dirty motel curtains.

"He's choking!" Hank cried.

Foam spilled from the man's mouth, and Lennon turned him onto his side. The back of his neck was wet. She withdrew her hand, finding her fingertips slick with blood, gleaming crimson in the yellow bug lights.

"What the hell is this?" Brighton asked.

Lennon recognized a scuttling form on the gravel with the long black appendages. She cringed. "It's one of them!"

She fired at it, but the alien spider sped away, rushing from the scene.

The man stilled.

Lennon expected the local authorities to be called. They were too late to save this man.

Rutger felt for his pulse. "He's gone."

Lennon rolled him over, and wiped the wound on his neck, finding three puncture marks. "We have more to worry about than just the Stalkers, it seems. I'll contact Dark Leader."

SEVEN

David

Chickaloon, Alaska

David sat on a couch in a cozy log cabin that they'd broken into hours ago, huddled around a wood stove with Kate and the kids. Private Reed guarded the front window, keeping watch with his targeting optic and the thermal scope on his rifle. The alien pulse weapon leaned against the wall beside him. The scanner was on an armchair, dormant now, in some type of power-saving mode, but David knew that touching the device would activate it.

"It's been more than six hours," David said, watching the private. "You can probably ease up."

Reed glanced away with a frown, lifted the alien scanner, and studied the holographic map that appeared. No sign of green alien blips, but David counted five yellow ones inside the cabin, corresponding to each of them. Even at night, that map showed the surrounding terrain as clearly as if it were day.

Private Reed sighed and sank to the floor with his back to the window and the front entrance. He balanced the alien scanner in his lap, using it instead of his actual eyes to keep watch.

"What's our next move?" Kate asked.

David caught his daughter and son looking to him, rather than the soldier, for the answer. He smiled and pulled Mark closer.

"We should stay here for the night," David suggested. "Get some rest."

47

"And what if they come while we're sleeping?" Kate demanded. "They were obviously after *you*, at the airbase."

"Were they?" David asked, even as he considered the possibility.

"We're expecting further orders," Reed reminded them. "So we sit tight."

"Nothing yet?" Kate pressed. "Can't you call and check again?"

Private Reed shook his head. "We wait," he insisted.

The logs in the stove crackled, throwing embers around. Outside a fierce wind blew, making the rafters creak.

"Mommy..." Rachel began.

"Yes, sweetheart?"

"What are aliens?"

"They're..." Kate trailed off. "Well, they're people like us, except that they come from another planet."

"Like from Mars?" Rachel asked.

"Yes, but Mars doesn't have any aliens."

"How do you know?" Rachel pressed. "Maybe they were hiding."

"That's stupid," Mark muttered. "They can't hide. There aren't even any trees on Mars."

"They could hide underground," Rachel insisted.

Mark frowned. "Stupid."

"*You're* stupid!" Rachel huffed.

"Quiet," Kate snapped. "Both of you. No one is stupid."

"They're not from Mars," David said quietly. "I've been to Mars. And I've never seen anything living there that didn't come from Earth. Besides, we would have seen their spaceship hanging around there. And they were in cryo. That wouldn't have been necessary if they'd travelled such a short distance."

"What's cryo?" Rachel asked.

David smiled and explained the technology for her as best he could. The kids' questions went on for a while. Rachel crawled into his lap, and Mark went to sit in the armchair by the door so he could put his feet up on the ottoman. Soon both kids were asleep; even Kate's eyes looked to be getting heavy. Her head sagged against his shoulder, and David listened as her breathing slowed.

"Hey," Private Reed whispered.

David answered with a lift of his eyebrows.

"Why do you think they were after you?"

"I don't know. Maybe they weren't? It could have been a coincidence."

"Helluva coincidence," Reed added. "They didn't do anything to you up there? Inject you with something? Or..."

That suggestion had him wondering the same thing.

"What?" Reed pressed.

"Well. They didn't inject me, exactly... but one of them bit me." David still had a ring of puncture marks on his ankle where the queen spider had pricked through his suit with the barbs on its tentacles.

"So maybe they put a marker in your blood? Biotech?" Reed suggested.

"It's possible," David agreed, but he wasn't convinced. "Or they might have seen me leaving their ship and followed me to the Long Island facility. Then from Long Island to Anchorage. It's even feasible that Stalker hitched a ride on the cargo plane. But the question isn't how they did it; the question is *why*. I don't have anything that they could be after."

"Maybe not, but you do now." Reed gestured with his eyes to the alien scanner. "This thing is tracking them. We could use it to hunt them."

"Assuming they can't just turn off whatever locator beacons the scanner is detecting?"

"I'm not sure that's how it works," Reed said. "It can detect humans, too."

"Good point," David replied. "Then I guess we'd better get that scanner someplace safe before they realize we have it."

Reed nodded gravely. "ASAP."

David let out a ragged breath. He allowed his eyes to close, and blurry flashes of the day's events to flicker through his mind's eye. He saw that Stalker lying dead on the airfield, its three buddies watching them leave.

And suddenly he was back aboard the *Interloper*, surrounded by a writhing carpet of spiders. They were slashing his suit and flooding in, tentacles spearing his flesh like hot knives. He hammered himself with his fists, trying to squash them, but that only made them burrow beneath his skin. He felt them squirming inside of him...

He shouted. His eyes flew open, and a hand clapped over his mouth.

"We have incoming," Private Reed whispered sharply, then turned the scanner so David could see. Three green dots were converging on the cabin from a kilometer away.

***

Reed made a pinching gesture, and the screen zoomed in. Those three green specks resolved into the more familiar outlines of Stalkers, their legs churning in oddly graceful movements, their long arms carrying the bulky alien plasma rifles.

David jumped from the couch, rousing Kate. She startled and blinked rapidly. He placed a finger to his lips and said, "We have to go. Quickly."

She woke Mark, and David picked Rachel up. She murmured sleepily and nestled against his shoulder.

"Ready," he said to Reed.

The private took point, flipping his targeting optic down and cracking the door enough to stick his carbine out. The alien scanner dangled from his other hand, making the task of aiming his rifle seem awkward.

"Clear," Reed said. He glanced at David. "Grab the pulse rifle."

David took the alien weapon, and they rushed down snow-dusted stairs to the cabin's driveway. Everyone was still wearing their winter clothes and boots, so it was an easy escape. It was barely two steps to the JLTV, since they'd parked right outside.

"How close are they?" David asked.

"Close," Reed breathed as he took the driver's seat.

Kate followed suit, crowding in the back with Mark. David dropped Rachel in. "Daddy!" she cried as she woke up suddenly, her eyes wide with terror and confusion.

"Shhh. You're okay, honey." He ran to the front passenger's seat.

Reed handed over his carbine and the alien scanner to focus on driving.

The three Stalkers were within a hundred feet of the cabin. Adrenaline sparked through David's veins. Were these the same three who'd watched them leave the Air Force base?

The truck roared to life and the wheels spat clumps of snow as Reed reversed, then threw it into drive and gunned it to the road. They bumped over a hump at the end, and the kids and Kate sobbed.

Something screeched against the side of the truck, and David watched in the mirror as a dark shadow tumbled away. Two more were bounding after them, hazy and indistinct from the cloud of snow they'd kicked up in their wake. It took David a moment to confirm that the Stalkers were losing ground rather than gaining it.

"They're falling behind," he said.

"Good," Reed breathed, but the truck's engine roared louder.

"You need to slow down!" Kate said as a sharp bend appeared up ahead. Reed hit the brakes briefly and drifted to the middle of the road to give him more room for the turn.

They raced along the dark, barely-plowed rural roads until coming to Glenn Highway, which was also just two lanes, but it was clearer than the rural avenues.

David sat in stunned silence, giving his sleep-addled brain time to catch up. It felt like he was stuck in a nightmare. How had those creatures pursued them all the way from Anchorage? He glanced at the scanner in his lap. The Stalkers were running inside the cabin, maybe to check if they'd left anything important behind, or some hint about where they were going next. *They're definitely intelligent,* David thought.

"What if they can track the scanner?" he asked, hefting the device.

Private Reed frowned. "It's possible. If so, we'll have to block the signal."

"Why don't we just get rid of it?" Kate asked.

David was tempted, but the nebulous fear that it might be used to monitor them wasn't enough to justify discarding something that had just saved their life.

"That tech's too valuable to throw away," Private Reed said, mirroring David's own thoughts. "We need to deliver it in one piece to the safe house."

"We have to survive to do that," David said.

"We will," Reed said. "We've bought ourselves some time. They might have followed us from Anchorage, but it took them the better part of a day to do it. And given how fast they move, I don't think they're homing in on the scanner. If they were, they would have found us sooner. Regardless, it's not my call to make. Major Keller will clarify the situation when we arrive."

"Major Keller?" David asked.

"Arrive where?" Kate added.

"My CO finally contacted me an hour ago. I wanted to let you three sleep, but then the Stalkers came. He's sending Major Keller and a Marine fire team to escort us the rest of the way to the safe house. We rendezvous a hundred miles from here, in a place called Glennallen. Earl's Roadside Diner."

David's stomach rumbled with the prospect of food. He hoped they'd be able to order something.

Once again, silence fell, and this time it lasted. David passed the minutes watching the sunrise, turning the sky from deep blue to blood-red and then peach. When they rolled into the diner's parking lot, it was nine AM. The drive from that cabin had taken almost two hours.

Private Reed killed the engine and grabbed his carbine and the alien device. He looped the rifle's strap over his shoulder and then pushed the scanner into a pouch on his combat vest.

David began reaching for the pulse rifle, but Reed gave David his sidearm instead. "We're trying to keep a low profile."

David smirked at the Army-issue pistol in his lap. Apparently in Alaska, walking into a diner with a handgun and an automatic rifle still qualified as a *low profile.*

The cold slapped David in the face as he jumped outside and tucked the weapon into the waistband of his jeans. Adrenaline had dulled the cold when they'd been chased by the Stalkers, but now he was really feeling it. A glimpse at his Holowatch told him it was minus two Fahrenheit.

"It's freezing!" Kate muttered as David held the door for her and the kids. Rachel whimpered and complained, while Mark insisted that it wasn't so bad.

They hurried to the entrance of the diner, where Private Reed was waiting for them. The scanner was in his hand, his rifle dangling from his neck by the strap.

"Are they here yet?" David asked, glancing at the vehicles in the parking lot. One was an old, rusty pick-up truck, the other an unmarked black van. Neither resembled something an Army major and a Marine fire team might drive around in.

"Doesn't look like it," Reed answered. "Guess that gives us time for breakfast and coffee."

"Thank God for that," Kate said, pushing past Reed. Soon they were seated in a booth, with Kate and the kids on one side and Reed and David on the other.

A waitress came by and the kids ordered pancakes, while he and Kate asked for coffee, eggs, bacon, and a stack of pancakes to share, while Private Reed went for a breakfast burrito and a black coffee to go.

"Coming right up," their curly-haired waitress said with a beaming smile.

"Odd choice—a burrito?" David commented to Reed.

Reed shrugged. "When you don't know if your meal will be interrupted, you learn to order things that you can carry."

David grimaced at that. "Didn't think of that."

"Don't worry. I'm sure we can spare a half hour or so. Besides, the major isn't here yet."

A bell on the door chimed as a tall, broad-shouldered man in digital white military fatigues stepped in.

"Speak of the Devil," Reed muttered as he slid from the booth and came to attention.

"At ease, Private." Four more soldiers followed the major in and occupied a booth near the entrance. They pretended to study their menus while Major Keller pulled up a chair.

"You have it with you?" Keller asked, his eyes never leaving Reed.

Private Reed frowned. "Have what, sir?"

Major Keller's mouth opened like he was about to say something, but then froze up, as though he'd forgotten what it was. His gaze seemed to swim out of focus, staring at the bottle of ketchup on the table.

"Major?" Private Reed prompted. When that didn't work, he waved a hand in front of the major's eyes. A muscle twitched in his cheek, and his head jerked. Half of his face drooped, while the other half ticked up in a smile.

"He's having a stroke," David said.

Reed hurried to his feet, ready to catch the major in case he collapsed.

Finally, the major shook himself, and the drooping side of his face joined the other half in smiling. "Sorry. Not a stroke, no. It's just a bit of Bell's palsy, I'm afraid. The scanner. You have it with you?"

Reed froze. "Um. Yeah, we do. It's in the truck."

David picked up on the lie immediately. The scanner was in Reed's vest, not in the truck. Something was wrong with this meet. Reed was playing it safe, but what exactly was he afraid of? That Keller was secretly working for another government and the tech would fall into the wrong hands?

"Good." Major Keller's smile vanished suddenly. "Go get it."

"We were about to eat," Reed said. "Can it wait?"

"Wait?" Major Keller asked. He blinked once, then stared intensely over Reed's shoulder for several seconds. "Yes, of course it can." The smile returned, but the major's eyes seemed to be rolling around aimlessly. "Eat first."

David felt a sharp trickle of warning creep into his gut. Kate shot him a bewildered look, and he gave his head a slight shake. She caught the hint, but his kids didn't. Rachel stared open-mouthed at the major.

"What's wrong with you?" she asked.

"Wrong?" Keller countered. "Nothing is wrong."

"Yes it is," Rachel said. "You're acting *weird.*"

Mark was more reserved, and he diverted his gaze.

"Rachel!" Kate whispered. "That's not nice."

"But it's true."

"Where is it?!" Keller demanded suddenly, making both of David's kids jump. The major's glance landed on Private Reed. "We need that tech! We must know if they're here!" he shouted, drawing sudden looks from the handful of other patrons in the diner.

The four soldiers who'd come in with the major had stopped staring at their menus and were now watching with their hands on their guns. For a moment, David thought they were reacting to the major's strange behavior, but then Reed said—

"Okay, it's no problem. I'll retrieve it."

—and the soldiers relaxed. They'd been waiting for Reed to offer resistance. At which point, they would have done what? Drawn their weapons and started shooting?

Major Keller smiled again, a switch flipped. "Good. Yes. It's better this way."

Rachel was right. Something was *very* wrong with the major. Not to mention those Marines.

Reed slowly exited the booth, and that sense of wrongness grew until it was like a klaxon echoing in David's head.

"Oh, David—didn't you say that you need some fresh clothes from your luggage? The kids have to change, right?"

"Yes," David said, sliding out after him. "Kate, maybe you'd better join us and bring the kids so they can choose their outfits. You know how picky they are with what they wear."

Kate smiled. "You bring the wrong pair of jeans and you'll be hearing about it all day!"

"I am *not* picky!" Rachel huffed.

"Are so," Mark added, selling the bizarre pretext.

Major Keller peered around with glassy eyes as Kate and the kids left the booth. "Be nimble. Torpor is death becoming."

"Hesitation's a hole in the head, sir," Reed agreed, smiling blandly at him.

David let Kate and the kids walk in front of him, falling behind Reed as he hurried to the entrance of the diner.

"Hey! Where're y'all going now?" the waitress called after them as she hurried from behind the diner's lunch counter. "Your food is almost ready!"

"Oh, we'll be right back, ma'am," Reed said. "I can promise you that."

"Well, okay..." She angled to the booth by the door where the Marines were sitting. "What can I get you fellas?"

The soldiers addressed the waitress, and David caught a glimpse of something strange. Three dark red punctures and red, swollen skin on each of their necks. He couldn't tell if all four had the same wounds, but it was enough that two of them did.

His mind flashed to the puncture marks on his ankle that had been left by that giant spider on the *Interloper*, and a shiver of apprehension rocked through him.

David burst outside to see his family and Private Reed running for their truck. He sprinted to catch up. Within moments, Private Reed was spinning the tires in the snowy parking lot.

"Here they come!" Kate cried as the soldiers exited the diner. One of them drew their sidearm and opened fire. Bullets plinked off the truck while Private Reed gunned the engine to rejoin the highway.

"Take it!" Reed said, drawing the scanner from his vest and tossing it at David.

He caught it awkwardly and checked the holographic map. It showed the diner with multiple yellow-shaded, human signatures inside. In the parking lot five green-shaded people were busy cramming into a second JLTV.

Green. The Stalkers had been green, too. The scanner's color-coding system was no coincidence. And it explained a lot.

"Those soldiers aren't on our team," David said slowly.

"No shit," Private Reed replied. "And they're giving chase."

David watched their truck reverse, then plow onto the highway.

"They're gaining on us!" Kate screamed.

"I see it!" Reed shouted. He glanced at David, and his gaze landed on the alien pulse rifle. "You know how to use that?"

"No!" David replied.

"You'd better figure it out quick."

EIGHT

Atlas

Montpelier, Vermont

"This is the place?" James Wan asked, sliding his sunglasses down the bridge of his nose. He seemed impressed.

"My brother's done well for himself." Atlas hadn't visited in a couple of years, and now that he was here, he recalled why.

The house, while technically not a mansion, was immaculate. The yard, despite the time of year, remained pristine, ready for the inevitable first snowfall. It was an old colonial restored to its former glory, complete with the white picket fence. It reminded Atlas of everything he'd missed out on.

"You two close?" James parked, glancing in his mirror before opening the door.

"Not particularly."

"I know your line about needing your files was crap," James told him. "You want to protect them."

"Wouldn't you? Don't you have any family?"

James shook his head. "Just my team members."

"I'm sorry."

"For what? We aren't that different, Atlas."

Atlas got out, imagining how this conversation would go. It was midday, the sun high, descending to the West, and he squinted as the front door swung wide.

"Atlas?"

"I told you I was coming," he said.

Hayden walked toward the sidewalk, scanning both directions before staring at James. "Who's this?"

"My friend. James, meet Hayden."

They nodded at one another, but his brother had a skeptical expression. Even after all their years apart, Atlas could still read him like a book.

"It's good to see you." Hayden hugged Atlas, patting his back twice before letting go.

Atlas had borrowed clothing from Booth's facility, and he felt slightly foolish in the dark blue pants and white dress shirt. He left the cuffs rolled up, and followed Hayden into the house. "Where are the kids?"

"It's a school day. They'll be home with Lisa in an hour or so," Hayden said.

Atlas sighed in relief. The moment the door closed, he moved into the kitchen. He smelled coffee, and saw Hayden's Holoscreens propped on the island. Financial numbers were streaming over the displays. "Working from home?"

"I *am* the boss," Hayden reminded him.

"Right. There's something I need to discuss with you." He glanced at James, who stayed in the front entrance.

"Who the hell is that, really?" Hayden whispered.

"He's here to protect me."

"From whom?"

Atlas had done the speech in his head over and over, but now he realized it wouldn't work. "Aliens have landed on Earth."

Hayden stayed rooted, a twitch on his lip; restrained amusement, waiting for the punchline.

James stepped in, his boots loud on the hardwood. "Atlas, you were ordered..."

Atlas lifted a hand, and James stopped. "Hayden, I'm not kidding. That big flash over the Atlantic... the meteor shower. That was their ship crashing. It's all being covered up."

"No. You've finally lost it." Hayden rubbed his stubble. "Lisa warned me this would happen."

"What would?"

"That your delusions of grandeur would grow worse. That you might require medication, or hospitalization."

Atlas slammed a palm onto the table, knocking a glass over. The water spilled onto the floor, but neither of them moved to clean it up. "Listen to me. There are a thousand nine-foot giants roaming this planet, and countless other monstrosities. Any one of them could kill you and your family."

Hayden grabbed his shirt, dragging him closer. Atlas let it happen. He wasn't here to fight his brother; he came to protect him. "That's enough. Either you get some help or I'll get it for you."

"He's telling the truth." The words surprised Atlas as much as they did Hayden. "Atlas means to give you a shot at survival."

Atlas staggered back when he was released.

"You're saying that aliens actually crash-landed on Earth?"

"Technically, our own people may have crashed their ship, but that's not important," Atlas mumbled.

Hayden paced the kitchen, glancing to the door like his wife might enter at any moment, catching him red-handed. "Unbelievable. You've always had one foot on another planet."

"We think Atlas might be able to help us," James told Hayden, and now his brother started to laugh.

"This has to be a joke."

"As we speak, there are covert teams spread around the world, trying to clean up the mess. The Stalkers escaped the *Interloper* in pods, and they're searching for something important," James said. "Atlas and I are going to find it first, but you have to cooperate, because the longer you delay Atlas, the worse our odds become."

Hayden just stared at James, then gawked at Atlas. "No way. This is a setup. I don't know what you're doing, Atlas, but it's wrong. If you need money, just come out and ask for it."

A shiny chrome handgun appeared from nowhere, and James aimed it at Hayden. "If you're going to impede our progress, I've been authorized to... oblige your cooperation."

"What the hell are you doing?" Atlas stepped between them, the gun pointed at his chest now. "Put that away." He turned to Hayden. "We'll go to the cabin. You still have it, right?"

Hayden nodded once. "Of course. Dad left it for me. I'm not selling it."

"Pack their things. I'll box the food." Atlas went to the cabinets, rifling through the pantry.

Hayden lingered for a moment. "Lisa's a doctor. My kids have school, and I have a business to run. This is absurd."

"There won't be any money flowing if we fail," Atlas said. "James... please convince him." This was his last-ditch effort, and he wished there was another way, because once you saw a Stalker, you'd never unsee it.

James Wan wasn't supposed to reveal the aliens to any civilians, but he must have realized it was the fastest approach to keep them moving. "This is a Stalker." He rotated the Holo so Hayden could see it. Four legs. Black exoskeleton. The body was on the ground, killed by a Dark operative. The image shifted to a map, and he zoomed on Vermont. "A pod landed forty miles away. There are four of these creatures on the loose nearby. Will you risk it?"

Hayden went white, and he sat in a kitchen chair. "This is insane. Why isn't this on the news?"

"Because the Association doesn't want people to know. It's our job to intercept this before the world turns to shit. And mark my words, it will... and soon. We can only contain things for so long."

The front door burst open, and Atlas heard the patter of children's footsteps as they rushed in after a day of classes. Wyatt was the first to enter, tossing his backpack to the floor. "Dad?"

"You remember your uncle?"

"Uncle Atlas!" Paige ran at him, hugging him tightly at the waist.

He crouched, smiling at the girl. "Hi Paige. Did you have a good day?"

Lisa walked in, wearing her scrubs from her shift at the hospital. "Atlas." She glanced at James. Luckily, he'd concealed his weapon. "What's going on, Hayden?"

"We have to go."

"Go?" Her eyes flicked between them. "I brought a roast chicken for dinner. And I had a tough day. I need a glass of wine and a soak."

"Lisa," Hayden hissed. "Get your things from the room. I'll bring the luggage."

"What's gotten into you? And who is he?" Lisa jabbed a finger at James Wan.

Paige's lip trembled. "Daddy. What's wrong?"

"I'm a friend of Atlas', and you should listen to your husband," James said quietly.

"This is weird." Wyatt was a skinny kid, all arms and legs. "I was supposed to go to Fred's..."

"No devices," James said. "Turn off your Holos."

Lisa frowned, fury boiling beneath the surface. "If someone doesn't explain..."

"We're leaving for the cabin," Atlas said. "A few days of rest and relaxation. Doesn't that sound fun?"

"But I have school tomorrow," Paige whined.

"No devices, no screens. We can read a book. Go fishing," Hayden told his family.

"Kids, go grab your things. Toothbrushes. Clothes. Jackets. Okay?" Atlas suggested, and they ran off.

"Will you tell me what the hell is going on?" Lisa kept her voice down.

"I'll tell you when we arrive," Atlas said.

"At the cabin?"

James checked his Holo. "Our ride is close."

Hayden's yard backed onto a playground, and Atlas peered through the windows, seeing the incoming helicopter. It lowered, sending fall leaves twirling in the sky.

"They're here for us?" Lisa whispered, then looked at her husband. "It's that serious?"

He nodded, and touched her cheek. "We'll be safe."

"Safe from what? Please tell me we're not running from the SEC. What did you get yourself into, Hayden?"

"No. Nothing like that. I'll clarify everything later."

"Let's move out," James said.

***

David

Rural Alaska

61

David leaned out the door, balancing the alien pulse rifle in his lap and holding the strangely curving butt of the weapon against his shoulder. The wind from their passage hammered the door, pinning him in the opening. He squinted through a swirling wall of snow from a fresh storm as Private Reed roared down the highway. David couldn't see their pursuit, but Major Keller and his Marines couldn't be far behind. What was *wrong* with them? He recalled the puncture wounds on their necks. The strange, almost illogical way the Major had been talking. It was as if he'd lost his mind.

"Any sign of them?" Reed called.

"They fell back!" David shouted. "Visibility isn't good enough to see if they're still there!"

"Just take a shot!" Reed cried. "Guess!"

"I could hit a civilian!"

"Or, you could waste so much time waiting for a shot that you get us killed!"

David grimaced and took a moment to steady the weapon in his lap. He'd found what seemed to be the trigger—a small, cylindrical button about a quarter of an inch long, shielded from accidental misfires by a curving metal plate. The trigger was situated in the middle of the four-foot length, making it uncomfortable to fire one-handed, but he managed by jamming the stock of it under his armpit.

Sighting down the top of the barrel, David worked to slow his breathing and peered through the shifting veils of snow, hoping to catch a hint of a shadow that might indicate their pursuers.

A glimmer of headlights strobed the murky walls of snow. Still, David hesitated, not wanting to pick off some local family by accident.

"You're going too fast!" he called to Private Reed.

"What?"

"Just ease up!"

The truck's frame dug into his chest as Reed hit the brakes. A boxy outline snapped into focus, too large to be a civilian vehicle. David squeezed the trigger.

The weapon went off with a sharp crack and a bright flash. Recoil kicked weakly into his armpit, and a ball of superheated plasma burst across the hood. It glowed orange, then faded. Nothing happened.

One of the doors flew wide, and a rifle appeared. A rattling hail of bullets plinked into the back end of their truck. David ducked into cover.

"What happened?" Reed demanded, pressing the accelerator again.

"I connected with the hood. It didn't do anything, though."

"The batteries and motors are in the chassis, between the wheels. You have to aim lower!"

A deafening roar of bullets peppered their armor, causing Rachel and Mark to scream. Kate held them close, covering their ears. "David, do something!" she cried.

He winced and steeled himself. He dropped his aim just as Private Reed suggested.

David pulled the trigger. Another crack and flash burst across the trailing vehicle's bumper, and a thick, greasy cloud of smoke gushed out, as they swerved into a snowdrift. A split second later, bright flames illuminated the swirling haze, followed by the muffled roar of an explosion.

David forced a grim smile. "Got 'em."

"Nice work," Private Reed replied, a muscle twitching in his jaw. "Now we need to find a new place to lie low while we figure out what the next step is."

"Can't we just go to a military base?" Kate asked.

"Where do you think Major Keller came from?" Private Reed countered. "If he was compromised, there's no telling how many other people are. We don't know who to trust at this point, and that's a big damn problem."

"Compromised by *what?*" Kate asked. "What was wrong with him?"

David and Reed stared at one another in silence.

"What?" Kate demanded.

"I believe we're looking at an alien parasite," David said. "I saw a pattern of puncture wounds on the Marines' necks. Like bite marks."

Private Reed nodded gravely. "Exactly."

"From what? The Stalkers?" Kate asked.

"Spiders," David replied.

"But I thought they crashed with you off the coast of Boston?" Kate countered. "They can't have crawled all the way to Alaska in such a short time."

"No," David agreed. "Which means either the Stalkers brought some in their escape pods, or..."

"Or?"

"Or they hitched a ride with us," David finished.

Kate shivered violently with the thought. "Our bags are in the back. Are they still ... in there?"

"Let's not jump to any conclusions," Private Reed cautioned. "We'll check our gear soon as we can, but since none of us has been bitten yet, I'd say we're probably okay. If we brought the parasites with us, how did they find Keller? He wasn't on the cargo plane with us."

"True," David admitted, and he sighed in relief. They had enough to worry about without adding the lurking threat of alien hitchhikers to the mix.

***

Atlas

Rural Northern Vermont

The place looked identical to the last time he'd visited. The wooden shingles and siding were slightly more deteriorated, but otherwise, it was filled with memories of his childhood.

His mom sitting on the front porch for hours, mending their torn pants. Dad out back, chopping wood, and wasting hours like you could only do at a cabin.

The helicopter's rotors slowed, and the pilot stayed while they all exited.

"This is awesome," Wyatt said, jumping to the pine-needle covered ground.

Paige had a smile on her face. "Why don't we use helicopters every day?"

Atlas just shrugged, grabbing a bag of food, and stalked toward the house. He glanced to the side, seeing the old bird house he and Hayden had built when they were ten and twelve. It was crooked, but remained after all these years.

Hayden unlocked the door, and James went in first, likely fighting the urge to sweep the premises. He did walk through it, checking the rooms quickly before Hayden let his family enter.

"What was that all about?" Lisa asked. "Can you tell me now?"

"Hayden, why don't you set up the family?" Atlas motioned to the bedrooms, and his brother took their luggage.

"Come on, kids."

When they were out of earshot, Atlas told her the same story, expressing how important it was to stay discreet.

"And I'm to believe this? Aliens are on Earth? And you're involved?"

"I understand your hesitation, but..."

"Atlas, you were never a good brother. And you're an even worse uncle. The kids don't even know you," she said, and Atlas felt the sting of her words.

"I'm sorry." He had nothing else to say.

Lisa sighed with her hands on her hips and stared at the sky while the sun lowered in the distance. "I won't say anything. But if aliens are upon us, please don't let my family be harmed."

"I'll do my best."

"That's not good enough," Lisa said. "Promise me."

He cleared his throat and glanced at the front porch where James was waiting impatiently. "I promise, Lisa."

"Okay. Get what you came for and leave." Lisa walked away.

Atlas left through the back entrance, going to the bunkhouse behind the cabin. He and Hayden had spent half their summers there, reading comics and playing with toys. It wasn't even locked, and he tugged the handle. The room was musty, the ceiling stained from water damage. But the trunk was right in between the pair of cots. The lamp perched on the flat top of the chest had a frayed wire, and Atlas spotted rat pellets on the floor.

He tossed the fixture aside, and opened the lid. It was stuffed full of newspaper articles, beige folders, and journals. It looked like a hurricane had torn through it, but Atlas recalled his own filing system. He dug into the lower section and collected anything pertaining to the Amazon.

Atlas sat on the mattress, the rusted springs groaning from his weight. He skimmed the papers, and grinned when he uncovered the map. Three marks were highlighted with red stars, and he recalled the information Booth had given him.

Atlas reached for his Holo, finding the proper program, and compared the two maps. His three markers perfectly coincided with some of the general's. These locations were where they would begin the search.

He took the map, and shoved the rest into the trunk. With a final glance around, he closed the lid and walked to the front of the cabin.

"I'm ready." Atlas watched his brother's family at the kitchen table. Lisa was preparing dinner, and Hayden sat with his kids, smiling and engaging with them.

"It's getting dark. We can leave in the morning if you'd like," James said.

"No. Time is of the essence."

NINE

Carter

Somewhere in Northern Alaska

C arter sank into his chair and arched his aching back. He stretched his arms above his head, then inverted the posture. His eyes hurt from hours spent staring at his screen. It was late. Everyone had clocked out for the night and gone to bed, including Doctor Nielson. Even Chris, the alien captive, was snoozing in his giant glass cube.

But Carter couldn't sleep. He was too busy working on the problem. Trying to decipher a puzzle that didn't make sense. The Grazers could mimic human languages almost perfectly, yet they didn't use sound to communicate. Instead, they relied on pictures for a written language, and on modulated vibrations as a form of spoken language. In a sense, that was the same as any other spoken language, just that they perceived it more through touch than hearing. Vibrations and sound were one and the same, after all.

But alien humming and purring noises weren't exactly the easiest codes to crack. Carter had thoroughly examined the work Nielson's team had done so far. They'd assigned sequences to various English *words* with some reasonable degree of confidence, but their dictionary of the Grazer language was depressingly light, considering how long they'd been at it.

When he'd asked Doctor Nielson about it, she'd given him a cryptic answer. "Go ahead and see if you can do any better."

So he'd devoted his day to showing the alien images of people, places, and objects from Earth, attempting to convince Chris to put names to them. An apple. A boat. A tree. A lake. Grass... Doctor Nielson. The Grazer had played ball for a little while, giving him a few new words to work with. *Lake* was one. So was *boat*. And roughly a dozen other words. As it turned out, Chris already had a word for Doctor Nielson. It was the same as his word for *human excrement*, which for some reason, had already been logged in the dictionary.

The next one hundred words that Carter tried to establish all received the same response. *Human excrement. Human excrement. Human excrement.*

Eventually, Carter gave up. It seemed that Doctor Nielson's lack of progress with translating the aliens' language wasn't a result of the Grazer's inability to communicate with them, but rather of his unwillingness to do so.

Throughout the day Chris had made one or two attempts of his own to communicate with Carter, each time placing his three-fingered hand against the glass and giving him a unique string of vibrations to record and process. Of course, Carter had studied them and translated what he could from their dictionary. Despite vast gaps in their lexicon, several words had been translated from those sequences: *Signal. Grazers. Death. Home. Earth. Stalkers. Humans.*

Carter could infer any number of things from all of that—and none of them good. But he was at his wit's end with what the Grazer was trying to communicate. Was this so-called Signal good or bad? Was it a physical item, or a message that had been sent ages ago? Where was home, and why had this Grazer left?

It was frustrating, to say the least. Carter looked up from his screens and his desk, his sight lingering on the Grazer's cell.

To his surprise, Chris was standing and observing him. Like the Stalkers, he didn't appear to wear any clothes. Then again, he didn't have any dangling bits that might correspond to genitalia. Just glossy black skin. A pair of long, thin legs with two sets of knees. Skinny arms that dangled precariously close to the floor.

Carter rose and walked to the glass holding cell.

Chris placed his palm on it, and Carter matched the action, feeling a fresh sequence of vibrations pulsing through the barrier.

"If you want me to understand what you're saying, you have to put in the work!" Carter said. The Grazer clearly understood what words were, and he could *see*, so he definitely knew how to assign vibrations to visible stimuli.

Four big, black eyes blinked slowly at him, the translucent lids sweeping over them.

The nose in the center of Chris's forehead dilated suddenly and fogged up his side of the glass, as if he'd sighed, or snorted with disgust.

"Yeah, I'm frustrated, too," Carter muttered. On a whim, he pulled out his Holo and opened his old translator app. He activated it, giving the AI a chance to listen and learn from the Grazer's language.

He watched a blue status bar run in circles above the word: *Analyzing...*

Chris stopped sending vibrations through the glass.

And Carter's program dinged with a result.

More input required.

Carter made a face and sighed. "No kidding. Apparently that's been the problem for the past decade. More input required."

Chris smacked his lips, then opened his jaws wide and gave his sideways imitation of a smile. It was a creepy jack-o-lantern expression, but a smile nonetheless.

The Grazer seemed to be searching for something. Or someone.

Chris touched the clear barrier and spoke once more.

"Human excrement?" a computerized voice asked. It was the lab's automatic translator. Any time it detected a word that was already in their dictionary, it translated it audibly for everyone to hear.

"Not funny," Carter said.

Another vibration. *"Human excrement?"*

Carter sighed and rubbed his eyes. Back to this. "I have to go to bed," he muttered.

When Chris didn't react, Carter mimed the action. Yawning, and putting his hands together to lay his head on an imaginary pillow. He shut his eyes.

"Sleep," Carter explained.

69

The Grazer grew agitated, and raised an arm, pointing to the side of his cage.

At least he knows a few human gestures, Carter thought bitterly. He followed the alien finger's trajectory.

The airlock. Chris jabbed in that direction once more. Then swept his arm around and aimed at Carter's chest. The message seemed clear.

"You... want me to go inside?" Carter asked.

Chris repeated the gestures, more emphatically this time.

Doubt and fear wormed through Carter. The very first rule Doctor Nielson had established was that direct physical contact with the subject was strictly prohibited. The only ones who could enter the cube were the alien's handlers, and even they had to enter in hazmats after knocking Chris out with gas.

But maybe their work was stalled for a reason. They were treating Chris like a prisoner rather than an equal, and somehow, they expected his cooperation? No wonder he was calling everything *human excrement*.

Carter smiled wryly. "You've got an attitude, haven't you, Chris?"

The alien dropped its arm and slowly blinked, as if waiting for him to respond to its request. Carter glanced at the hazmat lockers. He'd never be able to put one of those suits on and enter the cube before security came running to stop him. The lab was monitored twenty-four hours a day from a watch station right outside. The reinforced glass of the observation window illuminated with bluish light from the screens within. He couldn't see the pair of guards, but they could see him.

Would they be fast enough to stop him from climbing into the cube with Chris?

There's only one way to find out, he thought.

***

Lennon

Rural Bayou, Southeast Louisiana

Lennon wished they had full wetsuits on, but had to settle for the half-masks and covered hands. The bayou was a horrible place for hunting Stalkers. Her footsteps were tentative, never certain if she'd find solid ground or fall through the moss into the swamp.

Dark Twenty spat, wiping his mouth. "If I swallow another mosquito, I won't need dinner."

They'd arrived early in the day, but now, traversing the harsh landscape in the dark was proving a challenge.

Rutger was quieter than normal, and Lennon could tell from his posture that he was pissed off.

"It should have been here," he whispered. He opened his Holo for the tenth time in the last hour and stared at the screen. "It's supposed to be right there."

"This sucks," Dark Thirty-Four said. Brighton turned a flashlight on as the tree cover grew thicker. Lennon was glad to have waterproof boots, but the dampness had begun coating her uniform.

"There it is!" Hank roared, and Lennon slapped a palm over his face.

"Would you keep it down?" she hissed. "Where did you find this guy?"

"It's hard to tell how loud someone is from a file," Rutger explained, and Hank cast his gaze to the swamp.

The nose of the escape pod protruded from the water about a quarter-mile away.

"How do we get to it?" Brighton asked.

Rutger stepped in, sinking up to his waist. "We wade."

"Twenty, stay here." Lennon gestured to a nearby tree, heavy with vines. "And check for snakes before you settle in."

Dark Twenty's eyes darted around. "Snakes?"

Lennon followed Rutger, holding her alien gun above her head. Brighton mimicked her, moving silently in the rear.

They got to the pod a few minutes later, and she glanced up, seeing the crescent moon. For a moment, the entire region was peaceful. Just the sounds of nature. Insects buzzing, the occasional chirp of a bird finding food.

The door was submerged, and Rutger dove below. Lennon stayed alert while Dark One descended into the murky water.

She spotted the eyes before she could warn Hank.

The giant beast lunged, but this was no Stalker.

"What the..." Hank shouted as the alligator clamped onto his arm. His armor protected him, but the gator thrashed and rolled, dragging him into the swamp.

"Stay here!" Lennon bellowed at Brighton just as Rutger breached the surface, looking around.

Lennon hurriedly pointed her gun at the alligator. Hank was underwater, and she exhaled to steady her aim, then fired.

The blast of light shot from her weapon, striking the animal in its flank. It let go, its tail flailing behind it. Lennon didn't bother wasting her gun's energy cell with another shot. Half of the gator had melted away from the pulse.

She grabbed Hank and lifted with all her might. He gasped for air and struggled to his feet. "You saved me."

Lennon heard a noise, a chittering she was far too familiar with. "Don't be so sure."

Three of the Stalkers dropped from the trees, the nearest landing directly in the water between Rutger and Lennon. The other two were farther away. Their shrieks carried over the bayou, making her cringe. "With me, Hank!" She crouched in the water, trying to make herself smaller-looking. Brighton had already climbed onto the nose of the pod, and she fired a high-caliber semi-automatic rifle at the pair of Stalkers. Rutger's attention was on the closest one.

It all happened so fast. Lennon used the second to last shot on her weapon, hitting the beast in the legs. It hobbled away on two, blasting the water directly in front of her into steam. Hank shoved her back, his hair singed from the heat.

Brighton's bullets plinked off their armored bodies, the distance making it impossible to target their eyes. Lennon had to do something. She dragged herself from the swamp, running as fast as she could toward the Stalkers. This caught them off guard. They probably assumed their prey would flee, but they were dead wrong.

Lennon heard a scream from Brighton, and a splash as a fourth Stalker arrived, descending from the trees. Rutger yelled, firing his own gun and cursing the aliens.

She tried to remain focused. One of the Stalkers moved away, creeping toward Rutger from the opposite end of the swamp. The second was injured from her blast, and she dropped the depleted alien tech, opting for her sidearm instead as she barreled into the beast.

Lennon slammed the butt of the gun into its face while she sat on its chest, and it bucked, trying to throw her off. Lennon hit it again and spun the barrel around, shoving it into the thing's gaping nostril. She pulled the trigger and slid off while the Stalker went limp.

Despite the exhaustion in her muscles, she wasn't done. Lennon saw the team was struggling to survive. The Stalkers were much better in the water than they were. All three operatives moved into the swamp, and Rutger hid behind the pod with Brighton, popping off the odd shot in the alien's direction. They were running out of time.

Hank was already facing one of them, and she watched as he tossed his giant gun to the side, pulling a bowie knife from his thigh. He held it up, and Lennon dove, knowing he wouldn't stand a chance.

She kicked hard, swimming below the surface, and opened her eyes. The water looked like pea soup in the light of the lamp attached to her scuba mask. She saw the flicking tail, the glowing eyes as she arrived, and reached for Hank as the Stalker rose, aiming its weapon at Dark Twenty.

"Get under!" she called, and Hank did.

The alligator lunged, grabbing the Stalker's gun arm, and Lennon smirked, firing her gun at the ugly head while it was distracted. She blasted it in the eye, and the massive beast flopped into the water. The alligator still had hold of its appendage, dragging and rolling the corpse into the swamp.

Lennon scrambled to solid ground, sitting on the moss and gasping from the exertion. Hank came after, and the sounds of gunfire had faded to ringing echoes in her ears.

She stared across to the pod and spotted Dark One holding someone.

"No," she whispered.

Rutger met her gaze, and it told her everything she needed to know.

Brighton was dead.

TEN

Carter

Somewhere in Northern Alaska

Carter hurried into the airlock. The security codes Dr. Neilson had given him to access the project files worked, which was a stroke of luck. He held his breath as red warning lights flashed and decontamination sprays misted the little cubicle between him and the Grazer's living space. As soon as the indicators turned green and those sprays ended, he reached for the access panel to open the inner hatch.

Hesitation arrested his arm. He wondered if there might be another reason that the handlers used hazmats to go inside the cube. Was there something about the Grazer's atmosphere that was toxic to humans? Or maybe it simply wasn't breathable.

"Hey!" The muffled shout startled him, and Carter sucked in a stinging breath of lingering chemicals in the airlock. He turned to see security guards running at him from the watch station. No time left to hesitate. He slapped the access panel, and the door sprang open. Carter stumbled through as Chris stepped into view. The smell smacked him in the face. It was like a fish market in here. But so far, at least, he could still breathe.

Chris hummed, and Carter spun around to shut the airlock behind him— to find that it had already closed.

The security guards were gawking at him, their rifles drawn and aimed.

"What? He's harmless!" Carter shouted. He smiled reassuringly, then faced the alien.

Chris gave him a slow, eerie smile, and then reached for him. Carter experienced another moment of doubt. *Maybe this was a bad idea...* He backed up against the wall of the cube. Chris curled his fingers around Carter's wrists, seizing them in an iron grip and pinning them to the sides of the chamber.

"Hey, I'm on your team!" Carter yelped. "You wanted to talk, didn't you?"

Vibrations pulsed through the alien's hands, making Carter's teeth ache and his bones shiver. The creature's head lowered until it was at eye level with him, and its mouth slowly parted, revealing dull rows of translucent teeth, designed for munching grass or some alien equivalent, not for tearing flesh.

Taking comfort in that, Carter tried on a shaky smile. "Very nice. You must brush after every meal."

"We need a containment unit in the lab!" he overheard one of the guards saying.

A shadow flickered inside the alien's throat. Legs curled around both sets of lips, and a familiar, fist-sized creature crawled out.

"What the..." Carter's smile vanished as the spider rotated its body to confront him. "Help! Somebody help me!" It sprang from the Grazer and landed on his face. Carter screamed continuously as it crawled over his eyes and forehead, into his hair... then onto the back of his neck. Something sharp pricked through his skin, followed by a spreading warmth and sense of calm. His body grew numb, and his eyes dim. He felt like he was floating on a cloud.

The Grazer's language shuddered through him. Sequences and patterns flickered through his mind like musical notes, accompanied by flashes of light and bursts of color. His whole body had become an instrument, resonating with combinations of pitch and frequency that somehow coalesced into vivid meaning. Suddenly he *knew* what the Grazer had been trying to say for all these years.

Carter gasped, and his eyes shot open. He was lying trembling on the concrete floor of the lab, his clothes drenched with sweat.

Doctor Nielson and three others were crowded around him. One of them, a woman with gaunt cheeks and hollow blue eyes, was holding the paddles of a defibrillator.

Nielson's gaze sharpened. "What the hell were you thinking? You almost died in there!"

Carter sat up, for the moment ignoring the signs that he'd just suffered a near death experience.

"I felt it..." Carter whispered slowly. Remembering the creature that had emerged from the Grazer's mouth, he shivered and hesitantly reached for the back of his neck. There were three raised and crusted indentations where chunks had been bitten from his flesh, but the spider was no longer there.

"We removed it," the one holding the defibrillator said. Carter seemed to recall her name was Leslie and she was from Austria. "But it escaped."

"Felt what?" Dr. Nielson insisted, drawing Carter's attention back to her.

"What he's been trying to tell us," Carter said. "I know why they're here. All of them. The Stalkers and Spiders. The Grazers. Those four-legged pods..."

Nielson's eyebrows shot up, waiting for him to go on. When he didn't, she grabbed his shoulders and shook him. "Carter! What are you talking about?"

He was struggling to focus through the cottony haze lingering in his head. That sensation of floating clung to him, but he was crashing fast. Whatever feel-good chemicals that spider had injected into his system, their effect was wearing off quickly, but the message lingered, emblazoned in his mind.

"The Stalkers sent ships to search for the Grazers' colonies," he croaked, his throat feeling suddenly dry and chalky. "Can I have something to drink?"

Nielson snapped her fingers at a guard standing behind her. "Water. Quick."

He rushed off and returned a few seconds later, holding a gleaming flask. Carter took it and gulped greedily.

"Thank you." He wiped his lips on his sleeve. With a glance at Dr. Nielson, he went on. "The *Interloper* found Christopher's home world, but before it could activate its Signal and call for the others to come, the Grazers stole the device and hid it on Earth. The Stalkers tracked them here to retrieve it. But..." Carter trailed off, struggling to remember.

A humming sound trickled to his ears, drawing his attention to the cube. Chris was staring at them with both of his hands touching the glass. It droned another sequence, and Carter realized that he actually understood what the Grazer was saying.

"They didn't know that Earth was habitable. Or that it was already home to so many different forms of life. Now he's afraid that the Stalkers won't bother looking for his people anymore, and that they'll simply activate the Signal to bring their fleet here, instead."

Dr. Nielson started to speak, then promptly shut it, looking troubled. She tried again. "Where did they hide the Signal?"

More humming resonated from the cube.

"Forest... ship... crash... find... Stalkers... Death... Humans.... Grazers." the lab's automatic translator said.

"Get him up!" Nielson snapped at the guards. "Bring him to the cube."

"It's okay," Carter said, waving them off and coming to his feet on his own. "I can hear Chris just fine from here. He said, it's in the big forest where the other ship crashed, and that we need to find it before the Stalkers do, or else they'll do the same thing to us as they did to his people."

"And what did they do to his people?" Nielson asked, her eyes flicking between Carter and the alien in the holding cell.

More murmurs issued from the Grazer, pitching up and down sharply. The lab's computer picked out and translated known words once more: "Death... Grazers... End..."

"Deactivate automatic translation!" Nielson snapped, and silence rang in the wake of her command. "Well?" she demanded, pointing at the Grazer. "What did it say?"

"He said the Stalkers hunted them to extinction. They only survived because they fled into space."

Dr. Nielson scowled and drew her Holo from a pocket in her lab coat. "Call Dark Leader."

Carter blinked. "You have his number?"

Nielson looked amused. "Why wouldn't I?"

"Doctor, I hope you have good news for me," a familiar voice answered.

"Good and bad. You were right about the Signal. Carter made a breakthrough."

"I had a feeling he might."

Nielson held out the device to Carter. "You want to tell him yourself?"

He swallowed thickly and reached for it. "Hello...?" Carter tried.

"Doctor Robinson. Let's hear it. What have you learned from our friend?"

Chris spoke again, and Carter couldn't help but smile. "He says he's not your friend."

"Says?" Dark Leader muttered. "You mean you can understand him? Fluently?"

"Yes, sir." But Dark Leader gave no reply. He went so long without speaking that Carter had to ask, "Are you still there?"

"Tell me everything."

ELEVEN

Atlas

Burlington International Airport

"Ever get used to flying like this?" Atlas asked James. Their handful of possessions was stowed away on the private plane.

"Sure. If it suits you just the same, I prefer to travel in silence," James Wan said, boarding the jet. Atlas nodded, stepping after him.

It was nice. Roomy. The kind of luxury he could never afford. He flopped onto a seat and grabbed his Holo, scanning the feeds. The top story revolved around a presidential address from Carver, a few short hours ago. Atlas checked the time, seeing it was well after two in the morning. They were already later than he'd hoped.

The pilot didn't bother with any of the pleasantries, and the only uniformed staff was a dour-looking woman who didn't offer Atlas anything but a glare. That was fine. He could sleep, and maybe compile the best beginning locations to choose from. If Booth was correct, and Atlas presumed he was, the Signal wouldn't stay hidden for long.

The pressure building on his shoulders was immense. Booth promised to have his best and brightest prepared for extraction and support the moment he needed it, but Atlas was fully aware that the Dark Teams were currently spread thin across the globe, fighting Stalkers.

Atlas glanced across the cabin, seeing James' eyes were already closed. His chest rose and fell softly, indicating he was asleep. Must be nice to have that kind of control over your body. Even if he attempted to doze off, his mind would keep him up for hours.

Atlas linked his earbud with the Holo, and pressed play on the full address. The President spoke of staying vigilant in the coming days. That a war might be transpiring overseas. He kept the troubling comments full of diversions and hearsay. Conjecture and handwaving. It was classic President Carver. Atlas hadn't voted for the guy, even if the party was his first choice. There was something off-putting about his slicked back hair, his smile gleaming but never reaching his eyes.

Atlas didn't trust him. He watched the feed, not actually hearing anything of value, and near the end, the man lifted three fingers and stared into the camera. He said a series of words, Atlas could barely decipher. He cranked the volume, playing it above the sounds of the plane's vibrating engines.

"What's he saying?" Atlas muttered to himself.

He read the comments on one of the more liberal sites, and scanned through the common trashing, stopping on a later message.

He's saying numbers. Maybe code for something? 3581547.

It's an old code for a program at the Arecibo Observatory, another poster said.

Atlas wondered if that was true. He replayed it and mouthed the words.

There were several vague responses, mostly childish comments.

He took a screenshot and forwarded it to Booth, just in case the man's intel was as tired as James Wan, and closed the program. It was time to get to business. He only had a few hours to prepare. Once they dropped in Rio, a helicopter would be waiting, stocked with provisions, two backpacks, and hopefully an array of weapons. Brazil was huge, with immense regions of difficult terrain. Atlas wasn't prepared for what was coming; he could feel it in his bones.

Driving around Asia with a fake name was one thing, but contending with the wild in the Amazon was an entirely different skill set.

Atlas overlapped the maps he'd brought from his family cabin, and added them to the high-tech map provided by Booth. He clicked the three spots that were the closest, finding information about the regions. It had notes revealing any documented details on the areas, but one spot had nothing. It was as if the marker wasn't placed in a settled location. No one had walked or searched it, and from what he could tell, it was near the Amazon River, by the Peruvian border. His finger rubbed the side of the Holo. He trusted his gut, and it was guiding him to that last checkpoint.

He checked to see if Dark Leader responded, with no luck. Atlas was sure the guy had more important things to deal with than a midnight message from him.

The seat was comfortable, but his bladder had other ideas. He got up, walking quietly past Wan so as not to wake him, and the woman emerged from the cockpit. She stared at him, and he just smiled.

"Hello. Thanks for bringing us," he told her.

She nodded once, her lips a straight line.

"I'm Atlas."

Her eyes drifted to the sealed door on the side of the plane. "Nadine." The word sounded alien on her tongue.

"Are you sure?" he joked, but she didn't laugh. He proceeded, wanting to be as far away from *Nadine* as possible. She was probably just upset she'd been called in for a red-eye to Brazil last minute. Ten or so hours each direction, even at the speed the pilot was being paid to maintain.

He used the bathroom, splashing water on his face before returning to his seat. Nadine was gone, and he was relieved. Atlas yawned and thought about his brother as they flew. The occasional bump of turbulence kept him alert. Hayden had always been his parents' favorite, and Atlas knew why.

The man had lived his best life while Atlas worked tirelessly to obtain the artifacts. And now he'd learned it was all real, and that he might be able to help save the world. Booth was putting a lot of faith in him, but if he guessed right, there were other people searching for it too. There was no way a man of his means would be leaving it all in Atlas' hands. If he was, he was even crazier than Atlas had originally thought.

Eventually, as the plane flew over hours' worth of ocean, he fell into a slumber.

He dreamed of a glowing Signal, and a red sky flush with lightning.

***

David

Dot Lake, Alaska

David sat by a roaring fire with Kate cuddled in close. Reed was opposite them on an old, cracking brown leather loveseat by the front window. The log cabin was small, with two bedrooms and one bath, but it held the heat in reasonably well. Everyone was on their second cups of coffee for the morning. They'd already eaten pancakes from a box, courtesy of Private Reed. The mix was past its expiration, but they didn't tell the kids that.

"I've had worse," Reed had quipped while stirring in water from the tap.

Judging by the layer of dust over everything, David deduced that this cabin must have been empty for years, which made him feel better about breaking in. At least the owners wouldn't catch them here.

After escaping Major Keller and the Marines, Private Reed had driven north and chosen this cabin by its unplowed driveway, and its distance from other homes and roads. Sitting on ten acres by the lake and hedged with trees, no one would see if they turned on the lights or lit a fire.

Last night they'd eaten their fill of canned food from the cupboards. After the meal, even Reed had crashed, but before he did, he gave David first watch and set an alarm on his Holo to switch places with him at two AM.

David had settled by the window and used the alien scanner to search for intruders. As a result, he'd barely slept.

Rachel squealed, drawing his gaze to the sliding glass doors at the cabin's rear. The kids were outside making a snowman, having found more appropriate winter clothes in the coat closet. With a moment of reprieve from their pursuit, it was a good time to catch their breath and let Mark and Rachel be kids for a while.

No intruders had come knocking in the night—alien or otherwise. That had to be a good sign.

David struggled to process yesterday's events at the diner. "Those soldiers we met in Glennallen..." He directed his attention to Private Reed.

Reed looked up from the alien scanner in his lap and reached for a steaming mug of coffee. "What about them?"

"If the Stalkers managed to corrupt those soldiers with some kind of parasite or technology... how do we know who we can trust? You could be infected. Or *I* could be."

"Or me," Kate added in a shrinking voice.

"Let's not start jumping at shadows," Reed replied. "Keller was behaving strangely, using the wrong words in the wrong contexts, acting paranoid. Those are clues we can pick up on when someone is under their influence."

"I still can't believe this is happening," Kate said. "Just a few days ago we were in St. Ann. I was picking Mark up from soccer practice. Rachel pointed across the field to a couple of men in dark suits approaching from the parking lot. And now we're in Alaska running from aliens? It ... doesn't seem real."

David smiled sympathetically at his wife. "I was in space, on the *Interloper,* and even I find it difficult to accept."

"You two had better snap out of it," Reed said. "This is as real as it gets. People are dying, and if you don't want to be next, you'll keep your heads on straight."

Another scream interrupted their conversation, but the pitch was different this time. Not a playful squeal. Kate's coffee mug fell to the hardwood as she jumped to her feet. David snatched up the pulse rifle leaning against the couch, and ran. Reed tore after him, holding his gun with one arm and cradling the scanner with the other.

David was already halfway outside by the time Rachel screamed again. He burst from the cabin and flew across the deck, sinking deep into the snow.

Mark crouched by the edge of the lake with a big stick, poking at something black. It was slowly creeping in from the water. Ice hadn't fully formed yet, despite the recent snowfall.

Rachel backed away steadily from the creature. "Leave it alone!" she cried.

But he lingered with his stick, prodding it experimentally.

David's heart was hammering in his ears by the time he reached them. He grabbed Mark and yanked him from the shoreline. "Get behind me!" he snapped.

Mark dropped the stick and turned to him with big blinking eyes. "It's just a crab," he said.

"It's not a crab!" David said, struggling to drag Mark with one arm and aim the pulse rifle with the other. It was black as an oil slick *and* had too many legs to be a crab—all of them as jointless as an octopus' tentacles.

"It's not?" Mark asked, glancing at the creature. Its legs bent, the body dropping low. It was the size of David's palm with his fingers spread.

Realizing he didn't have time for Mark to snap out of it, David yanked his weapon up in a two-handed grip.

Too late. The spider sprang into the air. Mark ran, finally showing some sense—

And it landed on his back.

A hiss erupted, and Mark cried out, tripping over his feet and falling face-first into the snow with the spider clinging to his neck. Rachel screamed again, the sound primal and ragged.

"David, do something!" his wife cried.

David knelt beside Mark, dropped his rifle, and reached for the spider latched to his son's neck. His hands hovered above the alien's ovoid body, shaking with adrenaline. He hesitated as thin ribbons of blood trickled around the spider's jaws. Hair-like tentacles rose from the alien's back, questing blindly for him. David's mind flashed to a swarm of these things eating Zasha alive. He had to remove it.

"Wait!" Private Reed's voice stopped him. "We don't know if it's safe. It could have attached itself to his spinal cord or the brain stem."

The creature squelched, as if it were sucking Mark's blood. Or maybe digging in deeper.

"Step away, Mr. Bryce," Reed ordered.

It took every ounce of David's will to obey the command.

Mark stood and regarded them with glassy eyes. Clumps of snow were packed into the collar of his jacket and clinging to his dark hair.

"It's okay. I feel fine," he said. "It won't hurt me."

David glanced at the pulse rifle, which was closer to Mark than him.

Reed stepped by him, angling for the weapon.

Mark didn't seem to care. He blinked once, then looked to his mother and Rachel. Both were crying.

David hesitated. "Son, tell us what's going on. What do you feel?"

"Kinda numb. And... uh, really good actually." He smiled. "Excellence."

"Excellence?" Reed asked as he snatched the alien weapon.

"Excellent," Mark corrected himself, sounding distant. He wasn't watching Reed. He stared at the sky. "They're just looking for a home. They're not here to hurt us."

"Is that so?" Reed asked.

"Where is it?" Mark added, his attention fixed on the private.

"Where is what?"

Mark pointed to the alien scanner peeking from his army jacket.

Reed left his rifle dangling from the shoulder strap and slowly withdrew the scanner. "You want this?"

"Yes, please," Mark replied. "They need it. You're not supposed to have it."

"And if I give it to you, how are you going to get it to them?" Reed asked.

David realized he was fishing for information. Smart.

"It can transmit a distress call," Mark said. "The others will home in on it, and we can pass it to them."

"Thanks for the heads-up, kid, but we're not doing *that*," Reed said as he slipped the scanner back into his army jacket.

Mark looked confused. "Why not? They won't harm us. They've only been acting in self defense."

This was bad. Whoever was speaking to them wasn't Mark.

"We have to bring him to a clinic or a hospital," Kate said. "There has to be a way to remove that thing!"

"Army base. Fort Greely," Private Reed said. "It's not far from here. Assuming they're not compromised, it's our best bet. Bryce, bring the kid into the cabin and let's find something to tie him up with."

"Tie him up?" Kate echoed. "You're joking."

"Dead serious, ma'am."

"I saw nylon rope in the pantry cupboard," David said, stepping carefully toward his son. "Come on, Mark." David guided him by the arm, careful to keep as far as possible from the spider on his neck.

It seemed content where it was for the moment, but if it jumped to him or Reed and started waving a gun around, things would quickly turn ugly.

***

Dark Leader

Unmarked Building, Long Island, NY

The sun sat high and heavy in the west as midmorning greeted Allan Booth. The blinds had been closed, and he realized he'd forgotten to sleep. Again.

The pill would keep him up, but how long could he go on like this? He stood watching the skyline, wondering when he'd last lain down for some shuteye. He had no idea.

Instead of contemplating the issue, he swallowed the pill. If he trusted it to keep his Team members active in the field for days at a time, it had to be sufficient for him.

Allan lit a cigarette, knowing his wife would disapprove. But she was dead, and he supposed that didn't matter anymore. He took a moment, picturing her kind face, the soothing voice, her fingers on his chest.

Twenty-one years. Cancer didn't care if you were the spouse of a high-ranking general or didn't have a pot to piss in. It killed just the same.

He inhaled, letting the smoke sit in his lungs. What the hell was he doing? He stubbed it out, shoving the ashtray across his desk. It was the lack of sleep. He was fatigued, making poor decisions.

President Carver wasn't supposed to address the nation, and now, his cryptic code had been seen across the world. Why would he disrupt their people? And who was he giving a secret message to?

His Holo chimed, and Booth accepted the call. "Yes."

"I have the White House as requested," his secretary said.

"Thank you, Gail." He hit mute, and slammed a fist on the desktop. "About time," he muttered, trying to compose himself.

"*We apologize for not replying sooner, sir.*" The voice clearly wasn't Carver's.

Booth's patience had run out. "Sheila, where is he?"

"*He's gone,*" she said, her voice meek.

The words rolled around in his mind. "Gone? Where? Tell me he's just taking his dog for a walk."

"*He was acting strange. When he pulled that impromptu conference, we realized something was wrong. He was locked into the Oval Office with his security detail guarding him, but when the Chief of Staff tried to visit... he was... wasn't there.*"

Allan cringed. This could be trouble. "The Secret Service. Are they present?"

"*Yes, sir.*"

"Check them for bites." He'd been too slow in his efforts to thwart the Crawlers. He'd hoped they would stay hidden in the ocean until a later date, but it was possible he'd been mistaken. Reports had already described the infected near the crash sites, but there hadn't been any of the Stalkers at the White House. Hell, DC for that matter. How had they moved so quickly?

"*Excuse me, did you say* bites, *sir?*"

"Get them all in a line, and ensure they aren't infected."

"*Infected? I don't understand.*"

He should have made Sheila pass the call to someone with a higher rank within the Association, but they didn't have that kind of time. "You're aware of the Stalkers. Their little friends are wreaking havoc. Examine the necks first. Detain anyone with the marking."

"Just the Secret Service?"

"No. Everyone. Lock the White House down!" he ordered, unable to hold back. He was on edge, and the pills were making him even more jumpy.

"Yes, sir. Understood."

"I'll send my nearest team to assist." He scanned the maps and saw that Dark Eleven's squad was finished with the mission in rural upstate New York. Seven human casualties, but it was under wraps. He contacted them to rush to DC and sighed as he monitored Dark One's progress.

They'd lost a member. Dark Thirty-Something. He couldn't keep track any longer, not with the expansion of their efforts in the last few years since they'd discovered the idle *Interloper* floating through their solar system.

He received a message from a team in the French Guiana that there was an issue with the escape pod and the Stalkers. The note wasn't forthcoming, and since then, the feeds had gone cold. He decided to recruit his best, knowing they'd then be close to Atlas and Wan, should they require support.

Allan examined the stats, finding that seventy percent of the pods had been dealt with and covered up, but only about forty-three percent of the Stalkers were accounted for. This number was too low. He'd collected fourteen live subjects, which they could use for further testing. That was something he wished to avoid, but should the Signal elicit a response from the Stalkers' homeworld, they'd take every advantage they had.

Carter Robinson's confirmations proved Allan's own theories, to his dismay. If the Stalkers located the Signal first, they would use it, drawing an entire fleet to Earth. This was the worst-case scenario.

Against his better judgment, Allan lit another cigarette and messaged his secretary, Gail, for another cup of coffee. She brought it a moment later, as if she'd already anticipated the request. Of course she had. Gail had been at his side since he'd been appointed to lead the Association.

"Why don't you go home to your family?" he suggested, and she nodded, leaving him alone.

She knew well enough not to argue with him, even if she understood how grim their current predicament was.

He activated the feeds from Alaska, rewatching the interaction between Robinson and the Grazer. Amazing. The Brit had courage, that was for sure. Maybe he would have made a good Dark Team member.

Alan sent another communication, this one to the base commander. *Any word on David Bryce?*

The response was fast. *Nothing yet.*

We'll find him. Keep searching. Try the military bases in the area. And be on the lookout for suspicious behavior.

Copy that, sir.

Allan was tempted to light up another cigarette. He drummed his fingers restlessly on his knee. *Damn it!*

Everything was unraveling. He'd lost two dozen Dark Team members, and the human tally was climbing by the hour. The Stalkers were staying discreet while they searched for the Signal, but they were growing more brazen. Less patient. He could appreciate that. He felt the same way.

Finally, he saw the blinking dot of Atlas' plane destined for Brazil. He noticed it was off trajectory and sat up straighter. Something was wrong. He sent a message to James Wan, hoping he wasn't too late.

TWELVE

Atlas

Somewhere above the Amazon Rainforest

The sun glared through the plane's window, and Atlas checked how long he'd been dozing. Hours. He must have needed the rest, but he felt better for it, even if the sleeping position had been unpleasant. He stretched his neck in both directions and heard a crack.

"James?" Atlas called, not seeing the Dark operative.

The sound of the toilet suction carried to his ears, and he saw the man exit the bathroom down the hall. "Are you that codependent?" James asked with the hint of a smile. So the guy could offer a joke every now and then.

"We should begin our descent soon," Atlas told him, tapping his Holowatch.

James looked out the small window, his brow furrowed. "Something's off."

Atlas tried to understand what he was seeing. "What?"

"We're too low."

It was a canopy of green below them, but James was right. They were far too close to the ground.

James used his Holo, searching for their location and cursed himself. "The signal's been jammed. We're a thousand miles from our destination."

Atlas glanced at the cockpit. "Are you armed?"

"Of course I..." James searched his pack, but came up empty. "Shit. They must have..." He checked his arm, and Atlas saw a small puncture mark.

"They drugged us?" Atlas didn't understand. "Why?"

James tapped his toes, like he was trying to solve a puzzle, and quickly. "Maybe there's some other agency trying to welcome the Stalkers to Earth."

"Why didn't they kill us, then?" Atlas asked, grateful it hadn't come to that.

"They need us to find the Signal." James opened an overhead compartment, and then the one across the cabin. "I..."

"Looking for this?" Nadine appeared, holding his gun.

"Who are you working for?" James demanded, stepping in front of Atlas.

"Wouldn't you like to know?" Her grin was sadistic, almost comical.

The plane lurched, and the engines screeched as they began to plummet.

"What do you plan to achieve?" James asked, but Nadine shook her head, limp hair falling in her eyes.

"Your world will be ours."

Ours? Atlas saw the lump on the back of her neck now, black legs protruding beneath her hair.

Atlas slowly bent at the knees, picking up his Holo. He threw it. The tablet spun through the cabin, and he yelled, "Now!" as it struck Nadine in the chest. The gun went off, striking the window. It cracked but held.

James shot forward, tackling the woman, and she fired again, this time hitting the ceiling. They crashed into the exit door, and Atlas called a warning as he saw her grip the handle and turn it. She ducked into a row ahead. Atlas clung to the seat, his papers sucked past him and outside as the plane continued to plummet.

"Parachutes! They're in the back!" James told him, and Atlas fought for each purchase as he climbed using the seats. His arms ached when he got there, and he searched for the pouches. He opened cupboards, and anything small enough was sucked to the open door.

Finally, he saw them, the tiny parachute logos on the packs, and he hefted one up, strapping it around his shoulders. He moved fast, peering at the window to see nothing but green as the plane dipped sideways.

Atlas let the pressure differential and the angle of the plane assist his exit. He bashed into the partition between the cockpit and cabin causing a sharp pain to erupt in his knee. He shoved the second chute at James, who was clinging on for his life. Atlas managed to peek into the cockpit, and saw the dead pilot, his head hanging to the right. Several screens were broken.

"We have to jump!" James shouted, but Atlas had never done anything like this in his life.

James went first, letting go of the handhold. He was sucked from the door, shooting into the air. Atlas had no choice. He did the same and lost his breath as he raced into the clear blue sky.

The airplane continued on, screaming toward the dark green canopy as he pulled the ripcord, causing the chute to catch and slow his descent. James was some distance away, using the controls to get closer to Atlas. He stayed put, not trusting his ability to maneuver.

From this incredible vantage point, he saw the snaking river gleaming in the sun, and the jungle thick and green around it. He turned and looked in a full three-sixty, attempting to gain a lay of the land. His research went down with the plane, as did his Holo, but if he could find a landmark, there was a chance he'd be able to figure out where they were. It was the ship's key's loss that bothered him the most. But he could worry about that later.

James instructed him on the landing from twenty yards away, passing orders, and Atlas robotically obeyed, still mapping the region in his mind.

The water below was brown and murky, a small tributary that fed into the larger Amazon River. Atlas cringed, dwelling on the countless dangers lurking in the dense rainforest. But there were bigger threats to be encountered. Stalkers.

The plane's explosion was muted, a plume of fire leaped up a few miles to the south, followed by a gush of smoke, then a gentle trail as the debris smoldered.

They neared the top of the tree canopy, and James caught himself on a high branch. Atlas tried but missed, and his chute snagged, leaving him to dangle thirty feet over the ground.

"I'll help," James said. He used a pocketknife, slicing through the ropes of his own parachute, and crawled along the thick branch before jumping to land on Atlas' tree. James' grip almost slipped, but he recovered, and soon he was scrambling over to Atlas, the knife between his teeth.

"You guys are no joke," Atlas said while James cut.

"You better hold on."

"Huh?" Atlas dropped another ten feet when the first side was cut, and James laughed, moving to the middle of the tree to descend the trunk.

He passed Atlas the blade, telling him to do the rest. Atlas wrapped the free rope around his left arm, and when the chute finally broke free, he swung closer to the jungle floor, dropping the final eight feet.

His knee protested, but after a quick stretch, he decided it was fine to walk on. "Where to now?"

James put a finger to his lips. "Did you hear that?"

Atlas swallowed. They were alone in the Amazon rainforest, with nothing but a pocketknife and the clothes on their backs. "We're screwed."

***

Lennon

Remote French Guiana

"We should have requested a replacement for Brighton," Hank said glumly.

Lennon slapped a mosquito and ignored the big man's incessant commentary.

"Dark Twenty, we're here to locate the missing team. So focus on the task, or I'll be sending you to Dark Leader in a box." Rutger was in a mood, and Lennon had seen it enough to understand why. He was worried.

They'd already been sent to five Pods, and had successfully captured or killed every last Stalker from each of them. But that still left hundreds of the monsters creeping around the world. People were starting to talk. To share videos of mutilated herds of livestock. Entire villages in the remote Himalayas were unresponsive.

It was only a matter of time before the entire population was aware of the Stalkers, and if that happened it might be too late to save themselves.

The afternoon was hot. She'd never been to French Guiana and assumed that under different circumstances, the French settlement might be enjoyable. In the cities. At a resort with a slushy cocktail. Not in the middle of the rainforest after a deluge.

Her boots squashed into the earth. A soft mist rose from the puddles as it evaporated into a light fog. Lennon checked for the missing team's last location, and saw they were standing at it. After this, the Holo tracking went off.

Rutger gestured forward and crouched, picking up a cracked Holo. This was Dark Six's team, and she was as capable as any of them. *Maybe more than some*, Lennon thought, and glanced at Hank, who was poking the barrel of his alien pulse gun at a thick vine hanging from the distant canopy.

"They were here. That's a start." Lennon heard a bird cry and spun to the right. Colorful wings flapped as the toucan flew higher.

They kept walking. Eventually, they found the Stalkers' escape pod. The simple shell was damaged, and Lennon peered inside, finding one of the aliens dead at the controls. "Hard crash." There was a puddle of milky slime near the exit, and she deftly avoided it.

"They landed. Dark Six's team came. But where are they?"

"It's a lot of jungle to cover," Rutger said.

Dark Twenty sniffed the air. "I smell smoke."

Lennon took a deep breath and picked up on the scent too. "We need a better view." She jogged to a thinning in the trees. From there she could spy the gentle offshoots of a controlled fire to the east. "Follow me."

The trip took twenty minutes, and there was evidence the Stalkers had come through. Deep footprints. Four tracks per Stalker. The occasional patch of drool, or maybe some other bodily fluid, on the ground. Eventually, the forest gave way to a clearing. Across the village, she noted a rough road leading north. This was an old town, miraculously still in existence.

The buildings were likely built in the early 1900s, with none of the creature comforts of modern society. There were water pumps. White plastered walls, and thatched roofs. It was like they'd traveled back in time.

"Where is everyone?" Rutger asked with his gun raised as he slowly crept to the town's edge.

All Lennon heard was the constant singing of the tropical birds in the vicinity. They were oblivious to the fact that their world had been invaded by creatures from a distant planet. It made Lennon question the Stalkers' origin. How far was their home from Earth, and what had brought them here in the first place?

Her experience on the *Interloper* was only a few days ago, but so much had occurred since then, she could barely recall specific details. Lennon clenched her jaw, remembering as she'd pressed that button to detonate the explosives. The sinking feeling of failure when it hadn't worked. This was her fault. She should have done a better job. If the *Interloper* had met its end in the deep recesses of space, no one here would have been the wiser.

Rutger nudged her with his elbow. "Dark Three?"

"Sorry. I'm here." At least now, when she heard his voice, it was really him. She smirked to herself and strode into town, slowing at the nearest building.

The smoke they'd smelled was coming from across town. A cooking fire with a metal grill above it. Something was simmering over the flames, and it smelled like roasting meat. Hank shrugged and went ahead, his alien tech searching for a target.

Lennon waved a buzzing cloud of small insects away from her face and saw the leg jutting from the fire pit. It was human. "Dark One, we have a problem."

Rutger grunted quietly. "We have to leave." He started to turn when they heard the voice.

"Help me. I need your help!" It was a woman's voice.

"Where did that come from?" Rutger's head whipped around, checking for hostiles.

Lennon's heart pounded. So far they'd hunted the bastards off grid. The aliens were becoming more brazen. Exposing themselves. "That way." She pointed to the largest structure in the village. It looked like a communal living space. She expected that multiple families, or generations, shared the home.

"Help me! Please!" the voice continued.

Dark Twenty hurried, his footsteps no longer silent.

"Hank, hold your position!" Rutger hissed, but he didn't listen.

A shadow fell over Hank's big body as he neared the entrance, and he peered up, Lennon following his gaze. Dark Six was hanging from a tree, a vine tied around her neck. She was naked and lifeless, with the other three team members in a similar position.

"Oh my God," Lennon muttered.

"We found them," Hank started to say. A bright flash erupted beside him, sending clods of dirt and gore in all directions. Lennon froze, her senses trying to understand what she'd just witnessed. Then she saw the second blue explosive, like the ones she'd brought to the *Interloper*. It bounced on the dirt road, flying toward them.

"Run!" she shouted, but Rutger was already way ahead of her. He spun as he rounded a hut, firing at the deadly device. It burped as the plasma ray melted it, and the detonation shook the entire village. Lennon was flung to the ground, her face skidding through mud and leaves. She rolled to her back, weapon up, and tried to avoid seeing the dead Dark Team in the trees.

"Help me!" A Stalker approached, weapon held high. Vertical lips peeled from sharp teeth, almost like it was giving her a smile. "Please. I need help!"

Lennon realized with horror that the monster was mimicking someone. And she recognized the voice. It was Dark Six's.

"You son of a bitch!" Lennon climbed to her feet, blood dripping from a gash in her forehead. She wiped at it, and realized her visor was gone.

The Stalker swung its weapon like a club, and she ducked, feeling the wind from the missed impact. She kicked hard, hitting one of the knobby knee joints, and the Stalker howled. But the giant alien recovered quickly.

From the corner of her eye, she noticed two more emerging from the building, each of them armed and stalking toward

Rutger. They were enjoying this. Toying with the prey caught in their trap. It was a sick game to the Stalkers, and it fueled Lennon's rage.

"You're all going to die," she said.

"You're all going to die," the Stalker repeated, but this time in her own voice.

"I'm the ugliest thing in the universe," she muttered, and it repeated the phrase, giving her a moment of joy. "At least you admitted it." Lennon faced off with the alien from ten feet away. They both aimed their guns at one another, and she noticed that Rutger was in a similar standoff.

"Lennon, do you remember Beirut?"

The question caught her off guard, and she tried to recall. There had been a particularly steamy night in the hotel after they'd nearly been killed. Was he referring to... No. He meant how they'd completed the mission. It was similar to this. A stalemate, with neither side wishing to die. "I do."

"On three."

She mentally counted down, and the second she hit one, Lennon dove to the right. Rutger went left, and they fired their weapons at each other's opponents, with Lennon choosing the smaller of Rutger's pair. The blasts melted the freak's exoskeleton, and the remaining Stalker shrieked. Lennon saw the tiny sphere in its grip, and she took aim with her sidearm, letting the heavy plasma ray fall. Two taps of the trigger and the blue ball exploded, covering Rutger with shards of black carapace.

Dark Twenty was dead, and so were Dark Six and her team. But Lennon and Rutger were alive.

She walked over to him, helped him to his feet, and took stock of their surroundings. The bodies of the villagers had been piled at the far edge of town. They were all gone.

Rutger gestured to the operatives hanging from the trees. "Come on. Let's cut them down."

"I'll make them pay," Lennon whispered.

"I believe that."

THIRTEEN

Carter

Somewhere in Northern Alaska

"To Carter Robinson." Doctor Nielson stood and raised her glass of grape juice for a toast.

Six other scientists and linguists followed suit, lifting their glasses in unison.

Carter smiled broadly from where he sat at the head of the table. He placed a hand against his chest in a gesture of mock flattery. "Gee, thanks, guys."

Nielson went on, "Ten years of slaving away to get a few hundred words translated, and you come along and blow our progress out of the water in a single day. Guess one of us should have been stupid enough to think about climbing in the Grazer's cage without a suit."

Carter frowned at the backhanded compliment. "Stupidity or genius? It's a fine line, ladies and gentlemen."

"So it is," Neilson replied, elevating her glass a little higher. "To your stupid genius." She took a sip, and then everyone sat to consume their meal of roast salmon and rehydrated mashed potatoes. Carter sipped his grape juice with a grimace. "Ash ley... Ash. Can I call you that? Rolls off the tongue better than *Doctor Nielson.* Quite a mouthful."

She cocked an eyebrow and regarded him with a look of strained patience. "What is it, Carter?" she asked.

"Well..." He nudged his glass with his index finger. "If this is a celebration, shouldn't we be breaking out the good stuff? Where's the wine? This wasn't exactly what I had in mind when I asked for a glass of red."

"It's lunchtime, Mr. Robinson."

"Call me Carter. I know it's lunchtime. But technically one o'clock, right? And I just came from the East Coast, so it's five o'clock there."

"We have work to do."

"Well, you want me to chat to the alien, right? I've always found liquor loosens up the tongue, haven't you?"

A wry grin crept onto Doctor Nielson's lips. "Oh, you mean giving you an adult beverage would make you *more* talkative?"

"Damn right it would!" Carter said, slapping his knee.

"In *that* case, you're sticking to grape juice. In fact, we'd better lock the cellar and throw away the key."

Carter was speechless. "Was that a joke, Ashley?"

She popped a bite of salmon in her mouth and smiled smugly at him.

"I didn't know you had it in you."

"There's a lot of things you don't know about me," she replied cryptically.

He leaned in conspiratorially close and raised his glass for another sip of the treacly-sweet juice. "Well then, perhaps it's high time we got to know each other better."

Ashley frowned.

Too far, Carter decided. He pulled back and glanced around the mess hall, taking in the faces of his co-workers. He barely recognized anyone here. The portly guy with the comb-over and glasses was Deacon. The rail-thin Austrian woman with sunken cheeks was Leslie. Then there was Hanz, the hulking German with blue eyes and bristly-short blond hair. Brock, the Australian, unremarkable but for his accent and shit-eating grin. Finally, Teresa and Rachel, the brown-haired American twins from MIT. Recalling the name of the latter twin brought another Rachel to mind. David's nine-year-old daughter.

"Ashley..." Carter trailed off.

"Aren't you going to eat your food?" she asked, gesturing to his untouched plate before he could continue.

He grimaced at the salmon. He hated fish, and the pungent smells of it aboard the *Interloper* hadn't helped with that aversion. For some reason, seafood seemed like the only thing they knew how to make. Halibut, salmon, tuna, octopus, calamari... "In a minute," Carter replied, looking up from his plate. "Ash, where are David Bryce and his family?"

"Who?" Nielson replied.

"The Commander of *Beyond III*. He was supposed to be arriving with his family. He should have been here by now, right? I thought he was due yesterday."

Doctor Nielson grabbed her napkin and wiped her mouth. Then she bit her lower lip, looking torn—and also incredibly cute.

Don't get distracted, Carter! he snapped at himself. "What is it?"

"They were intercepted in Anchorage."

"Intercepted? What does that mean? Intercepted by *what?*"

"Stalkers, we think. We're not sure. There weren't any survivors at the airport where they landed."

The rest of the crew stopped eating, peering up from their plates to give Doctor Nielson their full attention.

Carter gaped at her. "So are they..."

"We didn't find their bodies, no. We believe they're on the run. Mixed reports have surfaced of people matching their descriptions. We have teams tracking them inland as we speak."

"On the run... you mean the Stalkers are chasing them? Why would they do that?"

"I'm sorry, I really can't say more," Doctor Nielson said.

"Can't or won't?"

"Can't. I've told you everything I know. All we can do is hope and pray that they make it here."

"What if they lead the Stalkers to us?" Hanz, the giant German linguist, suddenly asked. A murmur of discontent spread through the lunchroom as the others contemplated his question.

"This facility is well hidden, off the grid, far from the nearest town or road... We're safe," Doctor Nielson replied.

"Are we?" Hanz insisted, his accent thickening. "Or are we trapped? The only access is by helicopter or plane. If the weather turns bad, we can't leave."

"Stalkers won't make it across the mountains," Doctor Nielson replied.

"Let us hope not," Hanz intoned.

Carter frowned while the others traded wide-eyed looks.

Leslie set her fork on the table. "I've lost my appetite," she said.

"Give it here," Hanz replied, reaching for her plate.

Carter pushed his own food away. "I think I've lost mine, too."

"You haven't even taken a bite," Doctor Nielson said.

"Nevertheless." He brightened suddenly. "But man, I could go for a burger and fries!"

"Check the freezer," Hanz suggested.

Brock crossed his arms over his chest and glowered. "So you *are* hungry."

"Sorry. I'm not cut out for this pescatarian nonsense. And I think a man should at least enjoy his last meal, don't you?"

"Don't be dramatic," Doctor Nielson said.

"Excuse me, but is your friend missing and on the run from alien predators?"

Nielson blinked at him.

Carter barreled on. "Did *you* almost get eaten a hundred different times aboard an alien spaceship? No? Thank you very much!" He stood up. "Anyone else want a McRobinson?"

Brock snorted and shook his head.

Hanz raised a hand. "I'll take one."

Nobody else took him up on his offer.

Carter nodded and turned toward the gleaming steel doors of the kitchen. "Two McRobinson specials, coming right up."

***

Atlas

Remote Amazon Rainforest

In the four hours since they'd landed, Atlas guessed he'd peered over his shoulder a hundred times. James walked with purpose, his steps sure, his posture confident.

"How do you do that?" Atlas asked, glancing up at a squawking bird. It watched their passage with mild interest, the red and white head bobbing with their steps.

"Do what?" James kept stride.

"We crashed into the Amazon, and you're stalking through it like you know where you're going. With a pocketknife to protect you." Atlas quickened his pace, trying not to be left behind. James was relentless.

"You pick up a few things with the Dark Teams."

"How long have you..."

"A few years. I was retired. But when Dark Leader knocks on your door and claims he needs help to save the world, you don't hesitate," James said.

"You were a Marine, right?" Atlas recalled the photos of a younger James Wan.

"I was, and my father fought in the Vietnam War. He hated it. Came back with that tattoo." James rolled up his own sleeve, showing his to Atlas. Three dots.

"Do you all have it?" he inquired.

"All the Dark do, yes. It's given to us after our first mission. If we're deemed worthy," James said.

"What happens if you're not... deemed worthy?"

James' blank expression told him the answer, and Atlas decided to drop the subject.

"My research suggested we should be following the river to the south," Atlas told him again, pointing in the other direction.

"We'll get there."

"What's over here?" Atlas was getting tired of being ignored. He reached for James' shoulder, and spun him around. The man finally stopped, facing him.

"Atlas, we can't do this unarmed."

"Do you have a secret weapons cache I should know about?" Atlas asked, quickly realizing his mistake. "No way. You have to be nuts."

"One of the Stalkers' escape pods landed nearby. According to the latest reports, before I lost my Holo, it has yet to be investigated. It's so remote, Dark Leader was waiting for the Teams to complete their current tasks before reassigning them."

"So we're going to head to an alien camp? Then what?"

"We steal their weapons." James dusted his hands off, and stared into the distance again.

"Just like that?"

"Atlas, I'm trained for this kind of thing. If you want to hide out, you can. Give me a couple of hours and we'll reconvene."

"Where?" Atlas peered around, hearing things in every nook and cranny of the rainforest. It was like being on another world.

"Right here."

"Not going to happen." Atlas didn't want to admit he was scared to be left alone in the middle of nowhere. He wasn't equipped for this. But he also wasn't a pushover, so he clenched his jaw and nodded at James. "I'm going with you."

"That's what I expected."

They hiked the rainforest silently for the next thirty minutes or so. Atlas' linen button-up was drenched in sweat, as were the bottoms of his khakis. He knew that in areas like this, you kept your pants tucked into your socks, even if it made you look like a fool. James' uniform seemed impervious to the heat or dampness. The man was as solid as a rock.

Atlas swatted a cluster of insects and caught the sounds of a slow-flowing river. The air grew mustier, and he knew they were close. He smelled their fishy aroma and dashed behind a tree trunk.

James's eyes widened, alerting Atlas to a threat. He didn't spot any Stalkers. "What is it?" he asked.

James' gaze drifted above Atlas, and a green snake lowered, tongue flicking in and out of a sealed mouth. He froze, unsure how to react. He thought it was a boa, large enough to eat a wild pig, should it cross paths with one. Atlas imagined the snake coiling around his chest, squeezing the life from his lungs as it constricted.

James had the knife in his hand, and he held the other up, as if signaling the snake to stop.

It descended further, coming face to face with Atlas.

"Move!" James roared, and lunged, jamming the blade through the serpent's throat, pinning it to the tree trunk. The rest of the body dropped from the limb above, and it thrashed and writhed, struggling to get free.

James propped a foot on the tree, grabbing a branch, and he tore it off. Without delay, he bashed the blunt object against the snake's head five times, each with increasing ferocity, and finally, the boa ceased moving.

"Is it..." Atlas kicked the tail.

"It's dead." James pulled his knife loose and wiped the blade on his vest. "They might have heard that. Let's go."

Atlas crouched and followed James to the riverbed. They turned left, and found a section narrow enough for them to jump the water. James' foot slipped on the far side, and Atlas caught his arm, pulling him up.

"Thanks."

"We're still not even," Atlas admitted.

James gestured to their right, and a few minutes later, Stalkers appeared as the river rounded a bend.

"There," James whispered, indicating two alien weapons that had been placed on a fallen tree.

Atlas estimated the guns were halfway between them and the Stalkers. It would be a tight race.

"Make a distraction. I'll retrieve them." James' voice was almost imperceivable.

"You want me to... distract... those?" Atlas stared at the giant aliens. They were in the river, dipping into the water. If he didn't know better, he'd say they were taking a bath. Rinsing off the accumulated grime on their black exoskeletons. Their movements were strange, the way their four legs shifted, seemingly independent of each other. Their arms were deadly, and those sideways mouths, with sharp, translucent teeth.

James nudged him forward, breaking his contemplation. How did one accomplish a task this difficult without getting killed in the process?

He committed, running closer to the river and waving his arms. "Over here you ugly sons of..." He tripped, landing hard on his knees, then his chest. Atlas didn't stay down, knowing that every second mattered.

The Stalkers emerged from the river, water dripping off their external shells. They shrieked, a terrible sound emerging from their vocal cords. Instead of rushing to their guns, they came after Atlas.

A weapon blasted, sending a pulse at the creature, and the first one slammed into a tree beside Atlas, his inner set of legs suddenly missing. Atlas jumped over a log, heading in the opposite direction while James trailed after them, carrying the alien weapon. He risked a peek, and the Stalker swiped at him. He picked up speed, and James hit the second Stalker square in the lower back. It screamed, the noise echoing throughout the rainforest. Birds flapped and flew away. If there were more enemies in the area, they'd just been alerted.

James arrived, aiming the barrel at the injured Stalker. He pulled the trigger, the pulse melting the upper half of its torso. It flinched and died a breath later.

Atlas shouted a warning as the first Stalker crawled up behind them, standing shakily on two legs. James lowered, spinning as his foot swept under the alien. It crashed to the ground, swiping a long arm toward James. Atlas saw the moss-covered rock, and hefted it up, bashing the weight over the alien's skull. It clanked off, but the momentary distraction was enough for James to fire again.

The pair of humans stood there, panting, and surveyed the area.

James had a cut on his temple, and Atlas noted that his own pants were torn, his knees bloodied.

They returned to the river's edge, and James passed him the second weapon. "Not bad for your first encounter."

Atlas held the gun, looking at the strange design. It was uncomfortable in his grip. "First encounter?"

More Stalkers shrieked in the distance, their cries reverberating under the forest canopy.

"Come on. If we're going to find the Signal, we can't let them surprise us."

Atlas wiped a sheen of perspiration from his face. "Meaning?"

"We're going on the hunt," James said as he continued deeper into the rainforest.

FOURTEEN

David

Fort Greely, Alaska

Two soldiers moved to bar the chain-link gates of Fort Greely as the truck approached.

Private Reed tapped the brakes, skidding to a stop on the snowy road.

A soldier approached the window, and Private Reed popped his door open to speak with them.

"Private Victor Reed, 25th Infantry," he said before the other soldier could ask. "I have four civilians with me. Two adults, two kids—one is in need of urgent medical attention."

"What is the nature of the emergency?"

"Uhh..." Reed trailed off. "Multiple puncture wounds to the neck."

The soldier glanced into the back of the truck. "Bleeding?"

"Stable for now."

He used his Holowatch to scan Private Reed's name tape. It glowed briefly, highlighting the name *Reed*.

"Copy that, Private..." The soldier outside spared a hand from his carbine to draw his Holo. He spent a moment studying the screen. "I have here that your last orders were to escort Commander David Bryce of the Orbital Development Group, his wife, Katherine Bryce, and their two children to an undisclosed location. Are those the civilians in your company, soldier?"

"Yes, sir."

"Hold tight." The soldier hurried off, speaking rapidly into the radio attached to his collar.

"I don't like this," David muttered.

"What's he waiting for?" Kate demanded. "You told him it's an emergency!"

"Easy," Reed replied. "It's just protocol. He needs to clear it with the base commander. We weren't ordered to come here, so they have to treat us with suspicion. Especially these days, after what happened with Major Keller."

"You think they know about that?" David asked.

"By now? Probably. Alaska's like a small town, and there aren't a lot of highways. By now news has spread of what happened to Keller and those Marines," Reed replied.

"Won't we be in trouble?" Kate asked.

Private Reed sighed. "We'll be asked a lot of questions, but you four are VIP witnesses. We'll be okay so long as no one gets cute with their answers."

David nodded along with that and glanced at Kate and the kids.

Kate smiled tightly at him. Rachel snuggled closer to her mother. Mark sat calmly, staring ahead with a blank expression. His hands were bound in his lap with bright yellow nylon rope. They'd left his ankles free, in spite of Reed's protests.

So far, the alien spider that had attached itself to Mark's neck hadn't made any suspicious moves. He wasn't entirely himself, but he wasn't showing signs of aggression either.

The soldier who'd spoken with them returned. "Private, you are cleared for entry! Report directly to the Family Medical Center. Straight down this road, last building on your left. Can't miss it. Do not veer off of your assigned route. Colonel Larson will be waiting for you at your destination."

"Copy that," Reed replied, and pulled his door shut.

The gate rattled open, and they roared down the snow-covered road. A few seconds later they were rounding a traffic circle, and then a cluster of buildings appeared up ahead.

A chime dinged. "Just in time," Reed said. "Looks like we're out of gas."

David frowned at that.

"Can we trade it for something newer?" Kate asked, her thoughts mirroring his. This thing had to be at least twenty years old. It didn't even have a Holo built into the dash. "An electric car or truck?" she added hopefully.

Reed snorted at that. "This is Alaska, not New York. It's easier to lug around spare gallons of gas than it is to find a charging station."

"Good point," David conceded.

They flew by the other buildings on the base, passing a pair of other vehicles along the way. At the end of the street, there was a sign for the medical center. Reed signaled and pulled into the parking lot. "Let's move!" Reed said, exiting hastily. Kate didn't have to be told twice. She and Rachel practically fell from the truck. Then Kate reached in, beckoning for Mark to follow.

Mark proceeded calmly, seemingly oblivious to his mother's concern. "Why are we here?" he asked.

"You'll see," Reed said.

David went last, and rounded the vehicle to find a group of eight soldiers lingering by the entrance of the clinic with their rifles at the ready. In front of them, standing at parade rest, was a man who must have been the colonel. He had thinning gray hair, pale, rugged cheeks, and a thick midsection.

"Welcome to Fort Greely," he said as they approached.

"Thank you, sir," Private Reed replied, stopping short and saluting smartly.

The colonel's gaze roved on, taking in each of them in turn. "We've been searching for you, Mr Bryce."

Kate tapped her feet in the snow. "Can we skip the introductions? Our son needs immediate medical attention."

"What is the nature of his injury?" Colonel Larson asked.

David nodded to his son. "Mark, turn around."

He did as he was told.

Colonel Larson took a step back, and the soldiers' rifles snapped up to their shoulders.

Kate jumped in front of him. "He's just a kid! Are you crazy?!"

"How long has he been like that?" Larson demanded.

"Maybe forty minutes," Private Reed answered.

"Good. There might still be time. Follow me."

Colonel Larson turned and strode for the entrance of the building. The soldiers parted to let them by as they hurried after him. David tried, but failed to catch a glimpse of their necks. Their winter clothes covered everything except for their faces.

"What do you mean by that?" Kate demanded. "Time for what?!"

The colonel turned as glass doors parted, letting them into the medical center. "Time to save your son."

***

David observed the doctor from a wary distance. He had Kate wrapped in a tight hug, with Rachel clinging to his leg.

"I can't watch," Kate whimpered.

Mark lay face-down on the examination table. The base doctor approached the spider with a syringe full of anesthetic, while Private Reed and another soldier held Mark down—one on either side of him. They both appeared ready to spring away at a moment's notice, but Mark wasn't offering any resistance. Maybe Colonel Larson was right. They could stop that alien from taking control of their son.

"What's that for?" Mark asked, tilting his head slightly to see the syringe.

"Eyes on the floor," the soldier standing opposite Reed snapped.

Mark averted his gaze.

"Take a deep breath," the doctor warned. "This shouldn't hurt, but all the same..."

He took a moment to examine the alien parasite, then injected the anesthetic into a soft seam in the spider's hardened carapace.

It went suddenly limp, and Mark whimpered as it rolled off his neck and fell on the floor.

"That got it," the doctor said, smiling broadly.

The spider came to life a moment later, dozens of legs flailing around drunkenly, scrambling for purchase on the smooth tile floor.

"It's coming to!" Reed cried. He lifted a boot and stomped on it.

The spider gave a sickening *squelch*, and translucent slime gushed around his boot.

"Yuck," Reed remarked, raising his foot to find tendrils of slime still clinging to it.

"Is it over?" Mark asked.

"It's over, son," Colonel Larson said, stepping closer to the table.

Reed and the other soldier released Mark's arms, and he sat up. "What... what happened to me?" he asked, reaching for his neck.

"Don't touch," the doctor warned. "I have to dress the wound to prevent infection. Here..." He went to a nearby cabinet to gather the necessary supplies.

"Sir," Reed began, standing at attention before the colonel. "I must complete my mission."

"It's being handled, Private. We have a helicopter fueling up and transport ready to escort you to the airfield. They have orders to take you the rest of the way."

Private Reed sighed. "Thank you, sir."

"Thank *you*, Private. They wouldn't have made it this far without you."

David stepped in beside Kate and Mark. He gripped Mark's shoulder while the doctor dressed his puncture wounds.

"We still have to test his blood before he leaves," the doctor said.

"Is that really necessary, Captain Willard? These people are tired, and they're being hunted. The longer we keep them here, the bigger the risk to them and to us. We removed it before it could lay eggs.

"We don't know that, sir," Willard said as he finished dressing Mark's neck.

"I *do* know that," Colonel Larson replied. "But they can scan him at the destination to be sure. I'll give the order. Either way, the incubation period allows us time for observation."

Kate stiffened and belatedly turned her head. "I'm sorry, did you just say *eggs?*"

The colonel waved his hand dismissively. "There's nothing to worry about, ma'am."

"But they..." Kate swallowed thickly as her gaze found the squished remains of the spider on the floor. "They lay eggs *inside* of people?"

"There have been a few cases."

Horror roiled in David's gut. "What happens to the host?" he asked.

The colonel held his gaze. "As I said, there's nothing to worry about. And even if there is, they're more equipped to help your son where you're headed than where you are now."

"How far is it?" Kate asked.

"That's need to know, ma'am."

"Can't be that far," David said. "If we're taking a helicopter."

Colonel Larson smiled tightly at them. "Speaking of, your transport is ready. Not to be rude, but I want you five off my base before we become ground zero for another attack."

"Another attack? How many have there been?" Kate asked.

Colonel Larson stared at her.

"Copy that, sir," Private Reed replied, moving for the door.

"I'll show you out," Captain Willard said.

They hurried through the bland, sterile gray corridors until they arrived at the entrance of the clinic. Outside, in the searing cold, another, much bigger army vehicle was parked. "I'll get our bags," Private Reed said.

"I'll help you," David added.

The two of them took off at a run. As soon as they reached the aging gas-powered JLTV, Reed grabbed his military duffle. Zipping it open, he searched his jacket to withdraw the alien scanner and then tucked it into the bag between his clothes and toiletries.

"Shouldn't we give that to Colonel Larson?"

Reed held a finger to his lips and shook his head. "Until we're certain who can be trusted, this stays between us, that clear?"

David nodded.

Soldiers came to help with the bags. A young corporal with puffy cheeks flushed red from the cold, offered to take Reed's pack, but he jerked it away, saying, "I'm good, sir."

"If you say so..."

The corporal and another private helped David with his family's luggage instead, leaving him with his hands free. He ran to Kate and the kids.

Willard stayed with them, despite not wearing proper clothes for the cold weather.

"Thanks again, Doc," David said, nodding to him.

"I'm glad that it worked. It was a gamble."

The puffy-cheeked corporal rushed to their side. "Mr. and Mrs. Bryce, we're on the clock here. I've been ordered to expedite your extraction as much as possible."

"I'll let you go," Willard said.

"Come on kids," Kate added, pushing them gently in front of her as she proceeded to leave. Reed and the rest of the soldiers jogged ahead of them.

David was about to follow when Willard stepped in suddenly and grabbed his arm. "Make sure they scan your son, Mr. Bryce," he said in a low voice.

"What..." David wondered why Captain Willard was repeating his concerns after Colonel Larson had promised Mark would be checked.

"Disturbing things are happening—at the highest possible levels. You can't trust anyone. And now that your son has been compromised..."

"Compromised?"

Willard nodded. "If he's incubating eggs, you *need* to know."

"Mr. Bryce! Let's move!" the corporal called from the transport.

"I have to go," David said, pulling away.

"Good luck, Commander!" Captain Willard called after him.

David climbed into the vehicle with a heavy frown.

One of the soldiers hopped in behind him and shut the door with a heavy *bang.*

"What was that about?" Kate whispered.

David pasted a smile on his face. "Nothing, sweetheart. Don't worry." No sense in both of them agonizing over hypotheticals. He'd wait to see the results of Mark's scans before telling her anything. And hopefully, there'd be nothing to tell.

FIFTEEN

Lennon

Santigo, Chile

"This is going against direct orders, Lennon," Rutger said. "I don't care. These things are getting closer to our populations. We can't have the Stalkers roaming our streets, Rutger." Lennon took a deep breath and stared at the cityscape. It was one of the most beautiful sights she'd ever witnessed.

The capital of Chile was a real metropolis, with millions of inhabitants. She couldn't let the Stalkers loose in a place like this, not if she had the ability to stop them. Dark Leader had been adamant they return to Long Island to regroup. More and more of the Teams were going missing, and Booth was grasping at straws. Lennon didn't care. They were in a position to help, and the region had two escape pods landed near it. There had to be a reason for it.

So far everything the Stalkers did seemed random, but the longer she tracked them, the better she felt she understood. "They're here for a reason."

"What?" Rutger asked.

"The Signal, maybe?"

"Booth says it's in Brazil."

"Might be. Then something else."

"I'll let you explain it to him when he kicks our asses," Rutger mumbled.

"You're scared of Dark Leader?"

"Aren't you?" Dark One asked.

"Hell no." But that was a lie. She'd heard rumors that explained the scar on his face. How he'd gotten it freeing himself from an enemy camp. The place had been locked down like a vault, and Dark Leader had left fifty bodies in his wake, returning home. But that was just gossip. For all she knew, it was a shaving accident.

Beyond the city, the Andes stood like stark, snow-capped monoliths, their presence a constant reminder of the Earth around them. The population probably grew complacent with the spectacular mountain range as they dealt with their daily grind. It was a shame. The sight was truly remarkable.

The sun began its descent, casting an orange glow over the view, and soon it was gone, the sky clear and brilliant despite the light pollution from the city center.

They remained on the outskirts of town, waiting for the cover of night. It was finally upon them, the sun down for more than an hour.

"Did you think of me?" Lennon asked him, leaning against the truck.

"Never," he said, but the way his lip twisted, she knew he was joking. "What was it like?"

"Which part? Being kicked out?"

"No. Flying with ORB on *Beyond III*."

Lennon watched him from the corner of her eye. She picked up her weapon, verifying the charge while she talked. "Exhilarating. Terrifying."

"Practically every mission we've ever done, hey?" Rutger grunted.

"Pretty much. Rutger, I saw Earth from up there." She gestured to the sky.

"And? Did it change your life?"

"I suppose. I get what we're protecting better now. Before... in Three Points... I didn't care about anything."

"I'm sorry."

"Whatever. Space was remarkable, but I'd rather be here." She tapped her toes on the concrete. "Solid ground."

"You went aboard the *Interloper*."

"That was another story. The whole time I concerned myself with Dark Leader's objectives. I should have been trying to stop the ship. Save the crew." Lennon counted their losses. First Akira, then Zasha, and finally Liu, having died on their crash landing in the ocean.

"Is that why we came to Chile? To disobey Dark Leader?" Rutger checked his own weapon and snapped a spare magazine onto his leg.

"It has nothing to do with *him*. I need to stop this invasion. I missed my chance up there," she said. "I won't let the Stalkers win."

The lid of a garbage can fell from a metal waste basket, making her jump. A cat's eyes reflected in the dark alley. They'd left a helicopter hidden in the wilderness an hour away, near the escape pods' crash sites, and had happened by a dead man's truck. He was on the ground, and from the looks of his injuries, had been killed the same night the Stalkers had landed.

Lennon had been on the road for the entire time and couldn't even recall if it had been two or three days since then. Maybe four. She was losing track.

"You really think they came into the city?" Rutger took a protein bar from his uniform and offered her half. Lennon didn't love the chalky taste, but accepted it anyway.

"We saw a string of bodies leading us to the outskirts," she said between bites. "They're here."

"But why?"

Lennon's gaze drifted over the section of the south side. It was rough, not like the tourist spots she'd seen online about the Chilean capital. This was dark and depressing, the apartment blocks crammed together with narrow stone roadways. The dumpsters were overflowing, and everything held the slight scent of rotten food.

She didn't know why, but she could sense the Stalkers nearby. Not in an ethereal, mystical way. She was trained for this kind of task, and the culmination of her experience had led her to this spot. Now all they had to do was wait.

The pair of them stuck out like a sore thumb, and a car drove by, slowing when the driver noticed them.

Lennon's weapons were stowed in the back of the truck, but they still looked like soldiers. She glared at the man, and he sped up. "News is popping up around the world, isn't it?"

"I'd say so. The Association can only keep a lid on it for so long." Rutger dropped the protein bar wrapper on the ground, and Lennon sighed, picking it up.

"We're the good guys, Rutger. We don't litter." She started for the garbage can, and stopped when the two men emerged from a doorway a few short steps ahead. They were smirking.

"*Qué tenemos aquí?*" the bald one asked.

"Keep walking," Lennon muttered. She glanced at the truck, but Rutger was gone.

The other guy said something she didn't understand, but she heard the word for 'drink'. He had a bottle in a brown bag and shoved it toward her.

Lennon lifted her hands. "*No, gracias.*"

They walked up to her, and she sighed, sensing they weren't going to let this go.

A knife appeared in one of their hands, and she actually laughed. The noise escaped her lips, and they looked startled. "Listen, you idiots. I'm trying to save the world, and you're seriously wasting my time with this?" She kicked the bald guy right between the legs. He dropped like an anchor. His friend had the knife, and he sliced at her arm while the bottle crashed to the ground. It shattered as she easily avoided his attack, and she caught a glimpse of four black eyes observing them from across the alley.

The Stalkers were here. The assailant was unaware, and she clutched his wrist, breaking it with a sharp thrust from her other hand. He screamed and dropped the blade, which clattered to the cobblestones. Lennon shoved him as hard as she could, and he stumbled into the waiting arms of the Stalker.

It emitted a strange sound, something that she interpreted as amusement. Lennon ran for the truck, reaching into the box to grab her gear. She shoved on the goggles, flicking the night vision off, and powered on the pulse gun, the charger giving a gentle whine.

"We have movement," Rutger said in her ear. She searched for him, and saw he was two blocks away.

"What if I needed back up?" she asked.

"You? Against humans? I don't think so."

"Your confidence is inspiring." Lennon searched for the Stalker, but it was gone. Both locals were dead, their guts torn from their stomachs. She had no remorse.

Lennon hurried, chasing after Rutger, and caught up at the edge of a huge brown apartment block. It was ten stories high, and the side door kicked in.

Glass shattered above as a man was thrown from halfway up, landing hard on the concrete. Someone screamed, and Lennon's worst fears had been realized. The Stalkers were no longer hiding in remote regions. They'd escalated the situation.

"What do we do?" she asked Rutger, hoping he could decide.

"Shit." He held his alien tech-weapon with two hands and nodded to the doorway. "We see what the hell they want."

Lennon rested a palm on her sidearm and entered first. The halls stank, like fish heads at a Seattle dock. The drywall was singed, and one of the suites billowed smoke from under the door. People were screaming, others crying. Lennon assumed the police would be here soon, and didn't desire being questioned by local law enforcement.

She stepped over a woman in a pink robe, her eyes staring blankly at the ceiling. The Stalkers were killing anyone in their path.

Lennon rushed down the hall, trying to keep her breathing level. She stopped at the end. "Only way is up." She kicked the stairwell open and ascended two flights. The blast almost hit her near the third story, and she ducked, pressing her back to the wall.

Rutger silently counted to three, and pushed off, shooting to the floor above. The pulse cut a hole in the stairs, and the Stalker fell through behind them. It tumbled down the steps, and Lennon grabbed her sidearm, dashing to the crumpled form. She tapped the barrel to its eye and shot just as it was recovering. The hulking alien stilled.

Eventually, they came to the final floor, and Lennon saw a tiny girl curled near the exit. Her arms shielded her head, huge tears dripping down her red cheeks.

"Did you see them? Where are they? *Dónde están?*" Lennon asked.

"*Ellos subieron por allí,*" she whispered, pointing at the window. It was broken, and she ran to it, seeing the Stalkers dashing across another rooftop. They'd made the jump, but where were they going?

Lennon climbed out, clutching the frame, glad to be wearing gloves. The fall would kill her if she missed. She braced a foot and kicked off, rolling as she settled on the adjacent rooftop. There were seven Stalkers, and one slowed, firing a shot at her. Rutger arrived and, from a knee, shot the enemy, striking him in the gun arm. Lennon aimed and finished the job.

Police sirens filled the entire community, smoke wafting from a few of the residences.

Lennon moved to the edge of this rooftop and crouched. The Stalkers were on a third building, and her gaze drifted to the huge metal edifice perched atop it. "Why do they need a Holo tower?"

"It's an old transmitter. Before they didn't need them any longer. Most places have dismantled theirs," Rutger said.

"What use could they possibly have for that?" Lennon asked.

"I don't know, but we'd better find out."

SIXTEEN

David

Somewhere in Northern Alaska

The helicopter dropped altitude swiftly on the far side of a soaring mountain range. David caught a glimpse of the welcoming orange glow of lights on the ground through his window. The scene swelled rapidly with their approach. It was well past sunset, making it difficult to see anything else.

The chopper touched down with a gentle jolt. Snow gusted and swirled in the wind, illuminated by the spotlights surrounding the landing pad. Gradually, the thumping of the rotors slowed, and one of the soldiers in the front exited and waved them out. Reed departed and slung his pack over his shoulders. He'd ridden with it in his lap the entire way from Fort Greely.

"Let's go," Reed called into the dying wind.

Kate helped Rachel, then Mark. David slid out behind them and stood in the freezing cold, searching for the welcoming party. The adjacent building had no windows, and the door was sealed.

Someone arrived a moment later, and a group of four heavily-armed soldiers wearing Arctic white camo suits approached them.

A civilian pushed by them, taking the lead. The soldiers objected with shouts of alarm. David recognized the man immediately.

"Carter!"

"David, what happened? You decide to go sightseeing with the family?"

"Not exactly." David led Kate and the kids to meet Carter.

"Get over here, you crazy old sod," Carter said, opening his arms for an embrace. David stepped into a backslapping hug.

"You two know each other?" Private Reed asked with a frown.

"We flew together on the *Beyond III,*" Carter said.

"He's practically family," David explained.

"Awww, shucks, Commander," Carter said.

The soldiers from the facility interrupted. "This way, please. Major Baker is waiting for you."

That reminded David of Major Keller, putting a frown on his lips. "Major who?"

"The base commander," the soldier who'd spoken explained. "He'd like to debrief you. Follow me." He gestured to the door they'd exited a moment ago. They proceeded through a short walkway, and another soldier held the entrance open. The inner facility sported sterile gray floors and scuffed white walls. Exposed conduits and light fixtures tracked the ceilings, and what few windows they saw were small and air-gapped, with six inches to keep the heat in. Even so, it was cold.

Before long they came to a door with a glowing panel, and an old-fashioned plate that read *Major Baker.*

The soldier flashed his Holowatch across the scanner. It crackled to life, and the soldier said, "Dark Sixty-Two, sir. I have Mr. and Mrs Bryce, as well as Doctor Robinson and one Private Victor Reed."

"Proceed," a deep voice replied.

The door buzzed and slid to reveal a well-appointed space, with a desk in front of a window, a sitting area, and what might have been a bedroom hiding behind a half-wall of decorative wooden slats. A figure sat behind the desk, staring out the window. The chair turned, and a man with bristly white hair and ice-blue eyes met David's gaze. Jutting cheekbones and deep eye sockets made the man look almost sinister. He steepled his hands in front of his chin, contemplating them as they approached the desk.

Dark Sixty-Two saluted, and said, "Major Baker."

"Dismissed, Sixty-Two."

"But—" The man glanced at David and Kate with a tight frown.

"I said, dismissed."

"Yes, sir."

The soldier withdrew, and the door slid shut, leaving them alone.

"Do you still have it?" Major Baker asked, rising from his chair.

"Have what, sir?" Private Reed answered, hooking a thumb under the strap of his pack.

The rest of their bags must have been brought in by the soldiers from the chopper.

"The scanner," Major Baker said.

Private Reed blinked stupidly at the base commander. "What scanner?"

"Is this a comedy routine you two have been practicing?" Carter demanded.

"It's in his bag," Mark said before the major could reply.

"Thank you, son," Major Baker responded with a tight smile. "Hand it over, Private." He made a gimme gesture.

Private Reed sighed as he pulled his arms from the straps, propped the bag on the major's desk, and unzipped the main compartment to remove the alien device.

"How did you know?" Reed asked, shaking his head and regarding the commander with a suspicious look as he passed him the apparatus.

"It's my job to know," Baker replied.

"The only people aware it was in our possession were already compromised," Reed added. "Major Keller, and a fire team of four Marines."

"Compromised?" Carter asked. "In what way?"

"That may be the case," Baker said. "But we've encountered other devices like this one in the past, and they recognize each other."

Major Baker opened a drawer in his desk and withdrew a matching tablet with a holographic map and colored blips to indicate nearby life signs. He laid both of them on his desk and gestured to the screens. "Look." He made an expanding gesture with his hand to zoom in on the unit Reed had given him.

A blinking green dot appeared, dead center of the map, surrounded by seven yellow-shaded human signatures.

"Green indicates friendly assets—friendly to the Stalkers, in any case," Baker explained. "The blinking signature represents other scanners. Stalker field teams usually have at least one of these scanners with them."

"If you already had one, then what do you need ours for?" Private Reed asked.

"Because ours was offline, collecting dust in a drawer until you arrived and woke it up. I suspect the power level was so low after all these years that it entered some type of power-saving mode, but it recognized the proximity of another scanner and alerted me by squawking like a damned smoke detector. If I'm right about the levels, it won't be long before ours powers off again. Yours is obviously fully charged, and that offers a unique opportunity to track the Stalkers movements."

"Can't you just recharge it?" Kate asked.

"I wish it were that simple," Major Baker replied. "I won't waste any more time. Dark Sixty-Two is waiting outside to escort you to your rooms and to help you with anything else you may require."

"Thank you," David said.

"Sir, what are my orders?" Private Reed asked.

"For now, you're to remain on station and await tasking. Hit the rack. You've earned it. I can see a promotion on the horizon after what you did to keep the Bryce family alive. Dismissed, Private."

"Thank you, sir." Reed stood at attention and saluted before turning on the spot and marching from the room. He didn't seem happy to relinquish the alien tech, but the major's explanations seemed to have mollified him.

"I'm hungry," Rachel said on their way out.

"We'll hit the cafeteria after you settle in," Carter suggested. "I'll whip something up."

"That'd be great," David said. He was exhausted, but his stomach rumbled at the mere suggestion of food.

Dark Sixty-Two peeled away from the wall to face them. He was a mountain of a man with short black hair. He wore his arctic camo suit, his rifle slung crosswise on his chest. "Follow me," he said in a gruff voice.

"Jeez, who stuck a beetle up his ass?" Carter muttered.

***

"Cheers," Carter said, raising his pint of beer. "To you finally making it, alive and well."

David smiled grimly and lifted his mug, tipping it toward Carter's. They each took a sip, then set their drinks on the bar where they sat in the station's rec hall. After Carter had served them a hasty meal of grilled cheese and fries from the cafeteria, he'd led them here for some R&R. Apparently, it was well past the station's usual curfew, but Carter seemed to have sway with the guards. Sixty-two had grudgingly left them to their own devices, while Private Reed had excused himself to 'hit the rack.'

David glanced around while taking another swig of his beer. The decor was sparse and cheap, the paint peeling off the walls, the cushions on the couches and stools were worn down to lumpy rocks, and there wasn't a single window in the entire room, but as far as David was concerned, this was the nicest bar he'd ever been in.

It probably had something to do with being alive, safe, and warm, and not having to flee at a moment's notice because the next mortal threat had just reared its ugly head.

"So what have you been up to while I was running from Stalkers?" David asked.

"Oh, not much. Eating, sleeping, and flirting with the ladies."

David snorted.

"Well, that, and translating an entire alien language single-handedly."

David regarded him in stunned silence. "You're joking."

Carter grinned. "Want to know how I did it?"

"Please."

Carter explained how he'd entered the alien "Grazer's" holding cell, breaking the rules, and making direct contact with a species that apparently communicated more by touch than sound. When he got to the part about being bitten on the neck by an alien spider, it jarred loose a memory that never should have been buried.

David spun around on his stool, checking to see where Kate and the kids were.

"What's wrong?" Carter asked.

Kate was tucked under a blanket on one of the couches, fast asleep with an e-reader on her face.

Rachel stood around, looking bored, by the foosball table where she'd been playing a game with her brother.

And Mark was conspicuously absent.

David jumped off his stool, almost knocking over his beer. "Where's Mark?" he asked Rachel.

"He said he wasn't feeling very good," Rachel replied. "He went to the bathroom."

"No," David muttered. "Kate, wake up!" he shouted as he rushed to the men's restroom.

"Mmmmm?" Kate stirred sleepily.

"It's Mark," he explained.

She sat up, suddenly wide awake.

"What's happening?" Carter jumped from the bar and hurried to catch up.

"One of those spiders bit Mark. We were supposed to scan him when we arrived. Apparently they can lay eggs in people."

"Eggs...?" Carter echoed in a shrinking voice. "You mean, I'm..."

"You weren't tested?" David asked, pausing briefly as he reached the door to the men's room.

Carter slowly shook his head.

David scowled and pushed through the swinging door. "Mark?" he called.

The sound of him puking his guts out carried to David's ears. He followed the noise to one of the stalls and rapped lightly on it with his knuckles. "Hey, buddy, are you okay?"

Mark groaned, and then puked again.

Carter made a face. Kate burst in, clearly worried. "Is he okay?"

"Sounds like food poisoning," Carter suggested.

David hesitated, feeling suddenly stupid for overreacting. If Carter had been bitten last night, and he still wasn't showing any symptoms, then this could be something else.

"Buddy?" David rapped on the stall again.

Mark emerged, looking pale and shaky. Kate hugged him tightly. "Oh, sweetheart," she said, stroking his hair.

"Must have been those pancakes Reed made," David suggested. "But we should take him to the infirmary and get him checked, just in case."

"I agree," Kate said.

"I'll show you the way," Carter added.

David was about to follow them, but on a whim, he stepped into the stall instead. He gazed into the toilet, expecting to find it full of vomit.

But the water was clean and clear.

David frowned. Had Mark flushed the toilet? He hadn't heard anything. Feeling the hairs on the back of his neck rise, David glanced around quickly. A skittering noise pricked his hearing. Adrenaline lanced through him. He tracked the sound to an air vent in the ceiling above the stall. A piece of plastic fluttered loudly in the grate. The slats were bent, forming wider gaps, as if someone had manhandled the cover while performing regular maintenance.

David shut the toilet and stepped up on the lid for a closer look. He touched the grate—

And his hand came away sticky with translucent slime.

David jumped from the toilet and burst out of the stall, running for the exit.

SEVENTEEN

Atlas

Remote Amazon Rainforest

The insects stopped buzzing the instant the sun began its ascent into the sky, rising over the distant horizon. From his position, Atlas couldn't tell the difference until he gazed directly east. Despite being in the middle of the rainforest, he had control of his internal compass. It was a gift he'd inherited from his mother, who rarely needed a map or landmarks to find where she was going.

His father, on the other hand, would drive for hours, too suspicious to use his electronic car's GPS system. Despite the twenty years between them, Atlas guessed James' dad would have fit the same mold. It gave them something in common, even if James wasn't aware of it.

They'd risked a small fire that James had somehow managed to start, despite the wood being damp and having neither flint nor a lighter on hand. He was a true survivalist, and he did it all without any pretense or bravado.

Atlas stretched and stood up, his head dizzy with the sudden movement. He was hungry. After a quick trip to relieve himself near their camp, he glanced at the plethora of supplies they'd acquired in less than a day.

James had tracked and located three separate clusters of Stalkers, somehow managing to end the threat on each occasion. By the final battle, Atlas killed a Stalker by himself, growing his confidence. They were nine feet tall, and ugly as sin, but they died just the same as anyone if you hit them in the right spot.

A twig snapped, and Atlas realized he'd left the gun near his makeshift cot. When he lifted an arm defensively, he caught sight of James and let it fall. "You scared me."

"Good. You have to be on alert." James shoved the large alien weapon into his chest, and Atlas stumbled with the impact. "Don't leave this lying around, or next time it might be a Stalker walking up behind you."

Atlas nodded, his stomach growling. "We have to eat."

"I know," James said. "We're almost done here."

"You think we got them all?"

"No, but we can't delay any longer. Which way?" James peered to the west, as if he'd known the answer.

"Can I see that knife?"

James tugged it from his pants pocket and unfolded the blade with the snap of his wrist.

Atlas knelt near a felled tree and scraped the moss from the bark. With the tip of the knife, he dug into the wood, drawing a rough circle. "This is the region. Twenty miles wide."

James nodded, listening while glancing to the trees beyond their camp.

Atlas continued. "Three sites are possible locations for the crash. If I go by Booth's intel, there are five, but I think we should go to the nearest town. The locals might have witnessed the Grazers' ship crashing."

"It was a long time ago, Atlas. Likely nothing is left," James reminded him.

"I know, but it's worth a shot." Atlas drew the snaking river that would later connect to the Amazon River itself, just out of the circle he'd carved. Then he marked their position with an X and added three other Xs. "This is us." He indicated the first. "And I think the village might be here." He stabbed the knife into the tree.

"That's five miles away. If your scale is anything close to accurate," James added.

"I was guessing four."

"We'd better hurry," James said.

"What about food?"

"I almost forgot." James reached behind Atlas and lifted a bright and colorful bird. It hung dead from its feet in his grip.

Atlas poked at it with the knife. "That? We're going to eat that? Aren't they endangered?"

"Do you prefer to be extinct instead?" James began plucking it.

"I guess not," Atlas sighed.

They spent the next half hour roasting the bird, and when they were done, it was time to move. Atlas licked his greasy fingers, and used a leaf pooled with water to wash his hands.

Despite the early hour, it was blazing hot, even in the shade of the jungle canopy. His shirt clung to his skin in the humid air, but James didn't seem to be bothered in the least, except for a light sheen of sweat on his brow.

James never complained about their situation, just stepped forward at a determined pace. After spending an entire day with nothing but their wits, facing the enemy head-on, Atlas had a new respect for the Dark Team members.

"What's Lennon like?" Atlas asked after they'd walked the first couple miles.

"Dark Three?"

"Sure, whatever you call her," Atlas said.

"She's solid. Strong-willed. I think she might be one of the best shots we've ever had, but it's close."

"With whom?"

James paused and gave him a grin. "Me."

"Of course," Atlas mumbled.

"Why do you ask?"

Atlas kept scanning the trees for signs of snakes, jaguars, or Stalkers, none of which he wanted to cross paths with today. "She seemed..."

"Don't even think about it," James said flatly.

"Why?"

"She's severely traumatized. Every psychology test has said it over and over," James told him.

"Then why is she still in the field?"

"She wasn't, until recently."

"Tell me," Atlas said as he adjusted the homemade pack on his shoulders.

"I shouldn't."

"Come on. It's just us and the Stalkers. It's not like I have anyone to tell," Atlas laughed.

"Lennon Baxter fell in love with Rutger. Dark One."

Atlas remembered the quiet German. The guy seemed unstable himself. "And that makes her crazy?"

"No. They grew too close, and Dark Leader took notice." James plucked a small branch from a waist-high plant, peeled the green part and used it for a toothpick.

"Is that frowned upon? Hooking up with other operatives?"

"Not specifically. But they started to get distracted," James said.

"Lennon was slipping?"

James shook his head. "No. Not her. Him. Rutger is a killer through and through, but he was easing up. Sloppy mistakes on missions. Dark Leader saw him trying to protect Lennon, even though we all knew she didn't need a man to defend her. If I was betting, my money was always on Dark Three. She's the best we ever had."

Atlas raised an eyebrow. "Better than you?"

"Yes. But..."

"You think she's nuts."

"We caught her talking to herself. And it was obvious she was on edge."

"She was a danger to herself?"

"Not like that... she would stick her neck out, try to test fate. It started to escalate. Even Rutger couldn't convince her to relent, and when Dark Leader heard about..." James stopped talking, probably realizing he'd already said too much.

"What? The *Interloper*?"

"He had Chris, the Grazer, in custody. The Stalker as well. Dark Leader suspected something was coming long before we saw it. He decided to get rid of Lennon, and the only way to do that was to fake Rutger's death. It was an elaborate ruse, done under the guise of a real mission. These guys needed to be killed anyway, so we doubled down, and when the dust settled, Lennon was Stateside, and we continued on about our business."

"Damn," Atlas muttered. "That's cold. No wonder she was so pissed when she saw him."

"They better have gotten over it," James said.

"Why?"

"Because they're Dark Leader's best Team, and our chance to win this."

"They're paired up?"

"Last I heard. But I wasn't really in the loop. Since I'm..."

"Babysitting me?" Atlas asked.

James slowed and turned to face him. "This is important, Atlas. Maybe the most important thing either of us has ever done."

"Why not send more? One operative and me?" Atlas pointed to his own chest.

"There were more escape pods than Dark Leader had hoped. They were spread thin as it was. Usually we used five-person squads, and that was cut to four. It's dangerous. I suspect when this is over, there might not be many of us left standing."

"Sorry," Atlas said. James had been torn from the action, forced to guard Atlas in the rainforest rather than help his own. "Thank you."

"For what?"

"Being here. I couldn't have done this without your help."

James laughed lightly. "That's for damned sure."

"Even if you tried to blow me up in China."

"That was my property," James said.

Something crossed his mind. "You never were trying to kill me, were you?"

James grinned and kept walking. "No. Do you think you'd be alive if I was?"

After seeing him in action against the Stalkers, he guessed not. "You were pushing me forward."

"Time was running out, and Dark Leader needed that ship. But the Signal wasn't on it. It's in this jungle, and the enemy knows it." James picked up his pace. "You were getting too comfortable."

Atlas hurried, and they kept silent for a while, traversing the difficult terrain faster than he'd have guessed possible. Finally, as he'd hoped, they found the river. It was wider than he'd expected, twenty feet, with no way to cross.

"We follow it. Should lead us to the village," Atlas told him.

"The village we don't have proof of," James said.

"That's the one. It'll be there." Atlas said it with more conviction than he felt.

Another hour, and his legs were burning. He slowed when they caught the first sight of thatch-roof huts on the opposite edge of the river.

"It's here." Atlas beamed, proud of his prediction.

"How do we traverse it?" James looked in both directions, the water flowing west to east. The river had narrowed, but was surging much faster.

"How deep is it?"

"You don't want to go into that water, Atlas."

"Snakes?"

"Snakes, piranha, caimans." James pushed against a tree, but it stayed firm. "We need a bridge."

They spent the next twenty minutes searching for a dead tree long enough to span the river, and finally, after a failed attempt, they dropped one, the far end thudding to the ground. James tried to roll it, and the log nearly fell into the water. "We'd better brace this."

"Good idea." Atlas found a few wedge-shaped rocks, propping them on either side of the tree, and it steadied.

"You go first," James told him, and Atlas stared at the moss-covered narrow length of wood.

"Why me?"

"You're lighter. You can brace the other end for me."

Atlas shrugged, hoping his feet wouldn't slip. He grabbed his pack, heaving it to the opposite bank before attempting the balancing act. He held the alien weapon up in two hands, almost using it like a balancing pole.

"Whatever you do, don't stop once you start," James suggested.

Atlas inhaled and began to walk. His footsteps were sure, and Atlas crossed the distance after a near miss. He was drenched in sweat, but he'd made it. He crouched and held the far end while James joined him. He made it appear easy, like everything he did.

"This is no ancient village," James whispered, gun held at ready. Atlas tried to duplicate his actions, and they strode into town slowly.

The buildings were small, covered in aluminum sheets, with seventeen structures in total. The thatched roofs were long and drooping from the eaves. A fire pit remained in the center of town, and it was filled with outdated electronics. He spotted a radio and picked it up. "I'd guess it's from the Sixties."

"Agreed." James motioned to a hut, and they found a huge generator, the gas cap and frame heavily rusted. A black and white TV sat near the edge of the room, facing a rotted couch.

"Whoever lived here left a decade ago." Atlas returned outside, and they continued the examination, hoping for any type of clue.

"Over here," James called, and he followed the operative a short distance from the town's boundary. Fourteen wooden crosses were formed, lined up in a row with about five feet between them. Atlas approached them, seeing names engraved into the bleached lengths.

The names were congruent with the region, but one stopped Atlas in his tracks. "Homem do espaço," he whispered.

"What does that mean?" James asked.

Atlas was a hundred percent certain. "*Homem* is man, and *espaço* is space. Man from space."

James didn't wait. He dropped to his hands and knees, and began to dig, using the stock of the weapon for a shovel. Atlas joined him, careful not to accidentally touch the trigger.

The ground was hard-packed, making it grueling work, and whoever had buried the body had used a layer of rocks to create a barrier with the earth. An hour later, they had the body exhumed, and stood above it, examining the remains.

Long bones, two legs, an elongated skull matching the Grazers. "This was the ship's pilot."

"That means the Signal is close," Atlas proclaimed, and heard a rumbling sound carry above the tree canopy.

"They found us," James said softly.

EIGHTEEN

David

Somewhere in Northern Alaska

David caught up with Carter and Kate inside the cafeteria elevators. It had to be early morning already. He checked his Holo, finding it was just past six AM. Time was passing in a blur. He'd lost track. They still hadn't slept, and he'd barely had a few hours the night before, and now *this*. He stared at the trail of slime on his hand as he entered the elevator.

"What was the holdup?" Carter asked as he held the door.

"I found this." David showed him the thick liquid.

Carter made a face as he leaned in for a closer peek. "What is that?"

"It's from the vent above the stall Mark used. Does that look like what we found aboard the *Interloper*?"

"Bloody hell, it does!"

Kate's brow furrowed with concern. "What is it?"

"Spiders."

"Like the one that was on Mark's neck?" Kate asked.

David nodded, and Rachel pressed herself into the furthest corner of the elevator, suddenly wary of her brother.

All eyes turned to Mark, and he smiled blandly at them.

"Honey... what happened in the bathroom?" Kate asked.

"I threw up," he replied.

David frowned.

"Yes, but *what* did you throw up?" Carter asked as the door rumbled shut and the elevator began rising to the medical level.

133

David shook his head. "You think they came from *inside* of him?"

"That, or puking his guts out was a handy pretext for having a meeting with a few of his buddies in the men's room. The Grazer used a spider to communicate with me. Maybe they had another one contact Mark?"

The elevator opened, and Carter ran ahead. When they didn't immediately follow, he stopped and waved impatiently to them. "This way!"

"Come on, honey," Kate said, urging Mark forward. "Don't worry. You'll be okay."

"I feel fine," Mark reiterated. "We can go to bed now."

The infirmary was at the end of the hall, guarded by a single soldier in an unmarked black jumpsuit. He stiffened with their approach.

"We need Doctor Leslie Hauser," Carter explained.

The soldier's gaze traveled briefly over them, as if searching for the source of the emergency. "She's off-duty. Unless it's a crisis, I suggest you wait until—"

"It is," Kate snapped. "My son is sick. Call her. Now."

"He looks okay to me," the soldier replied.

"Let me handle this." Carter stepped forward with a thin smile. He tugged on the collar of his sweater to reveal a big white bandage. "You see this? That's an alien spider bite." Carter jerked a thumb to Mark. "The kid has one, too. And we believe this facility could be infested. Not only that, but we've just received information that indicates their bite could be a means of implanting eggs that later hatch inside the host."

The soldier's eyes widened. "I'll call the doctor."

"You do that," Carter snapped.

David listened while the soldier spoke into his radio in low, urgent tones. A moment later, he flashed his Holowatch on the door scanner, accessing the infirmary.

"Doctor Hauser will be here soon. She's asked for you to stay in the examination room until she arrives."

"Thank you," Kate managed, grabbing Mark's hand and leading the charge into the infirmary.

David followed her with Rachel and Carter. The medical center was divided between a curtained exam room to the right, and a lab full of microscopes, computers, beakers, sample vials, and all manner of other health equipment to the left. Straight ahead was a corridor with another exit leading off of it.

Carter led them straight to the curtained area and yanked it open to reveal a medical bed.

"Why don't you lie down, honey?" Kate suggested.

Mark jumped up and sat with his legs dangling over the side, idly kicking the air. He really did seem normal. Suspiciously so for someone who'd emptied the contents of their stomach a moment ago.

David approached the bed with a heavy frown, his heart hammering with apprehension about what might have been done to his son. "It won't be long, buddy."

He nodded, saying nothing.

A few minutes later, the doctor burst in, wearing a lab coat over fuzzy red pajamas with reindeer and elves on them.

"Leslie," Carter greeted warmly. "Looking radiant as ever!"

"What do we have here?" she asked, stopping beside the bed and ignoring Carter's flattery.

"My son, Mark," Kate explained. "He was bitten by a..." she trailed off helplessly.

"Same thing that bit me that night in the lab," Carter explained.

"The same one?" Leslie asked sharply. "You found it?"

"No," David said. "This one crawled out of a lake. Not here. Wait—did you say, *found* it? The spider that bit Carter escaped?"

Doctor Hauser nodded gravely. Between her hollow cheeks and deep-set blue eyes, she looked haunted.

"That could be the source of the slime you discovered on the vent," Carter said. "It might have nothing to do with Mark."

"Then why was the toilet empty?"

"Dry heaving? Or he flushed it before we got there," Carter suggested.

"Hold on a minute," Doctor Hauser said. "You'd better start from the beginning. What's wrong with him?"

"He threw up in the men's room of the cafeteria," Kate explained.

"Just the once?" the doctor asked.

"So far," Kate replied. "We're afraid that creature might have laid eggs inside of him."

David zoned out as the doctor asked more questions, checked Mark's pulse and listened to his heart. What did his heart have to do with being infected with alien parasites? Finally, she studied the bite mark on his neck.

"It's the same as Carter's. Do you mind, Mr. Robinson? I'd like to compare the progression of the wounds."

"Of course." Carter turned around and let Leslie remove the bandage to examine the puncture marks. "It's looking a lot better already. And Mark's wound isn't showing any signs of infection."

"Then why did he throw up?" Kate demanded.

Leslie shrugged. "It could be unrelated. Stomach flu or food poisoning. We'll monitor him overnight to be sure."

"Wait a minute—that's it?" David thundered.

Doctor Hauser blinked at him. "What would you have me do?"

"The military doctor he saw before we came here insisted that we have Mark scanned. He said it was important. That people were being used as incubators for alien eggs."

"Scanned how?" Doctor Hauser countered.

"I don't know! That's your job! You tell me."

"Even if your son were infected by some type of bloodborne parasite, the eggs would likely incubate near the bites, in which case their appearance would be much uglier than it is. We'd see localized inflammation. Pus. Possibly an entry wound or an air hole for the larvae."

Kate blanched as if she was about to be sick, but somehow Mark was taking it all in his stride, glancing from one person to the next, waiting for the verdict. That, if nothing else, was proof that something was wrong with him. Any other ten-year-old being told that he could have alien larvae inside of him would be terrified.

"It's not good enough," David insisted. "You should run more tests."

"I'll do everything in my power to care for your son, but you need to calm down and consider the possibility that you're overreacting."

"Overreacting!" David roared, throwing up his hands. "To an alien biting my son? The same aliens who've been reported to take control of hosts and use them to breed more of themselves?"

Doctor Hauser frowned. "Relax, Mr. Bryce."

David scowled at her, suddenly wondering if there was a reason he was getting so much pushback from the base doctor. "How do you know my name?" he asked.

"The whole base was informed ahead of your arrival. Besides, you're famous. I've seen you on TV. And that brings me to my other point. If there were alien spiders on the loose all over the country, invading people and laying eggs in them, don't you think it would be covered by the news?"

"If I'm imagining things, then why did that doctor warn me about it?" David said.

"Perhaps *he* was overreacting," Doctor Hauser replied. "But I will scan your son if that makes you happy."

"Thank you."

The doctor addressed Kate. "You said this happened yesterday?"

"Afternoon," Kate confirmed.

"Then it's too soon for a scan to reveal anything. The eggs would be far too small to identify. I could take a sample from the punctures and hope that I catch something, but it would be hit or miss, even if he is infected."

"Do it anyway," David said.

"Hang on. A biopsy needle that close to his brain stem isn't a procedure to be taken lightly. There are significant risks. Which is why I think the best course of action is to simply monitor your son overnight. We'll check his blood for other signs. But for now, a more aggressive approach simply isn't warranted."

David blew out a frustrated breath and held up his hand. "Something is definitely on the loose here, whether it has infected my son or not. How else do you explain this?"

Doctor Hauser leaned in and examined the drops. "It's a type of mucous."

"Spider poop," Carter suggested, drawing a scowl from the doctor. "What? It might be fecal matter," he added.

"I'll need a sample of this." Doctor Hauser hurried to a nearby cabinet and withdrew an empty vial with a cotton swab. She approached David. "May I?"

He nodded, and she dabbed the swab in the sticky residue on David's palm.

"Where did you find this?" the doctor asked.

"In a vent, directly above the stall where my son was throwing up."

"So it *is* in the ventilation system," Doctor Hauser said. "Strange that we didn't detect anything yesterday. We sent in a maintenance drone to search for it."

"Must be playing hide and seek," Carter said.

"Yes..." Doctor Hauser appeared troubled. "I'll see what I can make of this. And keep an eye on your son. Would one of you like to spend the night here with him? We have a rollaway bed in the back."

"I'll stay," Kate said.

"I'm sleeping *here?*" Mark asked suddenly, as if he hadn't been listening until now. Maybe that explained his lack of a reaction to the discussion about alien larvae burrowing under his skin.

"Yes," Doctor Hauser confirmed. "It's the least we should do."

"Don't worry, I'll stay with you," Kate soothed.

"Carter, under the circumstances, you should do the same," Doctor Hauser added.

"What? But I was cleared!"

"It's too early to make any assumptions, and your progression will give us an important glimpse into the future of Mark's recovery, since you were bitten sixteen hours before him."

"Fantastic. So if I keel over, you might be able to learn from it and save his life?"

Despite the gravity of the situation, David smirked at Carter's melodramatic reaction.

"No one is dying," Doctor Hauser insisted. "Not on my watch."

David's estimation of the woman improved a notch. "Is there somewhere I can wash up?" he asked.

Leslie pointed to a sink. "I'd better test this," she added, holding up the vial with the swab in it. "Carter, would you fetch the rollaway bed?"

"Just one? Where am I supposed to sleep?" he asked.

"The exam rooms, down the hall," she explained.

"On my own? In the dark?" he squeaked. "I bet it has an air vent, too..." he muttered as he left the curtained area.

David washed quickly at the sink, using a dispenser of surgical soap and then drying his hands on his jeans.

"I have to leave you here," he said, striding to Kate.

"Already?" Kate asked, sounding only slightly more certain than Carter.

"I'll find Private Reed. We have to speak with the base commander."

"You think it's that serious?" Kate asked.

"I do," David replied. His gaze flicked briefly to Mark, and he frowned. "I'll check in on you later, buddy."

"Sure, Dad," he said.

"Take Rachel with you," Kate suggested, jerking her chin to indicate their daughter. "She doesn't need to stay."

Suddenly remembering their other child, David spun around to find Rachel sitting in a brown vinyl armchair with her knees drawn up to her chest and her arms wrapped around them.

David felt a sudden pang of empathy for her. Most kids were afraid of monsters. Most parents, including David, had wasted a lot of breath reassuring their kids that monsters aren't real.

But now she knew better, because she'd been chased by them. And she'd watched another latch onto her brother's neck. Stepping over to the chair, he scooped Rachel into his arms, and she buried her face in his shoulder.

Maybe he couldn't kill all the monsters and make the world safe again, but he'd sure as hell protect his kids from them.

NINETEEN

Lennon

Mar del Plata, Argentina

The waves rolled over the soft sand, dragging pieces of debris with them. It was hard to believe this city used to be thriving, full of tourists. This very beach had once been packed with delighted visitors and locals, each vying for position as the first rays of light crested beyond the horizon.

Now it was a husk, burned to the ground in an accident twenty years earlier.

"It's a shame," Rutger said. "I came here once. In my early tenure with the Marines."

Lennon hadn't ever seen Mar del Plata, but it had been a big enough news story when she was a teenager. The entire city had caught fire when a shipping freighter exploded in the docks. It spread so fast, because of the high-density construction and laissez-faire regulations.

"What do they want?" Lennon asked.

"If I was to guess..."

"The towers?"

"Yep." Rutger had his Holo out, and Lennon watched the screen as he brought up old telecommunication plans. He tapped the Holo three times, activating markers on the map. "There are three of those old towers in the area."

"What are they doing with them?" Lennon recalled the one in Santiago. She'd wanted to destroy it, along with the aliens, but their enemy had fled the scene. Dark Leader had suggested this was their destination, and he'd been right.

"That's for someone else to determine. We're here to record. Dark Leader thinks we'll find a lead soon." Rutger walked over the beach, kicking off the sand when he contacted the sidewalk. The air still held a tinge of smoke to it, even after all this time.

Lennon's gaze drifted to the damaged cityscape. The entire place had been evacuated, and the government decided not to rebuild. It was cheaper to leave it there and start fresh thirty miles down the coast, with better rules involving the shipyard.

Lennon gestured to their helicopter. "They might have seen us coming."

"Perhaps." Rutger held his gun close to his chest, and jogged to the road, looking in both directions. "One of the towers is a half mile this way."

"Let's do this," she said, joining him.

A couple of hours later, Lennon saw signs of movement in this godforsaken metropolis. The first two towers seemed burned beyond repair, and apparently the Stalkers agreed. But the third was potentially operational.

Rutger lifted a palm, and she stopped. The Stalkers were at the base of their prize, chittering in their own tongue. The ground vibrated slightly, and she wondered if they used that in addition to sounds to communicate. She wanted to know if they could feel her steps, should she run at them.

Lennon pictured the first one she'd crossed in engineering on the *Interloper*. She'd come damned close to freezing up at the sight. Commander Bryce had nearly died in the explosion. Lennon hoped he was enjoying his cozy hideout in Alaska while the rest of them were facing Stalkers and constantly risking their lives. She figured David had lived a life of privilege, so why not keep it up? She'd been forced to battle for everything she had, and that wasn't going to change any time soon.

Lennon counted seven of them, and swallowed, not sure they had enough firepower to kill this many. She was almost ready to suggest calling for reinforcements when Rutger retrieved a device from his pocket.

"What's that?"

"Dark Leader gave it to me. Said it'll pick up their comms."

"You had this the entire time?"

"Yeah. He's anticipated a few outcomes."

Lennon peered around the corner of the brick wall, seeing the aliens hard at work. Their tools sparked and hissed as they modified the tower to suit their needs. "And what does he think they're doing?" she whispered.

"If they can't find the Signal, they'll make their own."

Lennon stared at him, trying to process the words. "They're using our old cell towers? That's insane."

Rutger shook his head. "Dark Leader thinks there's more. They require a worldwide network, and a central focus."

Lennon considered this. "Where?"

"That's what we're here to discover. When they're finished, we might learn their objectives." He held up the pen-sized tool. "In the meantime, we better hide."

Lennon hated to leave these Stalkers unmonitored, but if Dark Leader's theory was correct, there was a lot riding on the success of this mission. She followed Rutger down the alley, and into an abandoned building.

***

David

Somewhere in Northern Alaska

"What do you mean you're already doing something about it?" David demanded, leaning forward on the couch. Rachel was asleep beside him, her legs draped across his lap. She'd been unable to resist any longer. Out of the window, he noticed the sun had risen over the snowy wastes around the compound. They'd stayed up all night without even realizing it.

"Just what I said, Commander Bryce," Major Baker replied, sipping a black coffee in the chair adjacent to him. They'd woken Major Baker up just before his alarm was set to go off, and he was still wearing fuzzy gray long johns and a white undershirt rather than his regular uniform.

David stared fixedly into the man's ice-blue eyes, trying to decide if he was simply an idiot or secretly compromised by the Stalkers.

Private Reed shot David a warning look and then cleared his throat. "Respectfully, sir, if you already knew an alien is hiding in the vents, then why haven't you found it yet?"

"Because it's not hostile. It's scared. Remember, this one came from the Grazer, not from the Stalkers. And it gave us key intel revealing their language and motives, vis-a-vis your friend Carter Robinson."

"It bit him in the process," David said. "What if it laid eggs inside of him? Or if it deliberately gave us misinformation?"

Major Baker shook his head. "Your son's curious symptoms aside, Carter has shown no signs of the same reaction, and he was bitten before your son was. Therefore, we must conclude that your son simply has food poisoning. Perhaps from the diner you ate at several days ago?"

"We didn't have a chance to eat," David replied. "And I never mentioned the diner. How do you know that?"

"Major Keller's body was found not far from the diner. Witness statements given to the police placed both you and Keller there together."

David held Major Baker's gaze for a moment, trying to decide how much of that story he could trust. What if the two majors were conspiring?

"If you don't mind, I need to shave and shower. I'm sure you can imagine that I have pressing matters to attend. Rest assured, we're still looking for the missing alien, and we won't stop until we find it."

"What about the scanner we gave you?" David asked.

The major's eyebrows shot up. "I'm sorry?"

"Can't you use it to locate the missing spider?" David clarified.

"No, sadly it doesn't appear to detect the Crawlers. Only larger life signs. Private Reed, please escort Commander Bryce and his daughter from my quarters."

"Yes, sir."

They stood up. Rachel stirred sleepily in David's arms as he followed Private Reed from the room.

Back in the hall, Reed shook his head. "You shouldn't have pushed him so hard."

"Why not?" David asked. "He's hiding something."

Reed grimaced and grabbed his arm, leading him farther down the corridor. "If Baker *isn't* on our side, do you really think it's a good idea to make him aware of our suspicions?"

"Well..." David frowned and spared a hand from holding Rachel to rub his tired eyes. "Shit. You're right. Sleep deprivation is making me sloppy."

"Yeah. Let's go to your quarters."

Reed directed them to the elevators. On the dormitory level, he took David straight to the room he shared with Kate. Mark and Rachel's room was right next to it.

Reed opened the door from the panel, and David carried Rachel in. He laid her gently on the lower bunk and then dropped to his knees to check the air vent along the floor. He ran a finger over the grate, but it came away clean and dry.

"Everything okay?" Reed whispered.

David placed his ear to the vent and closed his eyes to focus on listening. Nothing but the distant scraping of a dirty ventilation fan.

"I guess it is," David replied, and a siren came whooping to life. "What is that?"

Rachel woke up with a start. "Daddy?" she cried.

"I'm right here, sweetheart," he said, and shuffled to her side. She wrapped her arms around his neck.

Private Reed stood frozen, listening intently. "They're here."

A split second later, hidden speakers crackled to life, and the major's gruff voice said, "Calling all units, this is not a drill. Full station lockdown has been initiated. We are under attack. Repeat, Specter Base is under attack. Twelve hostiles approaching from the airfield. Civilians, stay in your quarters and remain calm. Soldiers, arm yourselves. Secure all entry points and stairwells. They cannot be allowed to reach the lab."

David's eyes widened sharply. "Under attack by *what?*"

"What do you think?" Reed countered.

"Stalkers," David decided.

"I have to go."

"Wait. I'm coming with you." David shot up from the bunk with Rachel in his arms.

"You heard the major. Civilians are to stay in their quarters!" Reed raced out of the room.

David stared blankly after him for a second before snapping into motion again. "The hell with that," he said, and ran for the open door.

"What are we doing?" Rachel asked.

"Getting your mother and Mark."

***

Dark Leader

Unmarked Building, Long Island, NY

"Thank you for the update. Keep me posted, Major Baker," Booth said, ending the call. He rubbed his temples, feeling the tension creeping into his lower back. The bastards couldn't take his Alaska base. He'd been remiss in his expectations of the Stalkers. It was the damned Crawlers that had caused all the issues. They were an unknown, an unexpected advantage of the aliens, and might just be the root of Earth's eventual downfall. But there was still time to prevent that.

Alan took a drink of his coffee, finding it cold. He chugged the remains and checked the readouts incoming from Dark One. His left eye twitched as the data streamed in.

Is this accurate?

He waited for the response. *The tower is operational. I did what you ordered.*

Rutger always had been a good soldier, in every aspect. *Get to San Juan. This may be disastrous.*

A pause in the reply. *Will there be backup?*

Booth studied the screens. Only twenty-nine percent of the Dark Team members were still alive after the initial few days of skirmishes with the Stalkers, and almost all of them persisted in the field. The Stalkers had switched their focus from facing off against the humans to building their towers. Now that Dark One had recorded the communications, he realized what they were doing. But it didn't make sense.

Booth brought up all pertinent information on the Arecibo Observatory, but he still didn't understand their motives. It had sat out of commission for decades, even though it had once been used for radar astronomy and the SETI program. How did the Stalkers even know of its existence? And what were they going to do with the broken facility? It didn't have the kind of reach they needed to relay a message home, wherever that was. Light-speed comms were too slow to travel outside the solar system in any reasonable amount of time, unless they knew how to upgrade it somehow.

It's Dark Three...

Booth's gaze snapped to the screen. *Go ahead.*

What are our orders, sir?

He pictured Lennon Baxter; her jaw set in grim determination. She'd been through hell, but had returned, and continued seeking vengeance on the Stalkers. She was perfect for this job. He felt bad to do it to her, but she was more qualified than any of the others.

Destroy it.

The screen remained static, but a moment later he smiled as the words appeared.

Consider it done.

Booth sighed and looked up when someone knocked on his door.

"Dark Forty-One." He nodded at her, and she stepped in, holding a glass container.

"Is it...?"

"It's alive," she said.

Booth tapped the glass, and the Crawler jumped, almost hitting the top of the box. He gaped at it as dozens of black tendrils moved of their own volition, almost like a wheat field in the wind. It settled down, returning to a resting position.

"Come in." He waved the woman forward and shut the door to his workspace. She had bags under her eyes, and her chin tilted toward her chest. "It's been difficult out there, hasn't it?"

"My team is dead," she said.

"What's your name?"

"Dark Forty..."

"No. Your name."

"Ashley. Ashley Young."

"I'm Alan Booth."

She looked shocked to have her call sign summarily stripped away. But he didn't have to ask her name. He already knew who she was, as he did all of his agents, but they didn't realize that. "Are you certain you wish to volunteer? I could use..."

"It's fine. I've thought it over. It's my destiny," she said.

"We've had confirmation they can be removed afterwards," Booth told her.

"Good. I hope it will help." Ashley met his gaze and offered a soft smile. "Anything to stop these bastards."

Booth opened the secondary door, across his office, and they walked into a well-lit sterile room. "Please, take a seat, Ashley." He motioned to the large chair, and she obeyed, while Dr. Hunter took the Crawler sample from her hands. They strapped her in. One around the waist, two on her arms, then ankles. A pair of soldiers lingered nearby, hands on their guns.

"Are you comfortable?" Booth asked.

"Yes, sir." Her eyes were wide, and a tear fell as the doctor slipped into thick, puncture-proof gloves.

"This may be painful," Dr. Hunter said. He was young but prematurely gray, making his appearance somewhat confusing. "But from what we've gathered, it's quick."

He opened the case and grabbed hold of the Crawler with metal pinchers. It was smaller than a balled-up fist, and the thing screeched, trying to clamber away. "No you don't..." He set the Crawler on the back of Ashley's neck, and she shrieked before biting her tongue.

Booth stayed near the door, not wanting to get any closer to the dangerous creature. He could only imagine if his own brain suddenly became part of a greater neural alien network.

Ashley strained against the tethers, her neck tendons jutting out, and she sank into the seat, her head lolling to the side momentarily. She gasped, making Doctor Hunter jump, and stared at Booth, her eyes damp and red-rimmed.

"Why am I here?" she asked. It was her voice, but the tone was relaxed.

"I have a proposition for you," Booth said.

She blinked, her expression filled with resignation. "Go on."

"You're trying to contact home with this... radio telescope. I might have a better alternative," Booth said.

"We cannot reach our world with it," Ashley said.

Booth glanced at the corner of the room, ensuring the blinking light was on, and that this was all being recorded. If they weren't trying to send it home, then...

"There's a second *Interloper*..." he muttered.

"We only need to access the recesses of your solar system. It awaits communication."

"So the Signal is to call home, and the facility in San Juan is to connect the closest starship," Booth said.

"How can you help?" Ashley asked. Booth saw the long legs of the Crawler stretch out as she spoke, and he cringed.

"Where is the second vessel?" Booth asked, stepping closer.

"You lied," she said.

"Tell me!" Booth shouted.

Ashley looked away. Her skin grew darker, the blood rushing through her veins so fast that Booth saw each tendril snaking through her face. "You will never win..." Her capillaries burst and blood leaked from her eyes and ears as the Crawler freed itself, hopping to the wall. It moved for Doctor Hunter, but he swatted it with his Holo.

The soldiers intervened, shooting at the little target. After four gunshots, it was dead.

Booth crossed the room, setting a hand on Ashley's cheek. She was dead, too. What a waste.

"Your sacrifice gave us a lot of information," he told her, closing her eyelids with his fingertips.

There was another *Interloper*, as well as the Signal. If the Stalkers were successful in getting word to their allies, nothing on Earth could stop this invasion.

Dark One, don't destroy the facility. Find out where they plan on sending the communication first. Then do what you must.

He waited for the response.

TWENTY

David

Somewhere in Northern Alaska

David slid to a stop in front of the infirmary's entrance and set Rachel on her feet. The guard was conspicuously missing, having been pulled away to defend the facility.

Private Reed flashed his Holowatch at the scanner, and they proceeded inside. Doctor Hauser jumped to her feet from a stool in front of a table full of microscopes and medical equipment.

"We have to go!" David said to her.

"We can't!" Doctor Hauser countered.

The curtain to Mark's cubicle flew wide open and Kate emerged, looking pale and tense.

"Mommy!" Rachel cried, and sped across the room to collide with her legs.

"They said the base is under attack," Kate said, with Rachel clinging to her. "Under attack by *what?*"

"We're leaving," David insisted.

"Major Baker ordered us to shelter in this place! We're not supposed to leave. We should lock ourselves in and let the soldiers handle it."

"If we do that we'll be cornered," David replied. He pointed to the entrance. "And that door won't keep Stalkers out."

Carter hurried from the corridor as Mark emerged from the curtained area. "Dave?"

Mark rubbed the sleep from his eyes. "Dad?"

Private Reed peeked from his position near the exit with his sidearm drawn. He turned towards them, shaking his head. "We're clear, but there's no telling how long that will last."

149

Kate's gaze darted between them. "Where would we go?"

"Helicopter," Reed said.

"Can you fly?" David asked.

"We'll have to find a pilot."

"Hang on a second," Carter said. "*Why* are we being raided?"

David hesitated.

"It's the Grazer."

"Who?" Kate asked.

"The alien! He's locked up in the lab. We have to take him with us. They must be after him."

"Or else they've been tracking our scanner," Reed pointed out.

Realization shot through David like a lightning bolt. If the old scanner that the major had in his desk had woken up when theirs came into close proximity with it, maybe the Stalkers had been tracking the stolen device all along.

But if that was the case, then why hadn't Major Baker recognized the risk it presented to his station? David was sleep deprived. He wasn't thinking clearly. But what was Baker's excuse?

"There must be a way to turn it off," David said. "Let's go to Baker's quarters and retrieve it."

"So they can track us again?" Reed asked.

"No, so we can track them and use it to lead the Stalkers away."

"Unless they're really here because of the Grazer," Carter said.

David frowned, his mind spinning with competing interests. "Where's the nearest chopper?" he asked, glancing between Carter and Dr. Hauser.

"There's one on the roof," Carter said.

"Bring the alien and meet us there."

Carter nodded slowly, then looked to Dr. Hauser.

"We don't even know if you're infected," she said.

"I'll risk it," Carter replied. "You can stay here if you want, but you're on your own."

She shook her head quickly. "I'm coming."

David nodded to the private. "Reed, find us a pilot and bring my family to the roof. As soon as Carter shows up, you take off. Don't wait around for me."

Reed nodded uncertainly. "Where are you going?"

"To the major's quarters. I'll escort him with the scanner to the roof if I'm able. If not, I'll find some other way out."

"You're acting like we've already been overrun," Leslie said.

A muffled roar of rifle fire echoed through one of the ventilation ducts.

"That came from inside the base. It's time to move." Reed held the door open.

Kate fixed David with an urgent glance. "Come with us."

He hesitated. "I won't be long."

***

David

David crossed the corridor to Major Baker's room. Weapons had been firing throughout the building since he'd left the infirmary, and the sound grew steadily closer with every passing second.

Before he reached the major's quarters, David noticed that the door was ajar. He slowed as he approached and peered around the corner.

A hulking soldier was there with a pistol in his hand, and a familiar man with bristly white hair lay at his feet in a spreading crimson pool of blood.

David sucked in a noisy breath, and the soldier's attention swung to him. David ducked just before he recognized the man's grim features.

"Commander Bryce," Dark Sixty-Two ground out. "What are you doing here?"

David's heart thudded erratically in his chest. Was this soldier infected? "Is the major dead?"

Dark Sixty-Two grimaced and nodded, lowering his gun. "I had no choice. He was calling on our forces to surrender. I came in and found this"—Dark Sixty-Two showed his palm, and David saw the squished many-legged black spider—"on his neck."

"He was infected," David realized.

A rattle of weapons fire sounded from the corridor behind David. "We have to go. They're already inside. We're evacuating from the roof. Can you fly a helicopter?"

"Of course," Dark Sixty-Two replied.

David rushed into the room, heading for the major's desk. He yanked open the drawer where Baker had placed the scanner. Both were present. Making a snap decision, he grabbed the pair, then hurried for the hall. He hesitated beside the major's body, spotting the gun. David tucked the alien scanners under his arm and retrieved the weapon.

"What are those?" Dark Sixty-Two asked.

"Alien trackers. Shows where the Stalkers are."

"Give me one."

David passed him the working device, and the holographic screen snapped on. "We're the yellow dots," he explained.

"And green is... Stalkers?" Dark Sixty-Two asked.

"Exactly."

"Shit. They're close. On me, Bryce, and keep it quiet."

Dark Sixty-Two led the way, pausing briefly in the entrance to check both directions before heading left. They came upon a stairwell and slipped in as someone screamed. A devastating explosion rumbled through the building.

"What was that?" David huffed as he raced up the steps behind the soldier.

"Probably a fuel tank."

More eruptions echoed in a series as they continued the climb. "Sounds like they're trying to destroy the facility," David said.

Dark Sixty-Two didn't answer. David struggled to keep up as he sprinted up the stairs, taking them two and three at a time.

"Almost there." The big soldier glanced at the scanner and came to an abrupt stop. David crashed into him, and he spun around with a finger to his lips. He pointed up, then at the screen. David caught a glimpse of something big and black waiting on the next landing.

He slipped the broken scanner into the waistband of his jeans and raised the major's sidearm. Dark Sixty-Two placed his scanner into a pouch in his chest rig and drew a frag grenade from his belt. He pulled the pin and tossed it up the stairs.

It exploded with a *bang* and the Stalker shrieked. A giant mass of black limbs tumbled down the stairs. It thrashed and began struggling to its feet. Dark Sixty-Two stomped on it and stuffed his gun into the gaping nostril at its forehead. He tapped the trigger twice, and the Stalker lay still.

"Let's go!" he cried. They erupted from the stairwell and onto the roof. The chopper's rotors were already spinning. Kate waved frantically from her seat.

David used his remaining energy and careened into the helicopter. Kate and Carter caught him and helped lift him in. Dark Sixty-Two hesitated briefly on the snowy roof, scanning for signs of pursuit before entering and tugging the door shut.

David's kids were in the next row, and Private Reed in the pilot's seat. So much for finding a chopper pilot.

"Hey, he doesn't know how to fly!" David said.

"On it," Sixty-Two replied as he squeezed past them, heading for the cockpit.

Kate hugged him, her arms shaking. "You made it," she breathed.

He nodded into her shoulder and caught a glimpse of a hunching shadow crouched on the floor behind Carter. His gun snapped up. "Look out!"

Carter batted the weapon aside. "That's Chris!"

So this was the so-called Grazer. It was smaller than a Stalker, with two legs rather than four. But otherwise, the similarities between the two species were unmistakable. It hissed and flashed stubby translucent teeth at him while smiling sideways. A deep humming sound filled the air and shivered through the floor of the chopper. David wondered if there might be something wrong with it.

"He says not to feel bad," Carter explained. "Your bullets would have bounced off him, anyway."

"Here they come!" Dark Sixty-Two shouted. "Hang on!"

Stalkers flooded from the stairwell, preceded by a familiar wave of spiders. One of the Stalkers opened fire when the helicopter abandoned the roof and veered sharply away. The rotors screamed as Dark Sixty-Two flew an evasive escape pattern.

Several tense seconds passed before the gunfire faded into the distance, and David realized that they were out of range. He exhaled a ragged breath and sat beside Kate. The Grazer observed him with big, beady black eyes.

Suddenly, David realized who was missing. "Doctor Hauser?" he asked, struggling to be heard over the rotors.

Carter put on a headset, and David found one for himself.

"She stayed behind with the others to hold them off while we escaped. Spiders, Stalkers..." Carter winced. "It was a bloodbath."

David swallowed thickly, suddenly glad that he'd ordered Private Reed to take his family to the roof rather than accompany Carter to the lab.

More humming filled the air, vibrating through the hull of the helicopter.

"What's he saying?" David asked.

"He's sorry that they died protecting him, but he believes their sacrifice won't be for nothing. He thinks he can help us."

"How?" David asked.

"He knows what they're looking for. And..." Carter waited to hear—or *feel?*—the rest. "He might be able to locate the Signal."

"Hold this," Sixty-Two's voice said suddenly in David's ear.

"Hey, I can't fly!" Reed objected.

"Just keep it steady!" Dark Sixty-Two frowned at them from the pilot's seat. "Ask the Grazer where the Signal is."

Carter nodded. "Okay."

***

Atlas

Remote Amazon Rainforest

Three hours had passed since they'd first caught the sounds of the helicopter above them, and James was tense. They'd fully expected an assault, but instead, they'd only encountered more empty rainforest.

"Where are they?" Atlas asked.

James forced a finger to his lips, silencing Atlas.

He heard them. Low, murmured talking. Footsteps on the damp forest ground.

Finally, they spotted the group, and Atlas counted ten men and women, each holding automatic weapons.

"Duck!" James shouted as he dove behind a tree.

Atlas didn't have to be told twice. Bullets thudded into the trunk. He clutched his pulse gun close, like it was a life preserver and he was about to drown. "What are they doing? Those aren't Stalkers!"

"No. But they've been infected."

Atlas recalled rumors of the spider-creatures from the *Interloper*. "Great, now we're fighting our own people?" A couple of days prior, he would have had qualms shooting anything that wasn't a Stalker, but after seeing the infected woman on the plane, he no longer had those reservations.

"Pretend they're nine feet tall, if that helps you." James took a sharp breath and listened with his ear tilted to the sky. "Now!" He rolled out, firing the gun. Atlas was a step behind him, but he found an incoming target and blasted the man as he pulled his own trigger. The shot went wide, narrowly missing Atlas' leg.

James made the kill and rolled to his feet, gun swinging around as he sought his next victim.

Atlas huffed his breaths as he searched for the rest of the enemies. They'd disappeared. "What the hell?"

James patted three fingers against his forearm, and Atlas didn't know exactly what he meant by the signal, but he guessed. There were three to the left. Atlas kept watch on his right, and they departed slowly, heading farther away from the town.

Another flurry of bullets hit a tree beside Atlas, forcing him to drop. One of them struck his arm, but he only noticed after it began to bleed.

James took off, and Atlas heard five quick pops of his handgun. He returned a half minute later, his expression dire. "You okay?" He barely glanced at Atlas' wound, which was agonizing.

Atlas grimaced as he put pressure on it. "I'll live. Where are they?"

"Four remain, but I think they ran," James told him.

"What are we going to do?"

James grabbed Atlas' elbow, checking the damage. "It went straight through."

Atlas felt queasy seeing the entry and exit wound. "That's good, right?"

"Yes." James tore a section from his own shirt, wrapping it tight and tying it on Atlas' bicep.

Atlas groaned, searching for signs of the attackers. The forest was quiet. "You didn't answer my first question."

For the first time since he'd met the man, James Wan seemed unsure of himself. "I don't know. We have to find the Signal."

"Then what?"

"You press the button, and every damned Dark Team assembles at our location," James said.

Atlas had nearly forgotten about the device Dark Leader had given him. He reached into his pocket, finding it was intact. The clicker had a chain around it, so he draped it over his head, concealing it beneath his shirt.

A gunshot sounded, and James perked up. "Stay here."

"I'd rather come with you."

"Follow your orders. I'll be right back." James stayed low, creeping from his position.

Atlas was glad the injury was in his left arm, but it ached when he lifted the heavy alien weapon in both hands, using the sights to hunt for signs of the enemy.

There was gunfire ahead, and Atlas stayed close to the tree. Leaves shivered noisily from above, and he glanced up to see a hulking alien lower from the giant palm. It landed a few feet from him, all four legs bending to absorb the plunge. The nostril in its forehead flared, and Atlas stayed frozen. The monster moved closer, but he was still in shock from its sudden arrival.

Atlas belatedly swung his weapon toward the Stalker, but it swatted the barrel aside and punched him with a ferocious three-fingered fist. The impact was powerful, and the gun dropped to the ground. Atlas rolled over as the enemy's foot stomped into the earth, and he kicked its knee. It shrieked, and Atlas attacked again, using the heel of his boot. While it howled, he managed to secure his gun and pull the trigger.

Nothing happened.

Another fist flew at him, grazing his bullet wound. He cursed and ran backwards, tripping on his own two feet. The Stalker chased him, diving at the same second as he clipped a spare energy cell into place. He tapped the trigger again, and it blasted the incoming giant. The Stalker landed on top of him, and the wind blew from Atlas' lungs.

It twitched as he felt the Stalker's insides oozing onto his stomach. "Get off me!" He shoved at the heavy corpse and eventually slid out, panting.

Everything hurt, but the Stalker was dead. He swept the gun around, expecting more company to be attracted to the noise, but none came.

Atlas wanted to rest, but lingering wasn't a good decision. He abandoned the dead alien, and hoped he'd cross paths with James Wan again soon.

He checked to make sure his beacon was unharmed, and continued on, heading deeper into the rainforest.

***

Lennon

Northern Shore of Puerto Rico

They cut the engines a mile from the coast and paddled, hoping the sound of their boat hadn't carried to shore.

"Apparently Puerto Rico has gone dark," Rutger told her, staring at his Holo. "No communications in or out for the last two hours. Dark Leader is concerned."

"Because other countries will start to notice we're being invaded?" Lennon asked.

Rutger's jaw clenched with determination as they rowed. "Precisely."

"It's been a while since we did something like this," she said.

"The mission?"

"No. Sat in a boat together."

"Venice... that was nice."

"That was another lifetime," she reminded him. The longer she spent with Rutger, the more she realized they weren't ever going to be a couple. They'd been together out of convenience. It had taken near death again to see the truth. Or maybe she'd changed.

"What do you think our chances are?" he asked her.

"For us or Earth?"

"Earth," he whispered.

"For Earth, not great. For us, even worse," Lennon said.

He laughed lightly. "Were you always so upbeat?"

They kept their voices low. The boat was totally dark, and the night sky revealed an expansive blanket of stars. "I've had to protect myself," she said.

The shoreline was close, and they searched for an isolated beach, floating west before shifting directions to dock. Rutger was the first one out, quietly splashing in the water. He pulled their boat, securing it a few yards up. Lennon doubted they'd return for it, but she couldn't be certain.

She helped him drag it farther up the beach, as the tide could steal their only means of escape.

They gathered their gear, and Lennon checked her charge and sidearm for ammunition. They hid a few supplies, in case they lost their weapons during this mission. She guzzled water from her canteen and left it, not wanting the added weight. Rutger did the same, and they were off, rushing down the rocky beach.

He slowed, and Lennon saw the resort ahead. There were people approaching the main road. "At least they're not all dead."

Lennon wasn't sure what she'd expected, but so far, there was no sign of the Stalkers. They moved closer, and Lennon gasped. The ground was seething with Crawlers, hundreds of them, streaming to the west. The people walked stiffly, and she sighted down her pulse rifle's scope, finding one of the Crawlers on each of their necks.

"Damn it. That's where all the stupid spiders went. They're everywhere. They used the ocean for cover and came here," she muttered.

"This might make our mission easier," Rutger said.

"How?" she hissed.

Rutger unslung his pack and opened it up. From it, he retrieved two black boxes. He reached into the first and removed a dead Crawler, its tendrils drooping low.

Lennon almost slapped it away, but refrained at the last second. "What are you doing with those?"

"Dark Leader requested samples."

"When were you going to tell me you were carrying those... *things* with us?" Lennon hated the aliens. Whether it was a Stalker or one of their many minions, she wanted them dead.

"It wasn't important. Come here. Let me place it on..."

Lennon protectively clutched the back of her neck. "You think I'd wear that?"

"It'll make blending in a lot simpler." Rutger turned her around and set the lifeless Crawler onto her skin. The appendages brushed her neck, and she hated every second of it. "Stay still. We need to prop it up, otherwise it'll be too obvious."

Once hers was in place, she did the same for Rutger, doing her best not to have flashbacks to the *Interloper*. Every time she closed her eyes, she thought about the horrors they'd witnessed.

They used a wire, almost like dental floss, to sew them into their collars. When they finished, it looked reasonably convincing. "Think they'll buy it?" Lennon asked.

"I sure as hell hope so," Rutger said. "Come on. Let's see what they're doing."

Lennon and Rutger exited the beach, trying to be inconspicuous as they marched alongside the infected. The humans walked with purpose, none of them offering the soldiers even a cursory glance. *This might work after all,* Lennon thought.

They met up with the road and followed the growing horde destined for Arecibo Observatory.

TWENTY-ONE

David

Anchorage, Alaska

Dark Sixty-Two landed in the snow-covered parking lot of an abandoned dock and shipping warehouse on the outskirts of Anchorage. David balanced the two alien scanners in his lap. Both screens were off. Soon after departure, Chris, the Grazer, had explained how dangerous they were, proving David's theory that the Stalkers might be able to use the scanners to track them.

In theory, they couldn't do that unless they were activated.

David watched as the thunder of the rotors slowed into silence. It was late afternoon, and the sun was low in the distant horizon.

"Now what?" Kate asked, yanking off her headset.

Mark and Rachel sat quietly, their eyes wide with shock as they stared at the alien sitting across from them.

"I can't contact Dark Leader," Dark Sixty-Two explained, twisting around in the pilot's seat. "I'll try again once we reach the airport."

"Airport?" David asked.

"We're catching a flight to New York," Sixty-Two said. "With Specter Base overrun, the facility in Long Island is our next best bet. And we need to share his intel with the Association," he added, nodding to the Grazer.

Chris still hadn't revealed the Signal's coordinates. He'd said he would only speak to their leader. David wondered if the alien meant President Carver, but he suspected that Dark Sixty-Two had taken it to mean his commanding officer, Dark Leader.

Private Reed observed them, and his gaze fixed upon the alien. "We're taking a commercial flight?"

Dark Sixty-Two nodded. "After your run-in with Major Keller, and mine with Major Baker, we can't trust military bases. They're targeting key personnel, and anyone could be compromised. Flying as civilians should help us to avoid further complications."

"What about Chris?" Carter asked. "He can't walk into an airport like that."

"We'll have to use some kind of disguise," Sixty-Two replied, frowning at the lanky alien.

It hummed and reached for Carter's hand. The two shared a bizarre moment, and then Carter said, "He says we should hurry."

"Agreed," Sixty-Two nodded. "Private, let's search that warehouse."

"Copy, sir."

The two soldiers jumped out, and a cold wind sliced through the cabin, bringing with it a fresh dose of the Grazer's fishy body odor.

"Gah," Carter muttered, holding his sleeve beneath his nose.

David distracted himself by watching the soldiers rush to the big cinder-block building. Dark Sixty-Two shot a padlock and rolled the bay door up before he and Reed disappeared inside.

David checked the scanners in his lap. He was tempted to turn one on, even if only momentarily, to search for any Stalkers in the area.

Mark glared at the devices, as if he was busy thinking the same thing.

"What's wrong, sweetheart?" Kate asked, misinterpreting the glazed intensity in their son's eyes as distress.

Mark shrugged and looked out his window. "Nothing."

David frowned, questioning if Mark's interest in the alien tech was more than idle curiosity. They hadn't finished testing him for signs of infection. He predicted that Mark's strange behavior was more to do with their equally peculiar circumstances, rather than some alien awareness silently growing in his son.

They waited quietly for the soldiers to return. Kate was wringing her hands. Carter made one-sided small talk with the alien.

"You're telling me you haven't even had a girlfriend?"

Chris hummed a few notes.

"Stop making excuses. Face the facts, Chris. You're basically a five-hundred-year-old virgin."

Chris hissed something at him.

"A virgin? Oh, that's a... how do I explain it to you..." Carter began to make a gesture with his hands.

David stared pointedly at Carter.

"What?"

"Let's not," Kate said, nodding to their kids.

"They have to learn about the birds and the bees eventually."

David sighed. "They already have, but I don't think they covered the alien version at school."

"Ewww, gross," Rachel said.

But Mark didn't even react. He watched outside, as if he were expecting company.

Feeling nervous, David reached under his seat for the gun he'd taken from Major Baker. He held it on the scanners with the barrel facing the door, and scoured the parking lot for signs of trouble.

"Did you see something?" Kate whispered.

"No." But David didn't relax his guard.

A few minutes later, Private Reed and Dark Sixty-Two emerged from the warehouse, carrying a long wooden shipping crate between them.

Carter frowned. "I'm not sure Chris will like riding in a coffin."

"I don't think he has much of a choice," David replied.

Ten minutes later, Chris lay in the crate with packing peanuts stuffed around him.

"You good, buddy?" Carter asked, shivering and rubbing his arms from the cold. None of them had been wearing jackets when they'd evacuated the facility.

The Grazer hummed.

"He says it's better than a cryo tube."

Dark Sixty-Two nodded, and he and Private Reed hammered the lid into place. The crate had metal vents in the sides, allowing Chris to breathe.

"It's freezing," Kate said, jumping up and down to stay warm.

"Don't worry. Our Uber is on its way," Dark Sixty-Two said.

"You called an Uber? Are we all going to fit?" David asked, dubiously eyeing the crate with the Grazer in it.

Dark Sixty-Two shrugged. "We're about to find out."

"Let us know when it gets here," Kate said, and returned to the helicopter.

When they arrived, Mark hurried to his seat, looking guilty. David glanced at the spot where he'd left the alien scanner with the depleted power cell. "What were you doing?"

"He was playing with that thing you told him not to touch," Rachel said.

"Mark, is that true?"

"No," he huffed. "I was just protecting it. Rachel's trying to get me into trouble."

David climbed in and closed the door.

"Hey, watch it!" Carter cried as David almost shut it on his fingers.

"Sorry," David muttered.

He watched his son with a growing sense of dread. He prayed that someone would be able to help them reverse whatever had been done to Mark once they returned to the facility on Long Island.

***

The Uber stopped in front of departures at the Anchorage International Airport. Their driver opened the trunk of the full-size SUV and helped remove the heavy wooden crate that had forced him to lower the rear two seats of the vehicle.

Reed, Carter, and Dark Sixty-Two hopped out of the trunk. They'd had to squeeze in with Chris. Not exactly a legal way to travel, but Dark Sixty-Two had managed to silence the driver's objections by threatening to commandeer the vehicle. That had been before he'd discarded his gun, so it probably hadn't been an empty threat. Not that David supposed the giant operative would need a weapon to overpower the much smaller man.

An ominous thump sounded from the crate as the driver failed to hold up his end, and it tipped suddenly. David stepped in and caught it before it could crack open on the pavement.

The crate began to vibrate, and the driver retreated with a curious frown.

"We've got it from here," Dark Sixty-Two said, edging the man aside.

"What's in there?" the man asked, scratching his reddish-brown beard.

"You don't want to know," Sixty-Two replied.

"Toys," Carter added with a wink.

The man's eyes widened. "Gotcha."

Inside the airport, they managed to balance the crate lengthwise on a luggage cart before lining up at the ticket counters, while Reed used his Holo to buy their tickets and Sixty-Two attempted to contact Dark Leader again.

The operative gave up with a sigh a few minutes later. "The first time I assumed it was the poor reception. But now, it seems like he's just not answering."

"Maybe he's on the toilet," Carter suggested.

Dark Sixty-Two and Kate both glared at him.

"You take your Holo in with you?" Carter made a face and slowly shook his head.

"How did you put up with him in a rocket for three months?" Sixty-Two asked.

David smiled tightly. "It wasn't easy."

"Close quarters makes for even closer friends," Carter explained, grinning and wrapping an arm around David's shoulders in a brotherly hug.

"You have the tickets?" Sixty-Two asked Reed.

"Yes, sir."

"Good."

They reached the front of the line, and Reed stepped forward to speak with the airline agent. She transferred their tickets to Reed's Holo.

When it came time for them to check their bags, the woman's brow furrowed with concern as she realized that their only luggage was the oversized wooden crate, and they didn't even have carry-on.

Reed and Sixty-Two placed it sideways on the scale, and the woman's frown deepened as she read the number.

"Excuse me," she said. "I'll be right back."

She returned with her supervisor, a portly man with thinning gray hair and a grumpy expression. David read the name tag on his uniform. Bob Hart.

"I'm afraid you'll have to open that," Bob said.

Carter looked worried, but Dark Sixty-Two stepped forward with a thin smile. "It's nailed shut."

"Either you open it, or you leave it here. Your choice."

Dark Sixty-Two scowled, then reached for a multi-tool on his belt and dragged the crate off the scale to pry the lid off.

David watched anxiously as the wooden cover came up, revealing a sea of pink and white packing peanuts. One glossy black arm was peeking out.

Bob sucked in a sharp breath. "What is that?" he demanded.

"A prop for Comic-Con," Carter said.

"Show me the rest," Bob said. "I need to see it."

Carter shrugged and placed a palm on Chris's arm. "It's pretty heavy. Kind of a dead weight. Guys?" He looked to Sixty-Two and Reed.

Dark Sixty-Two took Chris' legs, while Carter and Reed took his torso.

Chris emerged in all of his alien glory. His head flopped backward, and a long black tongue rolled out of his mouth. He was doing a convincing job of playing dead. Maybe too convincing.

A fishy stench filled the air, and Bob threw his sleeve up to his nose. "Smells terrible!"

"Cheap vinyl," Carter explained.

Chris's hand twitched, and the ticket lady yelped with fright. "I think it moved!"

"Animatronic," Carter grunted, struggling visibly under Chris' weight.

"All right, put it away," Bob said, waving impatiently at Chris' smelly form.

They laid him into the crate, and Dark Sixty-Two hammered the lid on with his fists. "Happy now?"

Bob glared at him. Seeing something else to complain about, he pointed to the multi-tool on Dark Sixty-Two's belt. "You can't take a Swiss army knife on the plane," he said.

"Here," Sixty-Two tossed it at him, and it almost struck the man in the face before he snatched it from the air. "You keep it," Sixty-Two said, smiling.

Bob pocketed the tool as he walked away, muttering that he needed a vacation.

A minute later, they left the ticket counter with Chris sliding down the conveyor belt.

"Well, that was easy," Carter said as they headed for security. "Who's hungry? I could murder a fish taco right about now."

Reed groaned, and Kate wrinkled her nose.

David's stomach did a queasy flip. After spending hours in that helicopter bathing in Chris' BO, fish was the *last* thing he wanted to eat.

"What?" Carter asked.

"I thought you hated fish," David said.

"I think it might be growing on me."

Dark Sixty-Two sighed and pulled his Holo out to busy himself with another call.

***

Dark Leader

Unmarked Building, Long Island, NY

Alan Booth glanced at his Holo, but ignored the incoming call. It was from an Alaskan operative, but he wasn't certain who he could trust anymore. The last thing he wanted was for one of the Stalkers' infected human agents to discover his location. This was far too important.

The door to the second-lowest floor slid to the side, and he smiled as he appraised the laboratory. Twelve of the world's finest biologists and chemists in the same room, working to help save humanity. The rest of the planet was finally learning about the Stalkers. It was impossible to avoid.

Booth had thought they could contain the Stalkers, and his Dark Teams had done an admirable job of that, but he'd never anticipated the Crawlers. With that horde of parasitic creatures sweeping across the globe and multiplying faster than anyone could have imagined, the Stalkers had been able to take over entire locations, towns, and even cities.

The information was slowly leaking: video footage, news reports. When he checked his Holo, there was always another horde of people in the streets, abandoning their families and workplaces. So far, nothing had turned violent, but Booth wasn't stupid. It was only a matter of time before the infected took up arms and fought to clear the planet for their incoming allies.

Booth couldn't let that happen. He smoothed his thumb and forefinger into his eye sockets. The tension and stress gave him a constant headache. It took him a moment to realize that Dr. Geoff had spoken.

"Can you repeat that?" Booth stepped farther into the lab, assessing the nearest clear glass container. A live Crawler scurried inside it, and the science team member pressed a button on the digital display, releasing a gas into the box. The Crawler twitched and fell limp.

"Sir, we have good news," Geoff said.

"It's about time. What is it?" Booth followed the doctor to the edge of the room, where a patient lay in a bed. Her eyes were closed, and he glanced at the machine displaying her vitals.

"We've been able to separate the patient from the invader," Dr. Geoff said.

"We've done that before. They also managed it in Alaska without issue."

"I know, but this is different. It's been successful with an airborne substance." The doctor grinned widely, and Booth patted his back.

"This is ingenious. Are you saying...?"

"With a series of trials, we could possibly deploy this over infected regions, effectively eradicating the Crawlers."

Booth pictured jets dropping clouds of the substance above cities, freeing the infected from their guests. "Great work. How soon can we—"

"Months. This was almost a fluke. It'll take countless tests, and the ingredients aren't easy to come by. The mining alone will..."

Booth shook his head and walked up to Dr. Geoff. "You will finish what you started. Send the list to Gail, and she'll transfer it to the proper people. We cannot fail, do you understand me?"

Geoff gulped and nodded, but Booth saw hesitation in his eyes. "This is the most important thing you'll ever do. That any of us will do."

"I understand."

The woman in the bed gasped, pulling tightly against her restraints. Her eyes were bloodshot, her face contorting in horror or agony. She screamed, the sound horrific, and Booth almost reached for his sidearm. She flopped down, refusing to look at them.

The machine beeped, and Booth saw that she'd flatlined. Dr. Geoff stood at the bedside, his hands shaking.

"She was doing so well," Booth said. "We can perfect it. This isn't over." But his optimism had already deflated.

"Yes. I'll work on it, sir." Two uniformed assistants rushed to help roll the patient from the lab. Dr. Geoff went to a separate room, and a second patient was brought in, strapped to a gurney. Another infected to test. A middle-aged man, still wearing an Army lieutenant's uniform.

Booth walked away, and Dr. Victoria Marcus beckoned him. "Do you have a moment?"

"Only if you have good news."

She gave him a grim smile and picked up a device. "This is wirelessly connected to my Holo."

"What is it?"

"Put your hand out."

Booth hesitated for a split second, and did as she asked. The round object blinked blue lights as she clamped it over his index finger. Something jabbed him, and the Holo flashed and chimed.

"Sorry, it takes a blood sample."

"For what?" Booth snapped.

She removed the tester, and he licked his finger where the blood welled at the puncture. Dr. Marcus smiled proudly as she showed him the results on her Holo. "You're not infected."

"I already know *that.* Try it on him." He pointed to the Army lieutenant they'd transported on the gurney.

"Yes, sir."

He followed Dr. Marcus there. The device flashed and buzzed. "What's it doing?"

"Using a proprietary UV method to sterilize the needle."

Booth resisted the urge to tap his foot. A few moments later, Dr. Marcus pressed the tool to that man's finger. Again lights blinked, and then her Holo chimed. She turned the screen for him to see the result. A single word was all he needed to see.

Infected.

"How accurate is this?" Booth demanded.

"Extremely."

"Test all of us. Now!"

"But..."

"Just do it."

"I don't have the authority—"

Booth cleared his throat, addressing the staff. "Everyone in a line."

They continued working.

"Line up, now!" he demanded, his heels clicking together.

This got them moving, and he stared down the row of twenty-five doctors and their assistants. Were any of them nervous? There were no visible Crawlers, but he suspected that didn't matter. For all he knew, they'd already laid eggs, or burrowed in. Some of the infected had continued to present behavioral anomalies even after the Crawlers had been removed. The mechanisms by which they overtook their hosts were still unclear.

"We require volunteers. I want to see firsthand that it's working so I can duplicate this prototype." Booth noticed a couple of them squirming near the exit.

The first few were quickly cleared, and the line continued shuffling forward while Victoria scanned them.

When only two remained, a man grabbed a woman, holding a scalpel to her neck. "It's too late!" he said.

Booth flinched but stayed calm. "Why is that?"

"Because we're everywhere." The assistant's skin was coated in sweat, his hair matted to his forehead. He hurried to a table, turning the butane lever, and used a lighter to start the flame. It hissed out, and he snatched a spare uniform, grinning sinisterly. His hostage matched that expression, and he released her now, revealing that she was also one of them.

Booth saw that they were planning to burn down the facility. He drew his sidearm and shot the man, then the woman, all in the time it took to exhale, and they crumpled to the floor. A Crawler emerged from the guy's mouth, scampering away.

Security arrived just as the sprinklers started, and Booth sensed something was off. The scent was familiar. He grabbed hold of Victoria with her Holo, and ran from the lab, diving through the open doors as the flames took hold. Judging by the smell, a gas valve had been opened.

He peered at the lab, watching it burn. Small explosions rattled the windows and glass as the people inside cried out.

"We have to go," he managed. He slid a miniscule memory stick from his pocket as they bolted to the stairs. He wasn't going to risk the elevator.

Victoria panted and stomped her legs. He hadn't even noticed her pants hems were on fire. They put it out, and she hesitated near the exit. "We can't leave them!"

The heat penetrated the sealed doors, and someone banged on the glass, barely visible through the smoke. "They're already gone," he said as a blackened arm slowly slid to the floor.

They sprinted, Booth's gun in his grip. "You have all of Dr. Geoff's data on that Holo?"

"It's on the server, but I can access it."

"Then transfer everything you two worked on with this." He shoved the memory stick at her as they breezed through the outer doors, stepping outside.

It was night, which almost surprised him, and he waved at a pair of Dark soldiers. "Prime my helicopter. We're leaving. Evacuate the entire building."

They stood there, and for a second he thought they might be infected, until one snapped off a salute. "Yes, sir!" One spoke hurriedly into his comms, and Booth ran around the building.

"There, it's done," Victoria said, removing the drive.

Booth grabbed his own Holo and sighed. Their base was compromised, which meant he needed to remove everything from the server. He found the hidden folder, let the Holo scan his eyes, and entered his personal code.

Years of work and information that not even the Association had copies of. He did have a backup, but it was across the world, stored in as remote a setting as you could find. He killed it, and the screen dimmed.

"Time to leave, Dr. Victoria," he said over the noise of the helicopter rotors.

He entered after the ashen woman, and saw another call coming in.

"President Carver," he muttered. Before answering, he told the pilot to take off. Below, a steady stream of his employees emerged from the warehouse, and the Dark Team had them filing onto a waiting bus. They were prepared for emergency protocols, but he'd hoped for more time.

He stared at the name on the screen, and finally accepted. "Carver, what do you want?"

Victoria sat up in her seat, probably shocked by how indifferent he sounded when answering a call from the president. But Booth only answered to the Association.

"I've been authorized to make you an offer."

"Convenient timing," Booth muttered.

"Yes, the facility. Sorry about that. We couldn't have you sabotaging us, could we?" Carver's smile was unnerving.

"Just give it to me."

"We ask that you lay down your arms. Meet us in Paris. You and the entire Dark organization. If you comply, you get to live," Carver said.

"Is that so? With Crawlers on our necks? Laying eggs and burrowing inside of us?"

"Is it not better than the alternative?" Carver asked, still smirking.

Booth glanced at the base from high above, the people resembled ants. "Go to hell. All of you." He ended the communication and saw another from Dark Sixty-Two. He answered it this time, and caught a glimpse of David Bryce standing next to the soldier.

"Report," he ordered.

Dark Sixty-Two looked tired, and Booth guessed they were at an airport. "We're leaving for New York. I have... Chris is with us. He says he can help."

Chris? It took Booth a moment to connect the name to the Grazer. "What about the scanner?"

"We have that, too, sir," he said.

"Excellent. Why not take a military flight?"

"Specter Base was overrun, and I believe it's not the first. There's no one left to trust," the Dark operative explained.

"Okay. Give me your flight number. I'll be waiting."

"Yes, sir."

"Don't fail me, soldier."

"I won't, Dark Leader."

Alan Booth stared at the Hudson River as they crossed over the Manhattan Bridge, and wondered if there was any chance they'd win this war. With the scanner and some assistance from the captive Grazer, their odds had substantially improved. Now they just needed to locate the Signal before the enemy did.

TWENTY-TWO

Atlas

Remote Rainforest

Atlas wiped the sweat from his brow and glimpsed the sun from beneath the canopy of trees. He'd spent the late hours of last night scouring the jungle, and he'd mentally marked off the first two locations where he'd estimated the Signal might be.

After a fitful sleep, worried about the local wildlife as much or more than about the Stalkers, he returned to the search, needing to check the final spot. He was close, but his legs moved slowly. Atlas wasn't used to this kind of adventure. He had no food, and his only water had been scooped from large leaves after a dawn rain. His limbs were covered in bug bites, and everything itched. The wound on his arm had stopped bleeding, but the rag holding it tight was soaked. It wasn't a romantic trek through the jungle in search of ancient treasures, like he'd seen in the movies. It was a living nightmare.

His thoughts kept drifting to his journey to this point, and he struggled to believe he was even in the jungle, hunting for the mythical Signal. If the Stalkers weren't able to locate it, why had Booth expected him to be? Was Atlas only a distraction, a red herring while Booth played some other game?

Atlas wished James Wan was with him, but he'd seen no sign of the cynical soldier since their separation. It only added to this morning's hesitation. Even if he found the Signal, how long would it take for the Dark Teams to arrive? Hours, at best. Days, at worst.

He patted his chest, ensuring the beacon stayed tucked under his shirt. He did this religiously, fearing he might lose it.

Atlas licked his cracked lips and stepped forward. "Don't give up yet," he said, but the self-motivation fell flat—until he spotted the first section of the crashed airplane.

Part of the wing was lodged into the top of a giant palm, and Atlas slowed, peering up at it. If the crash site was near, there was a chance of obtaining food and water...if it hadn't disintegrated on impact.

He tapped into energy reserves he didn't know he had and marched, eventually finding other sections of the plane, as well as items that had flown out the door when it had been in the air.

Atlas grabbed a neck pillow, tossing it aside. His feet were damp, his shins slimy from the terrain. All he wanted to do was leave, head home, and sleep. But even if he was able to escape with his life, there wouldn't be any moments of respite, not with the Stalkers still entrenched on their planet.

He kept going, discovering a food tray. Animals had opened this one, but a case of bite-sized pretzel bags remained un-scathed, and Atlas knelt by it, tearing the cardboard. He laughed while he ripped the top from one of the packets, devouring the contents, then another. Atlas stopped after he'd eaten six of them, and wished there was a nice cold beer to wash it down. He'd even settle for clam juice.

To his surprise, an entire rolling refreshment cart had plummeted from the plane, sticking halfway into the earth. Atlas rushed to it, almost tripping on a log. He jumped at the last second and landed hard. The cart was bent in half, but some of the drinks were still intact. He sifted through burst soda cans and found a bottle of water.

With a shaky hand, he drank, drops dribbling out the corner of his mouth. He tried to go slower, but his thirst took over.

He rattled the final splash in the bottle and finished it. Atlas spent the next couple of minutes gathering four more sealed drinks, and stared at the goods. He needed a way to transport them.

A noise echoed in the sky, and Atlas gazed to the sun in the east. The sound vanished, and he continued his quest, while cradling the box of pretzels and beverages.

The moment he saw the familiar carry-on bag, he paused. There was no chance it had survived. He rushed to it, dropping his supplies, and saw his Holo, the screen cracked. He attempted to turn it on, but nothing happened. It was broken.

His notebook sat inside. Atlas fished it out and thumbed through the pages.

Without another thought, he stuffed everything he could into the backpack, leaving the remaining snacks. He ate two more for good measure, and decided to head for the final destination where he and Booth had estimated the Signal might be waiting.

It was only a couple of miles, and under normal circumstances, that wouldn't be an issue. But Atlas had been hurt in his constant battles with these bastards, and everything was tender. He felt like he'd crashed with the plane, rather than escaping with a parachute. He removed the makeshift bandage on his bullet wound, wincing when he saw the angry entry point. After reapplying another piece of cloth, he kept going.

Two miles turned into an enormous obstacle, and there were still countless dangers to be wary of. But the sustenance gave more energy than he'd had since arriving.

A half hour later, Atlas stumbled upon the rest of the plane. The fires had dissipated by now. There was a section of the rainforest where tree limbs lay littered on the ground, and that's where he headed.

The hull was blackened, the nose smashed in. Part of the wing dangled, and he stopped at the door. There was no sense in entering, so he circled around it, leaving the mess behind him.

His heart hammered in his chest when he saw the nearest Stalker. There were a pair of them, perhaps more, and they walked by on all fours with casual disinterest. He paused to observe them: the rear two legs appeared to hold most of the weight, while the front pair leveraged obstacles and kept them balanced. God, they were ugly.

One chittered to its friend, and Atlas searched around, finding nothing in the way of a hiding spot. Unless he...

Atlas jogged to the aircraft, climbing through the charred doorway. Nadine, the infected cabin crew member, was there, the Crawler on her neck long gone. She was dead, her skin blistered, her clothing burned. Atlas checked to see that the

Crawler wasn't there, seeking a new host. When Atlas was confident it had fled, he rushed across the uneven floor. The entire section was tilted, making the trek to the bathroom a challenge. He kept the bag close and went into the compact space. He locked it, knowing that was fruitless, should a Stalker come for him.

He still had the alien weapon cradled to his shoulder when he set the bag down, planting a foot to the door. He braced against it, holding the heavy gun up.

Atlas steadied his breath, and as soon he stopped huffing, it became clear the Stalkers were inside the cabin.

One of them shrieked, probably asking if any allies were present. The only response was the litter of footsteps. Their weight and bulk made their passage noisy past the narrow rows of seats.

He held his breath when the floor beyond his bathroom door squeaked, and Atlas pressed farther back, his legs straddling the toilet. *Go away, nothing to see here.*

Something stroked the center of the accordion-style plastic. His finger skimmed the trigger. Then it was gone.

Atlas sighed and grinned nervously to himself. They were leaving.

He waited until they were gone before he lowered the gun. That had been far too close.

A drop splashed on his nose, and he peered at the source. A Crawler was upside down, legs flailing as it dropped. Atlas slapped a palm at it, bashing it into the mirror. It fell into the sink, but quickly recovered. He hoped the Stalkers had vacated the cabin as he bashed the stock of his weapon at the Crawler. It easily avoided impact and jumped to the floor. Atlas hated spiders, and now he was locked in a tiny airplane bathroom with one. And this wasn't just any spider, it was an alien.

He danced, trying to stomp on it, and failed. The Crawler seemed to be enjoying watching him squirm. It lurched to the wall, scurrying up to the ceiling, and once again, it attempted to land on him. Atlas finally understood its game plan, and the second it did the action again, he shifted his weight, opening the toilet lid. It fell into the dry bowl, and Atlas shoved the lid closed, stepping on it. The Crawler bashed against the underside of the lid in a vain attempt at freedom.

Atlas couldn't hear the Stalkers, but they might have been waiting for him to emerge after all the commotion. He searched for a heavy object to leave on the lid, but failed to find anything. The sink was fastened tight, and nothing here would do the job.

"Think, Atlas," he muttered, and grabbed his pack, testing it on the lid. The Crawler came close to knocking it loose, but couldn't. With that temporarily in place, he slowly unlocked the partition and investigated the plane. The Stalkers were gone. He rushed to the pilot's seat; fortunately, the door wasn't closed. The dead pilot stank, making him shove his forearm over his nose. Atlas found a metal crate in the front.

He replaced it over the bowl and took his things, creeping from the plane. Atlas checked the overhead compartment where he'd left the key. The latch was broken, the bin bent into itself, making it nearly impossible to pry open. With a grunt, he managed to get access, and smiled when he saw the bag. Atlas unfolded the cloth and stared at the pieces of the artifacts he'd found. They were still connected, and he peered toward the exit before shoving them into the pack.

He was covered in sweat when he departed, and didn't spot the pair of Stalkers he'd seen earlier. Moving as quietly as possible, Atlas rushed from the site, hoping those aliens had continued heading in the direction they'd been traveling. It was the opposite of his destination.

Atlas straightened the backpack, slung the pulse weapon higher, and went towards the sun.

He made it in record time, with every inch of his body thrumming upon arrival. This had to be the spot. The last of the intersecting radii from his data and Booth's. These were the only three locations where both data sets had suggested the Grazer ship had crashed, but that didn't mean they weren't wrong. He mentally taped off a quarter-mile section and scoured the entirety of it. There was only more shrubbery, fallen logs, and trees.

The entire endeavor was for nothing. Atlas sat on a moss-covered stone, resting his face in his hands. What was he supposed to do?

Atlas reached for a drink, finding his notebook. He checked the margins near the map, and realized he'd done something wrong. His fingers trembled as he flipped to another page: a missive from a villager thirty miles east of here.

"No way..." He grabbed the Holo, wishing it was operational. He tried to turn it on, but it didn't work. He felt a protrusion. Atlas rotated it, realizing the corner was peeled back. The lithium battery had been jarred loose. Atlas replaced it, snapping the frame closed.

The Holo chimed, almost causing him to drop it.

"Come on, be there..." Atlas retrieved the files Booth had given him. He took his old map, spinning it upside down. This had been drawn in the wrong spot. A simple misreading.

There was one more intersection, and Atlas estimated it was less than three miles from where he currently resided. With a grunt, he was on his feet, destined for that direction.

TWENTY-THREE

Carter

Alaska Airlines Flight 227

C arter sat in an aisle seat near the back of the airplane, his legs cramping from the tight space while sitting for the last seven hours. His Holowatch told him there were two more hours before their arrival at JFK.

David and his family were in the row ahead of him, with Dark Sixty-Two sitting diagonally across from Carter, his head leaning into a travel pillow he'd bought from a convenience store before boarding.

Carter's gaze drifted to the man directly beside him, on the adjacent aisle: a short guy with glasses and a blank expression. He was sweating visibly beneath a thick green winter jacket. The fur-lined hood was up, and his arms were crossed.

"Cryophobic?" Carter asked.

The man didn't respond. Carter frowned and reached over to poke him in the shoulder. The stranger flinched and regarded him with glassy eyes. "What was that?"

"It's just that you're wearing a jacket. In a heated cabin with two hundred ATP-powered heaters crowded in with you."

"Huh?" The man blinked. "ATP..."

"Adenosine triphosphate. It's the energy source that our cells use."

"Oh."

"You know, we're warm-blooded, so we generate our own heat. About a hundred watts each. Times two hundred. Short story long, it's kinda hot in here, don't you think?"

The man blinked, and a drop of sweat fell from his lashes.

"You could probably take off your jacket," Carter pressed.

The man shook his head. "No, thank you."

"See, that's what made me think maybe you're a cryophobe. You know, afraid of the cold? But then I thought: from Alaska? Now that would be ironic."

Dark Sixty-Two turned to glare at Carter. "Would you shut up?"

"He's wearing a jacket and sweating like a pig!" Carter said. "That doesn't seem odd to you?"

"Maybe he has a fever." Dark Sixty-Two faced forward.

"Are you feeling under the weather?" Carter asked.

He didn't seem to hear.

"Hey, mate? I asked—"

"Please leave me alone." The man unbuckled and stood. Popping open the overhead compartment, he rummaged around in his bag.

Carter sighed and stared at the seat in front of him. No one appreciated a good conversation anymore. It was a dying art, and people like sweaty-jacket-man were the last death knell in the coffin of high society.

The guy kept sifting through his bag. "Found what you're looking for?" Carter asked.

He jumped and tucked something into his jacket. "Excuse me. I must go to the bathroom."

Carter watched him go, leaving the compartment open.

If they hit turbulence, luggage could fall out and hit people. Carter unbuckled and rose to shut it. Before he did so, he noticed that the simple black satchel bag they'd bought was deflated.

Empty.

Carter patted it quickly, finding nothing inside. The contents had been the two alien scanners. Dark Sixty-Two had wanted to avoid drawing any unnecessary attention by carrying those scanners around in plain sight, especially given that infected humans were cropping up around them with increasing frequency. All it took was for someone to see those devices and turn them on.

Carter snapped into action. He smacked Dark Sixty-Two urgently on the top of his head. The giant man burst out of his seat, his eyes glaring and chest heaving.

"You have two seconds to explain before I—"

"Our bag is empty," Carter said.

Dark Sixty-Two scowled.

"It was the guy behind you. He's in the—"

"Move." Dark Sixty-Two shoved past Carter, forcing him into his seat. The operative stormed by the last few rows and tested the doors to both bathrooms. One folded open, while the other stayed shut.

Dark Sixty-Two pressed his shoulder and his considerable weight against the locked entry. It yielded, and the man yelped with surprise. The soldier reached in, and something cracked. Then he stomped on the floor, and Carter caught a glimpse of translucent fluid spraying out around his boot. The operative closed the stall and tucked both alien scanners into his pants.

Heads turned sleepily from the nearby rows to look for the source of the commotion. Dark Sixty-Two nodded and smiled, his back to the bathroom. "Stomach trouble," he explained, and jerked a thumb behind him.

People returned to what they were doing, their interest already waning.

But Carter knew the truth. Sweaty-jacket-man had been infected. Dark Sixty-Two had snapped his neck and trampled the Crawler before it could escape. Now he was guarding the stall to make sure no one discovered the body.

How long is he going to stand there? Carter wondered, with his heart suddenly slamming in his chest. Would they be arrested when flight attendants noticed the dead man in the bathroom? They'd been traveling together. At the very least, they'd be taken in for questioning, unless Dark Sixty-Two's sphere of influence was enough to get them out of it.

The intercom crackled to life. "Ladies and gentlemen, this is your pilot speaking. We are beginning our descent early, as we have just been advised of an unspecified situation on the ground at JFK. We are diverting to Newark instead. On behalf of Alaska Airlines, we apologize for any inconvenience, and we would like to offer everyone on board a free meal or transit voucher as compensation for your trouble. Once again, our apologies. Thank you."

Carter wrinkled his nose. "Newark?"

Dark Sixty-Two leaned against the wall between the stalls. A flight attendant hurried down the aisle and shut the overhead compartment. She strode purposefully toward Dark Sixty-Two.

"Do you need the bathroom, sir?" she asked.

"I'm waiting for a friend," he replied.

"I'm afraid you'll have to wait for him from your seat. The captain has turned the seatbelt sign on."

Dark Sixty-Two stood firm. "I'm good, thanks."

"Excuse me?" The flight attendant bristled. "Return to your..."

Dark Sixty-Two sighed and pulled his Holo out of his pocket. Carter saw a QR code flash up on the screen.

"Scan it," he said.

"Tickets have already been scanned, sir."

"It's not a ticket."

The woman withdrew her own Holo and did as he ordered. Her eyes widened, and she sucked in a sharp breath, her hand flying up to cover her mouth. Dark Sixty-Two leaned in and whispered something in her ear. She glanced to the bathroom, then at him. Wordlessly, she strode away, her cheeks pale.

Carter wondered what had passed between the pair. Whoever these Dark operatives were, they definitely had connections. What had he shown the flight attendant?

He settled into his seat as turbulence shuddered through the plane. Carter's gaze darted around the cabin, searching for signs of more infected. Would anyone else try to take the scanners from them?

And how had that man known where to look? The devices had been hidden in that satchel since before they'd even arrived at the gate.

The Stalkers had to have agents and eyes everywhere. Carter caught a glimpse of someone peeking between the seats. It was David's son, Mark.

The boy turned away quickly, but not fast enough to elude Carter's scrutiny. A sharp jolt of suspicion coursed through him. Mark knew where the scanners were hidden. Had he somehow communicated that fact to the nearest Stalker agent?

Carter's palms and feet began to sweat, and he shivered involuntarily. There had to be a way to detect infection—and, Carter hoped, to reverse it. If not, things would become very ugly. How many people were affected? A thousand? Ten thousand? Fifty? He hadn't had a chance to check the news lately. Nothing had seemed to be amiss in Anchorage before take-off, but that had been more than seven hours ago. The situation could have changed dramatically since then.

***

Lennon

Arecibo Observatory, Puerto Rico

"This is intense," Rutger whispered without moving his lips.

Lennon agreed. Seeing the old observatory restored to its original glory sent goosebumps up her arms. The spherical reflector dish was a thousand feet across, and the three towers were erect, with the telescope cables currently being repaired. The sun was up, casting a warm glow through the entire region, and Lennon admired the overgrown trees surrounding the radio telescope.

Workers cut away hanging branches, clearing the debris, and there were literally thousands of the Crawlers scattering on the disc, stopping to repair various sections. From the observation deck, Lennon now noticed what the spiders were doing. They dropped their bellies to the metal hull, releasing a liquid, then spun the material over cracks and fissures. It seemed to harden quickly, and they pushed on. The observatory itself was practically empty, with all the infected humans focused on the telescope itself.

"There." Rutger gestured to the other end, where two Stalkers strode, watching the progress. One held a tablet, which projected what she guessed were the blueprints for their finished product.

"We need to get our hands on that tablet," Lennon said.

"Good luck. Why don't you walk up to the Stalker and ask for it?"

"No. But that doesn't mean we can't access it another way." Lennon turned around, joining the ever-growing line of humans arriving for instruction.

"Where are you going?"

"When in Rome." Lennon waited with the group as a row of trucks backed into the parking lot. A thick-set man with extreme body odor flung a door open and revealed an endless stack of electronics.

"Everyone take something," the same guy called, and the laborers reacted.

Lennon trudged along with the crowd and picked up an old television. Rutger took an in-home Holo VR kit, and they brought them toward the disc.

The Crawlers were already on an existing pile, sorting through it. A group of humans argued over something Lennon wasn't privy to, and her gaze drifted to the left, directly in the center of the upside-down dome.

"What is that?" she hissed.

"Those are escape pods," Rutger answered.

She dropped the television and heard something shatter. No one confronted her as she slowly strode closer to the pods. They'd seen enough of them to recognize what they were, but these were different, and had clearly been modified.

They had glowing blue cables connecting them, and hundreds of Crawlers scuttled around the four pods, working tirelessly.

"I think we found our power source," she muttered.

"Now we know how to shut it down."

"You two!" someone called. The woman waved at them, suggesting they follow her.

"What can we do?" Lennon asked, trying to sound eager.

"They need these crates on the opposite end. Bring them." The woman touched her Holo, barely addressing Lennon and Rutger.

"Consider it done." Lennon pushed past Rutger, grabbing hold of one end of the heavy crate. It was stuffed full of microchips, resistors, capacitors, and transistors.

They trudged off, with Rutger grunting in effort. The cargo weighed more than her.

"What if we ditch this stuff?" he asked.

"Then they find more. That's not enough." Lennon slowed when she spotted a Stalker. His nostril flared, his four eyes blinking in unison. It took all of her focus not to reach into her jacket and retrieve her concealed sidearm, the only weapon on her. She closed her eyes, remembering the first being she'd encountered on the *Interloper*.

"You okay?" Rutger prompted.

"I'm fine. Let's keep going." Lennon placed one foot after the other, and eventually, they'd crossed under the disc. People of all sizes cleared debris from the worksite, dragging wheelbarrows full of branches and leaves deeper into the jungle.

It seemed as though the entire island had been infected. Lennon felt powerless. She'd already failed to destroy the *Interloper*, and now she was at this site, aware the aliens were determined to call for reinforcements.

"I know what you're thinking, Dark Three."

Dark Three. It felt so formal, like they were only numbers. Cogs in some great machine that she'd never seen from the outside. She didn't let the sting show on her face. Rutger didn't matter anymore, not in that sense. There were more important things in the world than love—if that's what they'd even had.

"I'm not thinking about anything. I am but a brainless infected," she mumbled.

They set the crate down, and Lennon saw the pair of Stalkers with the tablet again. They pointed at the construction, discussing it quietly.

"I think we..." Lennon checked behind her, but didn't see Rutger among the throng of workers. Where had he gone? The Stalkers moved away, and Lennon took her chance. She'd find Rutger again, but this might be too important to ignore.

She slipped through and rubbed her nose. Everything smelled so fishy, and it was beginning to roil her stomach. Lennon trailed the Stalkers, keeping in the shadows. It was hot, and the dead Crawler on her neck irritated her skin as sweat prickled from underneath its body.

Lennon couldn't wait to be out of here. She pictured a warm beach, somewhere far away, and imagined a shirtless server dropping off a fruity drink with an umbrella in it. In her daydream, she glanced at someone other than Rutger. It was the handsome artifact hunter... Atlas. His name was almost as ridiculous as her own.

Lennon was so distracted, she almost didn't notice that the duo had stopped. They'd reached the stairs and climbed them, idly chatting. It was strange to see these savage aliens in conversation. She found it easier to imagine them as monsters than people.

Almost silently, she emerged up the stairs thirty seconds afterwards, and saw them walking toward the observatory. More Stalkers lingered nearby, and Lennon cringed. If they discovered her, she was dead.

But that tablet would hold everything they needed to stop this, and to maybe even discover the location of the second *Interloper* that Dark Leader had suggested was in existence. If a fully functioning starship came to Earth, it was over. They'd already caused so much damage with the first one, and it had crash-landed in the ocean. Dark Leader was resourceful, but there were limits to what the Dark Teams could accomplish.

Lennon stayed near the outer walls, stopping at the first window. The tablet leaned against the doorway, the lights on it dimming until it went dark.

She crept closer, not daring to breathe.

It was warm in her hand, and she didn't risk looking at it yet. Lennon slid it into the back of her pants and pulled the jacket over the visible portion.

A Stalker came from nowhere, the front two legs landing on the deck right before her. It stared at Lennon, and she didn't make eye contact. Instead of acknowledging the Stalker, she turned and slowly walked off, making sure the Crawler on her neck showed.

It came after her, clomping at an even pace. She still didn't respond. Lennon smelled it directly behind her, and could almost feel its warm breath on her neck.

An explosion rocked the bridge above them, leading to the suspended telescope, and the Stalker shrieked, rushing off.

It took all of her restraint not to sprint away, but she did start jogging the moment she was out of sight of the primary building.

Lennon had the tablet. Now all she needed to do was find Rutger.

TWENTY-FOUR

Dark Leader

Financial District, Manhattan

I t was a hazard coming here, but Alan Booth was used to taking risks. He figured this was the last time he'd be able to visit his home.

It was empty, devoid of life. No plants to water. No pets to care for. It held memories of a past he struggled to remember.

A picture of his wedding day hung on the wall near the living room, and he stopped at it, squinting as he stared at this young version of himself. Before his scars. Long before she died.

Booth walked to his bar. That was one thing he kept stocked. With a drink in his hand, he strolled to the patio, opening the doors. He gazed west and felt the gentle breeze.

David Bryce and Dark Sixty-Two would be arriving soon. He needed to leave, but this was important to him.

He stared at the various military medals and accolades displayed on his wall. These were only a small assortment of them, since most were top secret. Even his wife hadn't known exactly what her husband had been through.

He felt for the scar on his face and took another drink. The couch looked inviting, and his entire body was exhausted, so he sat, sinking into the supple caramel leather. He turned the TV on, checking the local news, and wished he hadn't.

"*...just in from the northern coast of Ireland, where someone has caught an animal on film.*" The newscaster wore a pink pantsuit, her hair big and brown. The footage played, and Booth watched the grainy image of a Stalker walking through a field. It cut off, returning to the anchorwoman.

"This isn't the first of its kind. Social media is being flooded with images of similar creatures from all around the world. Entire cities have been cut off from communication grids, and no one has heard from friends and family in Puerto Rico for an entire day. While officials blame a solar storm for the communications blackouts, and an elaborate string of hoaxes cooked up by bored citizens for the so-called cryptid sightings, a former aide to President Carver has another explanation..." The woman stared off camera, looking startled. *"What... excuse me... I..."* She backed away rapidly from the camera. *"It appears to be a-a swarm of–"*

The feed abruptly switched to an advertisement. A minute later the woman returned, smoothing her jacket. *"Please excuse the interruption. We have just been informed that these videos are a hoax."* She smiled confidently. *"There's nothing to worry about. Everyone can remain calm. Now, let's go to Caroline at the Bronx Zoo, where we celebrate the birthday of..."*

Booth paused the feed and zoomed, seeing a black tendril extending from behind the anchor woman's neck. "They're everywhere," he muttered, powering the TV off.

He sat, unwilling to get up yet, knowing his knees would ache when he did so. Instead, he used his Holo, reading a message from the captain of the USS *John F. Kennedy.* He hit the response and nodded to himself, glad that the carrier group was in place. Things were coming together. This was why someone in his position relied on backup plans. His old military connections were paying off.

Now that his base and the one in Alaska had both been compromised, at least they had somewhere else to operate out of, a remote location that the damned Stalkers wouldn't even know about. He considered sending a message to the Association, but decided against it. Carver had implied that many were infected. And if the bastards had gotten to the President of the United States, Booth believed it. There was no telling how many operatives and mission leaders at the Association were under their influence as well.

A noise rattled his window, and he finally rose, using the couch arm to prop himself up. When had he gotten so old? People were in the streets, moving south. He peered to the north and saw a steady stream of New Yorkers crowding Broadway. Taxis gridlocked the road.

"It's happened." Booth cursed quietly and poured another drink. He needed to get to the airport to pick up Dark Sixty-Two and Bryce before the infection spread through all the boroughs. New York had seen enough over its course of time, but this might be the one that finally brought it to its knees, unless he could bring Dr. Geoff's research to his secondary team on the carrier. They might be able to finish perfecting that airborne cure.

He downed the liquor and wished he hadn't. Witnessing the hordes of infected had set his stomach on edge.

Booth walked to his guest room, finding the bed made, the place immaculate. The cleaning staff had kept the condo in order when he couldn't.

The artwork had always been his wife's favorite; that was why he'd chosen it. With a press on the corner of the gilded gold frame, he rotated the picture, revealing a hidden keypad. It scanned his retinas and clicked open.

The closet doors slid apart, and he stepped into the control room. The lights softly glowed as he grabbed the bag on the floor. It was heavy. The previous *Interloper* hadn't gone down with the batch before, but he would ensure they could destroy the second ship. He peeked inside and cringed at the sheer firepower within. Instead of the plasma-infused spheres, they were half the size, compact and square, but each contained five times the punch of the previous models.

Booth carefully lowered the pack to the ground and heard a knock at the door.

"What is it?" he asked his escort, Dark Fifty-Nine. The man was competent, but not his first choice.

"The flight's been redirected. Something about an issue at JFK."

"Where?"

"Newark, sir," Dark Fifty-Nine said.

"Okay. Take this." Alan Booth rubbed his shoulder, massaging it as he hefted the heavy bag. "And for the love of God, be careful with it."

The operative seemed to comprehend the danger it held, and carried it out gingerly.

Alan glanced into his condo from the hall, his gaze lingering on the wedding photo in the foyer. "Goodbye, my heart."

He locked up and headed to the elevator. The helicopter was waiting on the rooftop, and they had an important pickup. He hoped New Jersey hadn't been infected quite yet, but didn't think he'd be so lucky.

***

Atlas

Remote Rainforest

Atlas was in hell. Tiny black flies clung to him like sweat, and he tried to wipe them off while continuing closer to his target zone, but it was fruitless. He eventually gave up, letting them bite his skin. Everything burned from the heat, bites, and flora. But he was close, and that kept him going.

The landscape was all the same, making it difficult to navigate. Everywhere he looked, it seemed like he was walking in circles, but with the aid of his Holo, he could tell he was moving in the proper direction. It was his only saving grace.

He was about to step past a row of kapok trees when he spotted the Stalkers. Five of them. No. Seven.

They marched toward the west, with a group of humans trailing them. Even the Stalkers acted uncomfortable in the jungle. Their carapaces were shiny, as if they'd been oiled, and their movements were sluggish. The humans were worse off—red faces, their clothes drenched with sweat and exposed skin riddled with bites—but none of them seemed to notice. They carried advanced military-issue automatic weapons. Atlas briefly wondered where they'd acquired them.

He watched from the shadows of the treeline, ensuring complete discretion.

At first he hadn't seen the Crawlers, but when he spied one, the rest came into focus.

Atlas checked his feet, and the branches above, but couldn't find the spider-like entities near his position. He exhaled when the group eventually passed by and were out of sight.

His bag was at his feet, and he bent to pick it up.

"Finally," a voice said.

Atlas flinched, and accidentally pulled the trigger of his plasma gun. It missed and melted a thick branch twenty feet away.

James Wan rushed over, shoving his gun aside. "Are you crazy? You trying to wake up the world?"

"We have to leave," Atlas hissed. While he was relieved that James was alive, he'd likely just alerted the Stalkers to their location.

"Why?" James asked, his gaze lingering warily among the trees.

"They passed by a few minutes ago."

James didn't wait for more information. They headed in the opposite direction and stopped ten minutes later. Atlas huffed and rested on a log. "Where have you been?"

"Stalking the Stalkers. Seeing if they had any idea how to locate the Signal," James said, not even sounding winded.

"And?"

"They're grasping at straws. They have no idea."

"Good."

"What about you, Atlas?"

"I think I might have it," he said.

"Where?"

Atlas stood and walked around James, poking at his neck. The Dark operative swatted his hand away and glared.

"Had to be sure you're not infected."

"Just tell me. We're running out of time."

Atlas indicated a red X on his map. "It's right over there."

"The Stalkers are going in the wrong direction," James realized.

"That's correct."

"There's just one problem, Atlas. Can you see it?" James asked, eyebrow raised.

"The river."

"That's right. Only a two-mile-wide barrier to the Signal."

Atlas had planned to arrive at the river and consider his options before panicking. "Obviously."

"Okay, so we need a boat."

"Any suggestions?"

James grinned, which was unusual in itself. "There's a native village not far from here, near the water. The only access is the river, so you can bet they have boats."

"What are we waiting for?" Atlas gathered his belongings, and James noticed his pack.

"What's in there?"

"Supplies. I found the aircraft wreckage. Managed this as well." He extended the Holo to James.

"Can you contact..." James tapped the screen and frowned.

"No coverage. Just the satellites for the map and GPS location."

"But you still have the—"

Atlas pulled the beacon from his shirt, holding it up. "Ready when you are."

James stared thoughtfully to the north. "Let's push it now. Get them to come while we cross the river."

"Should we risk it?" Atlas asked.

"No. Better wait until we've succeeded. If the Dark Teams begin flooding the area, it'll draw the Stalkers' attention, and we can't have that until we have the Signal."

"We don't want that ever," Atlas muttered.

"Right." James sifted through the bag and saw the key. He rotated it in his palm. "You found it."

Atlas explained the situation at the airplane, and how he'd nearly been taken by the Crawler.

"You did well, Atlas." James ate pretzels and guzzled a can of soda. It was fizzy and warm, but the operative didn't seem to mind. When he was finished, they kept the litter, so they didn't leave a trail to be followed.

With the sudden reappearance of James Wan, Atlas felt like his fortune might be improving. Hopefully it held until they found the Signal.

TWENTY-FIVE

David

Newark Liberty International Airport

After the long flight, David couldn't wait to deplane. As soon as the seatbelt sign winked off, he burst from his seat, but Dark Sixty-Two beat him into the aisle.

David stood with his back hunched beneath the overhead bins, his aching legs cramping while Dark Sixty-Two removed their empty carry-on bag and stuffed the scanners into it.

"Here," he said, thrusting it into David's chest. "I need to keep my hands free."

David grimaced, remembering how the operative had used them to snap that infected man's neck. He shifted his weight restlessly from one foot to the other and glanced at the bathrooms.

"I'm thirsty," Rachel whined, squeezing into the aisle behind Dark Sixty-Two. Private Reed was stuck behind her, having chosen the window seat. Rachel had volunteered to sit between the two men when it became clear that they couldn't all fit in a row, because Dark Sixty-Two had insisted on taking an aisle seat.

David remembered experiencing a brief flicker of jealousy when he'd realized why Rachel had wanted to be close to the giant operative. She'd developed a harmless crush on the deadly mercenary, chatting endlessly to him in a stream of mostly one-sided conversation throughout the nine-hour flight from Anchorage. Apparently, superhero Daddy had been replaced.

"We'll grab something to drink in a minute, honey," Kate soothed from the middle seat.

"Don't worry," Dark Sixty-Two whispered. "We locked the stall from the outside, and the cleaning crew is on its way."

David noticed a few people giving them strange looks, but they kept to themselves.

"Hey, John!" Carter said, and Dark Sixty-Two glared at him. That was the name he'd finally given Rachel after several dedicated hours of insisting that he give her one.

"What did you show that flight attendant?" Carter asked as he squeezed out into the aisle behind Dark Sixty-Two, pushing an old lady into her seat in the process. She gave him a withering look. "Sorry, Grandma. Official business."

She huffed and muttered about his manners.

"Well?" Carter pressed, leaning conspiratorially close.

"That's not for you to know," Dark Sixty-Two said.

The line of people ahead of them began chugging forward, and Carter hesitated, giving David and his family a chance to escape first. Reed fell in behind them, leaving Carter to bring up the rear. At the front of the aircraft, the flight attendants gave them tight smiles and thanked them for flying with Alaska Airlines before exiting hastily.

David made sure to keep Kate and the kids in sight as he hurried up the sloping floor of the jetway. Dark Sixty-Two led the way, following the signs to pick up their luggage—Chris the Grazer.

Dark Sixty-Two yanked his Holo out and planted it against his ear for a call. Muffled screams and commotion came shuddering through the doors at the end of the corridor. A few passengers that David recognized from their flight came running from the other direction, their expressions filled with terror.

"This is it, man!" a long-haired kid said as he flashed by. "They're here!"

"Ahhh... John?" David asked, glancing around nervously.

"Something's wrong," Private Reed whispered.

"You think?" Kate asked as more screams roared down the corridor.

"Hurry up!" Dark Sixty-Two called, his Holo gripped tight as he stepped past the automatic doors to the concourse.

They emerged into a scene of utter chaos. Travelers raced around at top speed, dragging their rolling carry-on bags, while some simply dropped their luggage to run faster. People were knocked to the ground as they collided with each other.

Dark Sixty-Two led them to a relatively peaceful knot of people clustered around a bank of glowing screens that displayed connecting flights. Everything came up as red—*canceled*—but that wasn't what they were staring at. Their gazes were locked on live news feeds playing above the flight information.

Dark Sixty-Two gawked with them, his Holo slowly falling from his ear.

"David," Kate said sharply, clutching his arm.

"I see it," he said.

Armed Stalkers were striding brazenly down the streets of Manhattan amidst honking cars and fleeing crowds of pedestrians. People abandoned their gridlocked vehicles, scrambling to flee.

Every now and then one of the aliens lifted a rifle and popped off a blinding bolt of plasma to clear a path. The scene panned to show a growing crowd of civilians and police trailing in an orderly throng behind the Stalkers. And something else. David squinted at the screen—

And sucked in a sharp breath.

Crawlers poured out of manhole covers, jumping on people and taking control of them. There were at least as many people falling into line behind the alien soldiers as there were running away.

"We're too late," Dark Sixty-Two said, shaking his head.

Carter pointed to the operative's Holo, which was ringing and vibrating in his hand. "You going to answer that?"

Dark Sixty-Two stepped away and pressed a finger to his ear. Somewhere an alarm started ringing, and a group of security officers shot by, shouting into their radios.

David glanced sharply at Kate, relieved to see Mark and Rachel with her. Carter lingered on the side, gaping at the news feeds.

David followed Dark Sixty-Two, anxious to know what they were expected to do next. Wasn't his CO supposed to be waiting for them?

The operative slipped his Holo into his pocket and spun around. "We have to go!" he yelled to be heard above the mounting chaos.

"Where?" David asked.

"He's on the tarmac." Dark Sixty-Two gestured at the doors they'd exited a few moments ago. "This way!"

The *pop, pop, pop* of small arms fire interrupted David's reply, and more screams filled the air. David ushered his family and Carter through the doors, flying down the lengthy corridor, then the tunnel itself. They reached the end and stood near their plane.

David wondered if the Dark operative was planning to hijack the aircraft. But instead, he veered right to a narrow access for ground crew. It opened to a rickety metal stairway.

David paused at the top, and waved to his wife and kids. "Come on!"

Carter sailed past him, beating them to the stairs. Then came Mark with Kate and Rachel. Thundering footfalls and screams echoed after them as a group of terrified travelers materialized.

David ducked out of the jet bridge and hurried to the tarmac before they could catch up. The last thing they needed was for a civilian mob to swarm them and commandeer whatever ride Dark Leader had managed to secure.

At the bottom of the stairs, Carter grappled with a man in a bright neon yellow jacket. David tried to intervene, but Dark Sixty-Two beat him to it, snapping the man's neck with a sharp twist. A tentacled thing leaped from the body before it even hit the ground. Dark Sixty-Two batted it aside and stomped on it before it could land on Carter, and then he dragged the ground crewman's body out of sight, behind the wheels of the jetway.

"Let's go!" Dark Sixty-Two yelled above the nearby roaring of a flight taking off. A big black helicopter screamed overhead. The Dark operative pointed to it as it stopped to hover, dropping for an illegal landing on the tarmac.

"Wait! What about Chris?" Carter asked.

Dark Sixty-Two's expression blanked as if he'd only just remembered the Grazer in the hold. "Shit." He glanced at the 737 they'd flown in on. The cargo hold was open, and a conveyor belt rolled to a waiting luggage train below.

Wordlessly, Carter led the charge, but Dark Sixty-Two quickly outpaced him. David rushed after them with Kate and the kids.

He arrived in time to hear Dark Sixty-Two arguing with the baggage handlers. A group of four heavily armed soldiers in unmarked black uniforms marched from the helicopter. Rifles snapped up to aim at the baggage handlers. All three men raised their hands.

"Do what the man says," one of the four growled.

Two of them darted into the cargo hold to help a third, and within moments they had the wooden crate with Chris on the conveyor belt. A pair of operatives shouldered their weapons to carry it between them.

"This way, Commander Bryce!" one of the others called over a muffled explosion. A column of flames shot up above the helicopter, and Kate's hand flew to her mouth.

David felt sick. Two airplanes had just collided on the runway, but there was no time to delay. A few seconds later they all piled into the back of the helicopter behind the soldiers and Chris' crate. A familiar man faced them. Short, thinning gray hair, a trim physique, and a scar cutting from his right temple to his upper lip, giving it a permanent sneer. His demeanor was stoic, his deep-set eyes shadowed with dark circles.

"Commander Bryce! It's good to see you again," Dark Leader said.

Sirens erupted as emergency crews reacted to the crash on the runway. David nodded tightly in lieu of a verbal reply as he settled into his seat. He perched Rachel on his lap as he realized there wasn't enough room for everyone. Kate did the same with Mark next to him.

"Not the best of circumstances, I know!" Booth said loudly as another soldier hopped into the chopper and shut them in. It was standing room only. Carter and Reed leaned on the Grazer's crate. Booth twisted around to regard the pilot and made a twirling gesture with his finger. "Let's go!" he ordered as the rotors intensified and they leaped from the tarmac.

A thump sounded from the crate, and Carter jumped visibly with the impact.

"Free him!" Booth said. "We must locate the Signal before it's too late."

David frowned, peering out his window at the flaming wrecks on the runway and the swarm of emergency vehicles now gathered around them. Flickers of the madness inside the airport flashed through his mind's eye, casting Booth's words in a dubious light.

Wasn't it *already* too late?

TWENTY-SIX

Lennon

Arecibo Observatory, Puerto Rico

Work continued well into the morning, with more humans arriving every thirty or so minutes on tour buses. They filed out, Crawlers connected to each of them. They mindlessly wandered the processing line and accepted orders from a man with a tablet. A single Stalker hung behind him, watching over the area. After spending the last week hunting the Stalkers, it was nearly impossible to stay calm around them. Every one of her honed instincts told her to end the threat. But here, in the center of their camp, it would only mean her quick demise.

Lennon had pretended to be busy for the last couple of hours, searching for Rutger to no avail, which deeply concerned her.

She peered at the Observatory disc, seeing how many modifications had been made. Lennon walked away, carrying a half-empty crate, and took in the sight from a distance. The cables flashed and crackled with blue energy, the telescope burning a bright azure. Underneath it all, the power cell, made with four linked Stalker escape pods, hummed and fueled the entire structure.

Lennon tried to estimate how long before the radio signal would be operational, but couldn't tell. With the number of workers and activity in the area, she suspected they were half done, which gave her a few hours at worst to locate Rutger and destroy the cells.

But where was he?

Lennon heard a commotion from a nearby bus, as a girl lashed out at a man trying to keep her in line.

"I don't belong here! Let me go. What the hell is happening?" she cried.

Lennon wanted to intervene, but if she did, the Stalkers would realize she wasn't infected. The Stalker made a noise, and the supervisor strode to them. "Take her to the holding cell. We don't have time for this."

"Yes, sir," a guard said before shoving the girl. She fell to her knees, while he hauled her under the armpit, dragging her to her feet. "Would you rather I shot you?"

"Depends on my other option," the girl spat.

Lennon followed at a distance, holding the crate. A gun sat under a stack of control panel components.

She was led to a building that was once a gift shop. A second guard stood in front, an alien pulse weapon dangling from its strap. The pair of infected humans whispered to one another and unlocked the door. "Move it." He pushed the girl in, and a minute later, the man returned.

The girl's escort walked off without another word, and Lennon liked her chances.

With the guy alone, and lazily leaning at the entrance, she sauntered over, smiling. "I've been asked to discuss something with you."

He looked mildly surprised. "What is it?"

"They have an issue with..." Lennon waved him around the building. "It's better if I show you."

The guy walked with her and lifted a hand to block the sunlight. She jabbed her fingers into his throat, and his weapon clanged to the sidewalk. She kicked him in the crotch, then bashed the crate against his head. He flopped to the ground, eyes rolling up. The Crawler on his neck slid free, and she stomped it, squishing it into a sticky mess.

The keys hung from his pocket, and she reached in, grabbing them.

Lennon took his weapon, shoving the handgun from the crate into her pants. There were three keys, and she tried the first. It didn't fit. Lennon peered over her shoulder, sliding the second in. *Click*.

She rushed into the building to find thirty or more people behind an energy barrier. The wall thrummed with power. The gift shop hadn't been open in decades, but a spattering of items remained. Miniature replicas of the observatory sat in dust-covered boxes, and books lined a shelf to her left.

"Lennon?" It was Rutger.

She could make out his face through the crackling wall. "What is this?"

"Don't touch it," he warned. "Look what happened to him."

Lennon saw a charred corpse where Rutger indicated. "Noted. How do I shut it down?"

"I don't know. They used a tablet," Rutger said.

"Like this?" Lennon retrieved it and began swiping on the device. "It's all in their language. I can't..."

"That's okay," he told her. "Blow this place up, Lennon."

"Wait, what about me?" the girl exclaimed. She was probably sixteen, her cheeks red, her hair a curly mess. "Get me out of here. I was on vacation with my family and... Mom and Dad started acting weird."

"We're having a private conversation," Rutger said.

"No way. Don't leave me. Please. I'll help you. I can handle a gun!"

Lennon shook her head. Rutger was right, but she couldn't abandon him to die. Not again. The front door began to open. "I'll be back, Rutger. Be ready."

Lennon rushed to the far wall, clutching the tablet and gun in opposite hands. A Stalker walked in, inching toward the barrier. Lennon almost blasted it, when the Stalker stopped and went into another room. Lennon managed to sneak through the exit, slipping into the trees beyond.

She had to learn how to shut off the cell wall and free Rutger.

Lennon kept one eye on the gift shop and the other on the tablet, searching the programs. The files were listed as icons, symbols she didn't recognize. It was the same as everything on the *Interloper* had been, and she suddenly wished that Carter, despite all his flaws, was there to assist her.

The Stalker eventually departed, gaping around as if searching for the sentry she'd ended. It wouldn't be challenging for the alien to spy the dead body crammed near the old garbage cans out back. He spoke into a device strapped to his wrist while heading for the suspension bridge that led to the telescope. Hundreds of Crawlers dangled from its surface, working to fix the damages.

Lennon had to break Rutger out.

She returned cautiously so she didn't catch anyone's attention. The energy barrier persisted, and Lennon went closer this time, searching the edges for signs of weakness. The tablet blinked, and Lennon saw a pulsing icon on the screen. "What's this?"

"Maybe your proximity to the shield prompted it," Rutger said, glimpsing the display.

The others gathered around. Lennon touched the icon, and the wall of blue static disappeared. She rushed into the cell and hugged Rutger.

"Let's get the..." Rutger cut off, his gaze darting to the exit.

Lennon panicked and tapped the tablet again. The cell barricade reappeared, this time with her behind it. They couldn't fight everyone, not without being killed in the process, and she was too close to thwarting the Stalkers' operation to allow that to happen.

The girl grabbed her arm, tugging Lennon closer.

"What's your name?" Lennon asked.

"Winnie," she managed.

"Everyone be still." Lennon slid the tablet away, staring at the incoming humans. There were two of them, holding a clear box. She listened, picking up on their conversation midway through.

"... explosion killed the entire section. We need replacements," the lead woman said.

"That's what they're here for, isn't it?" the man responded. The box somehow permeated the energy field, and he dumped the contents. Twenty Crawlers hopped out, scattering around the cell.

"Want to watch?" the woman asked her partner.

"No. We'd better check on quadrant four. The relays are acting up." They departed, and Lennon backed against the far wall.

The prisoners screamed, others gaping in shock as Crawlers jumped on them. Lennon meant to help them all, but there wasn't time.

She brought the wall down. A couple of people escaped with her and Rutger, and Lennon saw Winnie being cornered by an alien invader. She kicked it, sending it flying, and Lennon lurched forward, snatching the girl. She hauled Winnie into the store lobby, using the tablet to seal the remaining captives in. They screamed as the Crawlers took hold, but quickly recovered as they became infected.

"You saved me," Winnie said, wiping hair from her face.

The others had already fled, and Lennon hoped they could escape. But she doubted it.

"Be careful. Get to a safe place and hide until it's over. And a word of advice," Lennon said. "Don't be anywhere within a mile of the observatory."

"I'm coming with you," Winnie said.

Lennon sighed and glanced at Rutger. "Whatever. You need a weapon."

"I know where they took my gear."

They couldn't delay. Someone would see they'd escaped, and the search would be on. Lennon wouldn't allow them to capture her.

They rushed into the jungle, moving south, until they caught a glimpse of the power cells beneath the disc.

Rutger gestured to a stack of electronics. "They put my things there."

"How are we going to find it?"

"What are you looking for?" Winnie asked.

"My Holo. It's the only way to communicate with Dark Leader," Rutger said.

Winnie frowned, clearly not intimidated by them. "Dark Leader? Who the hell are you guys?"

"We're the reason the world is still here to invade," Lennon muttered. "You two get the Holo, I'll scour for something with enough juice to detonate the energy source."

A few humans came and went, picking through the junk, and Lennon noticed that not all of them had Crawlers. She felt her own neck and looked at Winnie. Could she be infected?

Lennon tugged the back of the girl's shirt, searching for the three-holed puncture mark, but she was clean.

"What was that for?"

"Had to be certain," Lennon said, and Winnie nodded. "Spread out. We have to be quick."

The three of them walked with restraint, trying not to become targets. Lennon began to accumulate anything that might assist her cause. To her right, five hundred yards away, the escape pods began to hum and power on.

Lennon hastened her pace.

TWENTY-SEVEN

Atlas

Remote Rainforest

It poured from the heavens as midday approached, but Atlas hardly noticed as they walked. It reminded him of his arrival in Croatia only a couple of months ago. All his travels were a blur to him now. James had remained quiet, but he finally spoke, letting Atlas know they were close. His footsteps squelched on the wet grass, the foliage wiping nature's tears on his clothing as they tackled a thicket.

When they exited, he saw signs of life for the first time since encountering the Grazer's grave.

Except this village was occupied. Someone shouted in alarm when he spotted the two men approaching with guns. James' stayed slung on his shoulder, aimed at no one. He lifted his empty palms, indicating he wasn't an enemy. Atlas did the same, trying on a smile for good measure.

"Who are you?" the man asked in Portuguese.

"We're friends. We need a boat." Atlas did his best, hoping his rough translation was good enough.

The guy seemed to understand. "River?"

Atlas nodded.

"Trade."

"For what?"

"We see," the guy said, waving them into the village.

The rain intensified, and they were escorted into a home, the thatched roof holding the water at bay. Atlas struggled to imagine living in a place like this, and was surprised anyone could. But maybe being off the beaten track, away from society, would be a simpler and more carefree life. Instead of following world events and watching TV, struggling to pay your bills, you worked with your hands, every effort assisting your survival.

"Lucas," the local said, touching his chest.

"Atlas."

"James."

Lucas nodded. "Too wet for a boat."

"We have to go," James said, his Portuguese better than Atlas'.

"The river is too dangerous."

Atlas didn't want to delay any more than necessary.

The place was compact, but comfortable. A cookstove sat in the corner of the room, and they took the seats at the table. A woman entered, and she almost dropped a pitcher of water. Her husband whispered to her, and she nodded, stoking the stove's fire. Soon she boiled water, watching them with interest.

"Lucas, we really..."

James interrupted him. "It's okay, Atlas. We've been on the go for so long, we don't know how to stop. Take a minute. The storm won't last."

As soon as Atlas let himself relax, his muscles ached, and he felt a thousand different bruises and scrapes come to life. "We haven't even seen a boat," he said.

"I have. Near the water," James said.

"Then we could have stolen one," Atlas whispered in English.

"Is that what you want to do?"

"No." Atlas wasn't feeling himself. "I'm on autopilot, James. I thought I was going to die out there."

"So did I," James admitted.

"Really? You?"

"There's nothing quite like approaching a hard-shelled nine-foot-tall alien, and realizing it might be the last thing you ever do."

Lucas delivered two piping hot cups to them, sitting on the opposite side of the table. He grinned. "Trade?"

"What kind of boat is it?" James asked him.

Lucas feigned pulling an engine to life and held up four fingers.

"Big enough for four, and has a motor," James mumbled in English, then switched to Portuguese. "It can cross the river?"

Lucas nodded, and chuckled. "No problem."

"We don't have much," James said.

Atlas opened the pack, offering the last can of soda and a few pretzel bags.

Lucas gestured to the Holo. "That."

"No. We can't—"

James grabbed it, sliding it to Lucas. "Done."

Lucas licked his lips. "More."

"Listen here, you can have the boat back. We just..." Atlas stood and spilled his tea.

"Sit," James hissed.

He did so reluctantly.

"What else?"

Lucas indicated the cloth-wrapped object that contained the key to the Grazer's ship. "That."

"Not going to happen," James told him. "Give me another option?"

"Gun."

They each had one, and James nodded. He swung his around, removing the energy cell without Lucas noticing. He handed it over.

"Deal," Lucas said.

"I have a favor to ask. Do you have a tattoo kit?" James asked, jabbing a finger on his own arm.

"Yes." Lucas walked out into the rain and returned a few minutes later.

"What do you want this for?" Atlas asked.

"Roll up your sleeve."

"Why?"

"Atlas, you've gone above and beyond. You've fought the Stalkers, fended off Crawlers, and killed the enemy. You might have single-handedly pinpointed the Signal. For that, you're one of us. You're a Dark operative."

"I am?" Atlas swallowed and did as he was told, exposing his forearm.

James took the needles to the fire and held the points in the coals in an attempt at sterilizing them.

"I'd better not die from an infection," Atlas half-joked.

"It's fine. I got mine in a bunker outside of Cairo," James said, not explaining further.

Atlas didn't press him, respecting James' privacy.

When the ink-covered end pricked his skin, he clenched his jaw, letting it happen. The tattoo was small, and it didn't take long to be completed. The three circles were familiar to him, having seen them since his father had brought home the first relic. He'd spent hours touching the indentations, wondering where it came from.

"I'll wear it with pride."

"Welcome to the Dark," James whispered, and peered outside. "It's clearing up. Time to go." He turned his attention to Lucas's wife, who lingered in the kitchen. "Thank you for your hospitality."

Lucas led them from the village, and Atlas saw a young boy with the alien weapon aimed at another child, possibly his brother. He chased him, pretending to shoot.

"Kids," James muttered softly.

The boat wasn't far, and Atlas already heard the river. It was enormous. They'd only encountered its tributaries to date, but this was awe-inspiring. The water was brown, flowing quickly despite its impressive width. The edges rose to the vegetation, rather than cutting into a dirty cliff. Trees overhung the river, everything swathed in bright greens.

"It doesn't look like it's over a mile wide," Atlas said.

"That's because the trees are so big. Believe me, you don't want to swim it."

Atlas recalled the terrible stories he'd read describing the piranha and snakes, and nodded. "You're right, I don't."

Lucas flipped the motorized canoe, water spilling from the bottom.

"This is it?" The thing had seen better days.

"It works." Lucas crossed his arms, glaring at Atlas.

"Sure. We'll see about that."

Lucas tossed a single paddle into it, and they dragged it to the river's edge. "Just one oar?" James asked.

"You won't need it." Lucas tied the boat's rope to a metal rod in the ground and pushed it out into the current. He hopped in, helping Atlas and then James inside. He primed the engine, and it took four pulls for it to catch. The motor sputtered and coughed, letting a cloud of black smoke from the exhaust.

Lucas rushed off, holding the rope. "Goodbye."

With the boat free, they instantly began flowing along with the current. James took control, adjusting the rudder, and it worked, sending them toward the other side. It was a slow process, but the motor did its best to battle the mighty river.

Atlas clutched the edges of the canoe, trying to stabilize it as they hit a section of choppy water. He searched the shoreline for Lucas, but the man was gone. He sighed, focusing on his next task. If the Signal was anywhere, it was across the river waiting to be discovered.

Atlas kept his eyes peeled for Stalkers or the infected, but it was quiet on the far bank. More trees, more green shrubbery.

"You've got to be kidding me," James called.

"What is..." Atlas caught himself as the engine sputtered out. James yanked the cord, but nothing happened.

"It's out of fuel."

Atlas estimated that they had another half-mile to the shore. He glanced at the paddle and picked it up. "I should have stayed with my brother in Vermont."

The current tugged them, and he struggled to fight it. Each time the oar cut into the water, the river threatened to steal it. The job would have been difficult enough with two, but this was nearly impossible.

James grabbed Atlas' gun, using the stock to help, and after a grueling twenty minutes, they reached the shore. The boat stuck between two trees, and James grabbed a trunk, keeping them steady. Atlas exited first, splashing to the wet shoreline, and James chucked his pack at him before continuing. They lay on the grass, panting, and eventually, James laughed.

"Something funny?"

"No, just remembering what my dad used to say. 'Life's short, paddle hard.'"

"He was a wise man," Atlas said.

He didn't have his Holo to verify their location, but the water had carried them at least two miles off track. He climbed to his feet, shrugged his pack on, and started forward. He was going to end this journey soon. Whether they found the Signal or failed, he was pressing the beacon either way.

TWENTY-EIGHT

David

Aboard a Helicopter Heading South from Newark

The soldiers cracked the lid off the crate, and the nauseating smell of fish roiled out, along with Chris, who sat up quickly, scattering packing peanuts everywhere.

"Gah," Booth gasped into his sleeve. Most everyone was wearing headsets now, both to dull the thunderous sound of the chopper's rotors and so they could communicate.

"You get used to it," Carter said into the boom of his microphone.

David caught Booth's eye and shook his head. Maybe it had something to do with Carter's special connection with the alien, but he still hadn't gotten *used to* the stench.

Kate leaned away from the alien as it stepped out of the crate to hunch in the back of the helicopter. The soldiers closed the lid, and Chris sat on top. Carter joined him and took the alien's hand. The air began singing with subtle vibrations.

Looks of disgust and apprehension flashed between the soldiers. Dark Sixty-Two and Private Reed seemed less surprised.

"Chris says thank you for saving him," Carter explained, meeting Dark Sixty-Two's gaze.

"Just another job," the Dark operative grumbled.

"Ask him about the Signal," Booth insisted. "We need to know where it is."

More humming. "He wants to know if we have a... an *overseer*. Is that right? What is that?" Carter asked.

The Grazer hissed between its stubby teeth, then pointed at David's chest.

212

"Me?" David asked.

"I think he means the scanners," Private Reed said.

"Right." David checked under his seat for the carry-on bag with the two scanners.

Carter passed the functional one to the Grazer, who quickly set to work, powering on the device, then making pinching motions on the holographic map.

"Can't they track us with that?" Dark Sixty-Two asked.

"Yes..." Carter trailed off.

Booth looked worried. "So now they have our location?"

The Grazer thrummed deep inside his chest and let out a snort of air from the blowhole-like nostril in his forehead.

"He says he only requires a minute. And we're in the air. They have no aerial vehicles."

"They control plenty of *ours*," Booth grumbled. "There could be F-42s launching to intercept us as we speak."

Mark stared blankly at the device in the Grazer's clutches, from his seat on Kate's lap. David hoped his son's interest didn't have anything to do with a lingering alien infection that they had yet to detect. Rachel nuzzled into David's chest, as if she didn't want to look—or perhaps to *smell*.

"Then let's hope this is worth it," Carter muttered.

Chris the Grazer zoomed out until the entire globe appeared. David blinked in shock, surprised to see that the scanner could do that. Green dots were scattered around the planet, but mostly concentrated around the continental United States, Alaska, and... was that Puerto Rico?

"You getting this?" Booth asked one of the other soldiers. The man was recording everything on his Holo.

"Yes, sir."

Chris flicked a finger and indicated the Amazon rainforest. The air reverberated once more.

"He says it's there," Carter translated. "In the Amazon."

Booth deadpanned. "You must be joking."

"What?" Carter asked.

"We already know that! I need him to be more specific."

More humming issued from Chris. "He says you'd have to take him there to search for signs of the crash site."

"Fantastic," Booth muttered. "Turn it off. Tell him I'll think about it."

"Wait," David said. Booth and Carter both regarded him with eyebrows raised. "Give it here first."

"Why?" Carter asked.

David made a gimme gesture. "I have a hunch." Seeing the new capabilities of the object had given David an idea, but he prayed that he was wrong.

"Do it," Booth said.

Chris relinquished the device. David worked quickly, zooming out until Earth was nothing but a dot, vanishing among the stars.

Carter whistled between his teeth.

"How far is the range?" Booth asked.

Chris hummed.

"As far as light can reach," Carter said.

"Isn't that infinite?" Private Reed asked.

"I think he means that the tech is limited to the speed of light."

"As opposed to the Signal device we're looking for," Booth suggested.

David stopped zooming out when he saw the entire solar system reduced to nothing but slightly-larger specks against a gleaming backdrop of stars.

A single oversized green blip shone at the far edge of the void.

"What is that?" Booth demanded.

David's guts churned. He'd been right. The *Interloper* hadn't been the only ship of its kind in the area.

"Enhance it," Booth demanded.

David did so, and the details of the vessel came clear. It looked identical: black and windowless, with spiked projections on the hull and a massive weapon in the front.

Chris muttered, making the air inside the chopper sing once more.

"He says to tap it with your finger," Carter translated.

David nodded, and streams of data filled the screen around the alien vessel. The symbols were all alien, so he returned the device to the Grazer.

"Ask him if it's coming to Earth," Booth said.

Carter shook his head while the alien rotated the display first one way, then the other. "He says that it's not coming to

Earth. But he can't be sure. The data is more than..." Carter blinked. "It's over a year old. They're more than a light-year from here."

Everyone in the helicopter breathed a collective sigh.

"Then they likely don't know what happened to the *Interloper*," Booth said. "Which means we're safe, as long as the Stalkers don't find the Signal and transmit a faster-than-light distress call."

Dark Sixty-Two leaned in and whispered to his commander.

"The problem is we don't have enough Teams left to split between both locations," Booth replied more audibly.

Chris turned the scanner to face them. He'd zoomed to the jungle. Thousands of green alien blips were converging on one particular section of the jungle. Given how slowly they inched along, it appeared as though they were on foot, and still far enough away, but it definitely looked as if they'd found something.

Booth cursed. "Turn it off."

Chris did so, touching the three-holed button before handing the *overseer* to David. Booth's gaze tracked the device, as if he desired to ask for it. "Keep it safe," he said instead.

David nodded. "Yes, sir." He took the sleek black object and stuffed it into the bag with the depleted one.

Mark watched him intently from Kate's lap. "You need something, buddy?" David yelled at him.

Mark snapped out of it. "Oh, I'm fine, Father! How are you?"

Father? David wondered. He couldn't ever recall Mark calling him that.

Kate looked alarmed, but nobody else seemed to have noticed.

David stashed the bag under his seat again. He slid Rachel to the seat, but as he was about to stow the bag, he thought twice and withdrew the working scanner. He slipped it into a webbed compartment with the life jacket beneath the seat cushion.

He straightened and beckoned for Rachel to sit in his lap again. Mark couldn't have possibly seen what he'd done.

"Where are we going?" Kate asked.

Booth set his jaw. "A secure location."

"You sure about that?" David countered.

"Positive. We have a means of identifying the infected." Booth tilted forward. "Dr. Marcus!" he called.

A woman peered from the co-pilot's seat. "Sir?"

"How many people can we check with that device of yours before it needs replacing?"

"An indefinite number, sir. We just have to keep it charged."

"Good. That's what I was hoping." Booth smiled grimly. "We'll be screening everyone soon."

"The moment of truth approaches," Carter said, rubbing the back of his neck.

David couldn't be sure, but he thought he saw Mark stiffen. They were finally going to learn whether or not he was still infected.

TWENTY-NINE

Lennon

Arecibo Observatory, Puerto Rico

Two hours had passed since they began the search, and so far they'd sifted through over a hundred variations of old tablets and phones. Some were the previous models, before Holo had taken hold and forced the other brands out of the market. Now, if you wanted a mobile device, it was labeled with *Holo*. This made the task slightly easier, but they weren't prepared for the sheer amount of effort it took to evade discovery.

Lennon was glad the Stalkers hadn't inspected the area yet. Instead, she'd dodged suspicion by talking her way out of encounters with the Crawler-afflicted humans, and Lennon realized the alien hive mind wasn't great at spotting lies. They always accepted her reasoning, but it would only last so long.

"Is this it?" Winnie asked, but Rutger shook his head, discarding the object into a pile. Her hair clung to her brow, her shirt soaked with sweat. Lennon billowed her own black uniform, undoing the zipper lower. They needed water.

"I'll be right back," she said.

Rutger looked on silently.

The aliens were smart enough to realize their workers required sustenance, and a station had been erected near the observatory offices. She joined a line and pretended to be one of them, standing wearily without apparent concern like the rest of the humans. When it was her turn, she grabbed three bottles, and shoved a handful of power bars into her pockets.

"It'll be operational in an hour," a man told a nodding woman staring at a Holo.

"They're upset it's taken this long. We're going to send a test sooner."

"It's not ready," he said.

"It will be. Inform your crew. You have thirty minutes." The woman sauntered off, leaving the stunned infected man alone. He barked out orders and jogged away.

Lennon had to stop them. She hurried, and the second she saw Rutger, she knew he'd found the tablet. "You got it?"

"Yep." He flipped it to face her. "Sending Booth a message now."

Winnie downed her entire bottle, and Lennon drank methodically, trying to ration the liquid. Her head pounded, but this would help.

"Anything?"

"Not yet." Rutger's eyebrow raised. "There it is."

"What does he say?"

He met her stare. "Destroy it at all costs. And that we're wanted in the Amazon when we're done. If we..."

"If we what?" Winnie interjected.

"Survive. If we survive." Lennon handed out the power bars, and they each ate one.

"You won't let me die here, will you?" Winnie asked.

Lennon peered at Rutger and sighed. "No."

"Thank God." Winnie smiled, her teeth stained brown from the chocolate-covered oats. "I'm supposed to go on a date with Blake when I'm back, and..."

"Do you mind?" Lennon asked.

"Sorry, I talk when I'm–"

A bright light blasted from the center of the disc, shooting through the telescope and into the sky.

"Is that it?" Rutger asked, seeing commotion a couple of hundred yards from their position.

"No. They're running a test. We still have time."

"Time for what?" Winnie asked.

"To blow this entire observatory to hell," Lennon muttered. "Come on."

She'd assembled every explosive she could locate lying around, and was grateful the Stalkers and Crawler-humans were so careless. All they thought about was sending the signal to their other ship in deep space, and they were overconfident in their security. They were going to learn a brutal lesson.

The bag was heavy, and it took two of them to heave it from the ground.

"Winnie, I want you to run up the stairs, past the suspension bridge access, and head north. We'll be there soon," Lennon said.

The girl glanced around uncertainly. "Alone?"

"Listen, kid. Get out of here. We'll find you. Clear the area. Once you're gone, run as fast as you can. This is going to blow, and you don't want to be here when it does," Rutger insisted.

"Fine, but don't forget me." Winnie hesitantly left.

"How do we escape?" Rutger asked her. "I could bring the bomb, and you can leave. Protect the girl."

"Not on your life. Besides, I have a plan." Lennon grinned, and they hauled the pack closer to the workers. She placed it into a crate and tapped the woman she'd heard earlier on the shoulder. "New orders."

"From whom?" The Crawler on her neck twitched, a few of its legs stretching out.

Lennon grabbed the tablet she'd stolen from the Stalker and held it up, pretending to read it. The lady blanched at seeing the device. "What are we changing?"

"Take this crate to the power source. The test failed."

"No it didn't. It went smoothly," the woman said.

Lennon kept her composure at the bad news. Was it already too late? "But you fried half of the resistors in the process. Do it. Now!"

She shouted commands to a handful of workers, and they set the crate on a rolling dolly, rushing it toward the center of the disc. This was it.

Lennon turned on her heel, and Rutger joined her as they deserted Arecibo. When they cleared the steady row of parked buses, Lennon shot into a sprint. She'd linked the explosive detonator to Rutger's tablet, and he yanked it free, stopping momentarily. "We should be out of range here," he suggested.

The huge observatory loomed large, even though they were a couple of miles from the middle of the site where the explosives were brought. Someone was probably fumbling with the bag, attempting to untie the complicated knot.

"They're still people," Lennon whispered, realizing how many of the infected would die in the blast.

"Their sacrifice is necessary," Rutger told her.

"Press it," she said.

"No. It's all yours." He handed the tablet to Lennon, and she knew he wasn't passing it for any moral reasons. He was giving her a chance to rectify her earlier failure on the *Interloper*. From anyone else, it might seem like an insult, but from Rutger, it was almost sweet.

Lennon glanced to the sky, seeing a stream of light begin to emerge from the telescope again. She tapped the detonator icon, and for a heart-stopping second, she thought the connection had failed.

Her concerns were washed away in flames as the disc erupted in fire. The ground shook, and the screams were short-lived.

The shockwave thrashed the nearby jungle, shooting from the central point, and Lennon saw it was heading in their direction. "Run!"

The pair of Dark operatives retreated, pumping their legs as fast as they'd go, which wasn't quick enough, considering their exhaustion and dehydration. The wave of crumbling earth caught them, shooting Lennon into the air. She landed a second later, face-down in the fractured ground. Rutger stood, dusted himself off, and turned towards the blue sky. The sun burned hotly, reminding Lennon she was still alive.

"Nice work, Dark Three," he said.

"You too, Dark One." Lennon moved closer, and kissed his dry, cracked lips. She heard footsteps, and reached for her gun, finding the teenager watching them.

Winnie's eyes rolled as only a teenager could. "Gross. If you two are done, can we leave?"

Lennon laughed, knowing what lay before them. They needed their supplies from the boat, and a way to get to Brazil ASAP.

When she relayed the problem to Rutger, he nodded once. "I have an idea."

"When you say that, someone usually ends up dead," she muttered.

***

David

Unknown Location

The helicopter touched down on the carrier's flight deck. Rachel scurried off him, rushing to the exit, and David retrieved the bag with the broken scanner in it. Mark hadn't tried anything, so he was tempted to grab the working one, but decided against it.

David emerged on stiff, wobbly legs and joined the rest of them on the deck.

"Where's the welcome party?" Carter asked, sounding offended that the carrier's crew hadn't rolled out the red carpet.

David searched for Booth and found him in the middle of a hushed conversation with the doctor from the co-pilot's seat. The two of them strode over, and the woman produced a sleek-looking silver device from her lab coat.

"Give me your finger," she said, stopping in front of Carter.

He hesitated, staring at the silver apparatus. "Why?"

"We're screening everyone for infection," Booth explained. "We can't afford to take any risks."

Carter did as he was told and winced as the device pricked him. "Ow. You could have counted to three."

"Three," the woman said belatedly. She studied the result and nodded. "He's clear. Who's next?"

Kate went; then David volunteered, followed by each of the soldiers. Finally, it was time for David's kids.

"You sure that thing is safe?" Kate asked. "Isn't it re-using the same needle?"

"The needle self-sterilizes after each test," Doctor Marcus explained.

"Okay."

Mark took a step back, leaving his sister to go first.

"It's just a small jab, okay?"

Rachel's head bobbed, and she squeezed David's hand tight. The device clicked and Rachel blinked. "That was it?"

"Yep," Doctor Marcus confirmed with a tight smile. "She's clear."

"His turn," Booth said, pointing to Mark. He was busy slipping behind his mother's legs. David regarded him with a frown. "Hey, buddy. We need to know, okay? If you're infected, we can fix it."

Mark smiled. "I don't require fixing, Father."

David stepped closer while the soldiers circled behind. Mark's gaze darted, spotting an opening, and he bolted.

"Stop him!" Booth cried. Soldiers lurched after Mark, but they were too slow to grab him. David shouldered the bag with the scanner and sprinted after his son. An operative raised his rifle for a shot.

"Target locked. Should I take him out?"

"Don't shoot!" Kate screamed.

David slammed into him, sending the man sprawling to the deck.

"We need him alive!" Booth roared. "Non-lethals only."

"Copy that." Dark Sixty-Two raced by. Fearing that things might go badly if the giant man caught Mark, David hurried to catch up. Mark reached the flight control tower and flew down a staircase.

David squeezed past Dark Sixty-Two, pushing the man aside to beat him to the lower deck.

"You don't know what you're dealing with!" the operative yelled as he gave chase.

David jumped the last three steps and landed with a boom. Mark was just up ahead. Marines flooded a matching stairway twenty feet ahead. A gun emplacement lay midway between them on a semi-circular balcony. Mark darted into that balcony, climbing the railing.

David's heart leaped into his throat. If he fell from here, he could die on impact. They were at least sixty feet above the water.

"Mark, wait!" David screamed.

His son turned and slowly smiled. The soldiers rushed heedlessly toward him. "Stop! Or I will throw the boy over!" Mark shrieked, and climbed higher, balancing precariously now on the penultimate rung of the railing.

The Marines halted, half of them raising their weapons. Dark Sixty-Two approached slowly with David.

"You don't have to hurt him," David said, realizing he wasn't speaking with his son.

"If you want to save the child, throw the overseers into the water instead," Mark replied, pointing to the bag slung around David's shoulder.

David froze, shock rippling through him.

Dark Sixty-Two gave him a warning frown. "Don't do it. He's bluffing."

But David didn't think he was, and it didn't matter anyway. He snatched the bag from his shoulder and held it above the water.

"Drop it," Mark ordered.

"Step off the railing first," David replied.

Dark Sixty-Two seemed to realize he was buying time, and continued behind the gun emplacement.

"This isn't a negotiation, David. Drop the bag, or your son dies."

Shock coursed through him at the way his son was speaking and behaving. But maybe he shouldn't have been surprised. This wasn't his son anymore.

Mark stepped past the railing and leaned into the wind.

"Wait!" David cried.

He released the bag, and Mark grinned.

Dark Sixty-Two lunged as he let go of the railing, catching his wrist.

David grabbed his other arm, and together they hauled Mark to safety.

Mark laughed maniacally. "You fools!" he squealed, kicking and screaming and cackling himself to tears. Marines crowded in and took hold of him, ending his struggles.

Kate, Booth, and Dr. Marcus arrived, and the line of soldiers parted. David realized that they'd been holding Kate back.

Mark regarded his mother with a sneer, and Kate stopped short. "What's *wrong* with him?" she demanded.

"Let's see," Dr. Marcus said. She approached Mark with the scanner. He spat and tried to kick her, but a Marine held his legs.

The doctor smiled thinly and pressed the device to his finger. It beeped and flashed a warning.

"He's infected. He'll be a good test for our treatment protocols."

"Take him away," Booth said.

"Wait! What protocols?" Kate asked.

"It's for his own good," Booth insisted.

"I'm going with him."

Dr. Marcus looked to Booth for permission, and he nodded. "Make sure you test everyone on board. We need to learn if they have any other agents among us."

"Yes, sir," Dr. Marcus replied.

David trailed after them. He noticed Rachel watching from the bottom of the stairs with Carter and the Grazer as Mark was half-carried, half-dragged through a heavy metal door.

Booth stopped David from following his son with an open palm and a not-so-gentle shove. "Did you even stop to consider *why* the Stalkers wanted you to get rid of the scanners? If you'd waited a few more seconds, we could have saved them *and* your son."

David scowled. "Maybe. Maybe not. But I didn't lose both scanners."

Booth's eyebrows shot up.

"I only threw the broken one."

Booth's scar puckered as he grinned. "Good man. Where's the functional one?"

"In the helicopter, under my seat."

"We'd better retrieve it," Booth replied. "There must be something in it that they didn't want us to see."

David hurried after Booth.

"Is he..." Carter trailed off as they reached the stairs.

"Stay with Rachel," David said as he ran after Booth. Private Reed jogged behind them as they crossed the flight deck to the helicopter.

Booth recovered the so-called *overseer*, looking for the switch to activate it. David pressed his fingertips into the three-holed pattern on the back, and a holographic map swirled to life.

Booth handed him the device. "Show me how to use it."

David pinched the display to zoom out until they could see the entire planet. Swarms of green blips were still descending on the Amazon; otherwise it remained the same.

On a hunch, David expanded further, until Earth dwindled to a tiny blue speck. The second *Interloper* outside the solar system appeared, and David brought it into focus.

David's heart slammed painfully against his sternum, and he sucked in a sharp breath.

"What is it?" Booth asked.

"The ship," David said, gesturing at the vessel. "It was facing away from the sun before. Now it's headed towards us."

Booth scowled. "Are you certain? I thought the Grazer said this data was a year old. How can it possibly have updated that fast?"

A hum filled the air, and they both turned to see the Grazer and Carter standing off to one side with Rachel and a group of Dark operatives.

"What did he say?" Booth demanded.

"He says..." Carter hesitated. "If the positional data has changed, then it's because they have the Signal."

Booth paled, and the Grazer started for them. The Marines barred his way, and he snorted angrily and hummed.

"Let him through!" Booth said.

Chris reached them, and David gave him the scanner. He expanded the display rapidly. Stars wheeled around, and a map of the galaxy emerged. David noticed green blips encompassing a particular section of the Orion arm. The Grazer made a circle around them with one finger, and reams of data appeared.

Chris thrummed softly and smacked his lips.

"Well?" Booth demanded.

Carter stepped toward them. "He says the data is still old. The only one that has altered its location is at the edge of our solar system."

"What does that mean? When was its position last synchronized?"

Carter waited for the Grazer to speak, then translated, "A few minutes ago, but it's not functioning any longer. Chris thinks they must have temporarily created a relay."

"Puerto Rico," Booth whispered. "Damn it! We didn't take it out in time."

Chris spoke again.

"Apparently it was good for something," Carter said. "Chris says the other ships would all be directed this way, too, if the relay was operational, meaning they still require the Signal to contact the rest of their fleet."

"That second ship they called doesn't have a Signal device?" David asked.

The air shivered as Chris continued.

"No. Only their... ravagers? Is that right?" Chris hummed low. "A battleship," Carter concluded. "The one coming here is a support ship."

"Then it's not over yet," Booth said.

The Grazer zoomed to Earth and pointed to the Amazon. "He says we need to locate it before they do."

"My thoughts exactly," Booth replied. "And you two are coming with me."

Carter gaped at him. "Me?" he asked in a shrinking voice. "Why me?"

"Because I can't talk to Chris without you. This way!" Booth roared.

"I'll see you on the other side," David said.

"The other side of what?" Carter asked.

"Don't read too much into it," David replied, smiling tightly. He gripped Carter's shoulder with one hand and added, "Try not to die."

"Gee, thanks," Carter muttered as Marines herded him and Chris after Booth.

David scooped Rachel into his arms and watched Carter leave, wishing there was a way he could help. But maybe he already had. He'd saved the scanner. And because of that, they knew the scope of the threat humanity was facing.

"Where are they going?" Rachel asked.

"They have an errand to run."

"Where's Mommy and Mark?" Rachel added.

"Let's go find out."

THIRTY

Atlas

Remote Rainforest

The two miles off target felt like twice that distance. This section off the Amazon River was dense, the thickets almost impassable in parts.

"I wish we had a machete," James told him.

"We were too focused on getting alien weapons. The simple things slipped our minds," Atlas said.

"Good point." James held a branch aside, letting Atlas through, and he returned the favor.

"I'm glad you came."

"You'd be dead if I hadn't," James said.

"That's why I'm thanking you."

James slowed, nodding at the open area near the riverbank. "This it?"

"I think so." He searched for signs of the Grazer ship, but on first inspection, there was nothing out of place. "We should have asked that villager. This isn't far from their town. Maybe they saw something."

"He didn't know. He would have tried selling information. I asked him about a ship or an unusual rock in the vicinity. He was oblivious."

Atlas set his pack down, pacing the opening. Trees hung high above, blocking the sun's light, but it did little to diminish the sticky, sweltering heat of the rainforest. "Why can't anything ever be simple?"

"We fight on," James said. "The odds are stacked against us, Atlas. Every human that's born on this planet has countless obstacles to endure before we—"

227

"Before we what? Find happiness?"

"No. I was going to say before we bite the dust." James' expression was grim. "But we experience moments of happiness in between. If we're lucky."

"You're one bleak SOB, James Wan," Atlas said.

"So I've been told. Okay, we think the Signal might be here?"

"I was banking on it."

"Then we spread out. Search the riverbank." He indicated to Atlas' right. "And I'll go farther inland." James unslung his gun, holding it in his grip.

"What about me?" Atlas asked. He'd given James his gun after the operative had traded his own for the boat.

James grabbed a pistol from a holster, checked the magazine, hit the safety, and tossed the weapon to Atlas. He caught it and nodded. "Reconvene in thirty. Make it quick. Those Stalkers aren't going to stay hidden for long," James said.

Without speaking, Atlas went west, while James started north. "If I were a Signal, where would I be?"

The other had crashed into the ocean. Could this Grazer vessel be in the river? Atlas wasn't going to dive in there to see, but it was a definite possibility.

He examined the area, eager to find the nose jutting from the grass, or to stumble upon severed tree limbs. But he came up empty. Atlas continued to scour the riverbank without success, and found James where they'd separated.

"Nothing," Atlas breathed.

"Same."

Atlas stamped his foot, angry they'd reached a brick wall. He wished he knew what was happening in the real world. Were the Stalkers out there? Had the Crawlers infected more people? It was like being on an island out here in the jungle.

The beacon weighed heavily. Atlas touched it. The metal cylinder sat in his palm, and he squeezed tight.

"We can't send the troops in without the Signal," James said.

Atlas kicked a rock and stubbed his toe. The dirt was gray under the stone, and Atlas stepped back, observing it. "Is that..." He dropped to his knees, digging through the spongy soil. He found the rocky black hull beneath. "Give me a hand!"

James knelt, using the butt of his weapon like a shovel. Soon they had a two-foot section uncovered. "This is it!" Atlas proclaimed.

"Shhhhhh. They might be nearby." James' tone was grave, but his expression was joyful.

Atlas held the beacon. "Now can I try it?"

"Yes."

Atlas pressed the button, anticipating an immediate response. When nothing happened, he shrugged and continued digging. They'd found the ship they hoped contained the alien tracking device, but a trickle of doubt entered his thoughts.

With a glance to the sky, Atlas silently urged Dark Leader's reinforcements to arrive before the Stalkers discovered them.

***

Dark Leader

USS John F. Kennedy

The light on his Holo flashed, and Booth couldn't believe his eyes. All these years, he'd been on the hunt for the pair of Grazer ships, and this Atlas Donovan had found both within a couple of weeks. With his back against a wall, it seemed as though Mr. Donovan could accomplish just about anything. Booth might use him again, and likely would before this invasion was prevented.

He'd already asked the team in Panama to make the trek into the Amazon, and suspected they'd be the first to arrive. But even better news: Dark One and Three had escaped the clutches of the observatory and managed to destroy it before the Stalkers could alert their entire fleet.

Their quick report suggested the initial message that notified the second ship may have been sent during a test, but there was no means to verify that. Either way, it was bad enough that a second *Interloper* had been dispatched, but he couldn't prepare for that now. They nearly had the Signal, and it was necessary to protect it with everything possible. Should it be used, the Stalkers' entire fleet would be privy to Earth's location, and if Chris, the Grazer, was to be trusted, they'd send many more ships.

As terrible as it was, the second *Interloper* was favorable to a fleet, but they couldn't easily defend Earth against another flurry of aliens like this. The world was already being taken over by the Crawlers, with entire cities already under their control.

Regardless of how dire the situation was, Booth felt rejuvenated by the news from the jungle.

Booth sent the message out. Any operatives within five thousand miles of the Signal would be activated. All present missions were placed on hold. With the battles raging for the last week, that didn't account for enough Dark operatives.

Dark Sixty-Two entered the office. "I want to go too."

"You saw the orders," Booth whispered.

"We can't sit idly by while—"

"Don't worry about it, soldier. We're going."

"In what?" Dark Sixty-Two asked.

"You'll see. Bring the Grazer and the linguist to the main hangar deck. I'll meet you there in ten."

The soldier snapped off a salute and left.

Booth slid the scanner across his desk, powering it on. He checked their vicinity, not finding any green blips to indicate Stalkers. That was what he'd expected, but he wanted to be certain. Booth zoomed out, moving toward Brazil.

Hundreds of lifeforms were in the northwest corner of the rainforest. Most were yellow human icons, but likely infected, and there had to be at least four dozen green-shaded Stalkers in the area. So far none of them were moving for the two yellow dots in the center of that area. He'd bet anything that those two represented Atlas and James Wan. But... no, he'd spoken too soon. The green silhouettes changed trajectory.

Booth cringed, knowing they were only three or four miles away. He wished he could send James a message to warn him, but they'd lost contact early on.

Alan Booth rose and took the scanner, but hid the pack of explosives under the desk. He locked the door and gave the soldier standing guard orders not to let anyone inside.

He started to walk, then slowed, facing the young man. "If I don't return, you are to give the contents below the desk to Dark Three, do you understand?"

"Yes, sir. Dark Three."

Booth headed for the stairs and descended to the carrier's hangar.

THIRTY-ONE

Lennon

Northern Puerto Rico

The roads were filled with accidents, likely from the moment of the Crawlers' advancement. Some people lingered near the highway, and Lennon didn't know if they were infected or not. She didn't care. The word had come. They were needed in Brazil.

Atlas had done the impossible with the help of James Wan. He'd discovered the Signal.

With the destruction of the Arecibo Observatory under their belt, and the wonderful news that they'd beaten the Stalkers to the Grazer ship, Lennon was optimistic for the first time since the *Interloper* had crashed.

The 4X4 had the top off, and she clung to the door frame, wind billowing against her cheeks. Lennon was alive.

"Where are we going?" Winnie asked, breaking Lennon from her inner thoughts.

"*We* are going to the US air base. *You* are being dropped off," Lennon said.

"But my parents are infected, or whatever you called it." The girl rubbed the nape of her neck. "What do you expect me to do? Did you see the size of those monsters? What the hell are they?"

"Stalkers," Rutger said.

"Where did they come from?" Winnie asked.

Lennon peered at the girl occupying the middle seat. "We don't know."

"What do you mean you don't know? You guys are like... what? Military?"

232

"Kind of," Rutger muttered, steering past an overturned van.

"Please, take me with you," Winnie pleaded.

Rutger flicked his gaze to the mirror. "How old are you, kid?"

"Sixteen," she said, sitting up suddenly straighter.

Lennon tried to put herself in Winnie's shoes, but failed. "Winnie, we're heading to the middle of the jungle to fight those monsters. It's far safer for you here."

"Fine. Just leave me, then... with them." Winnie jabbed a finger out the open window at a group of ten humans, spinning in circles as if they were lost.

"I think the Crawlers are confused now that we busted up their little party. They're waiting for orders," Rutger said.

"Good." Lennon grimaced when she saw the dead body in the ditch. "Okay, Winnie, but you'll do everything I say, got it?"

Rutger's eyebrows rose, as if he was shocked by her sudden bout of empathy. "You sure about this?"

"No."

"We need something that'll get us to the rainforest without stopping to refuel. With firepower," Rutger added. "And enough space for the three of us."

Lennon hadn't considered the details yet, and that told her how tired she was. Dark Three didn't make mistakes, and she wondered if it would cost her in the jungle. An idea sprang into her mind, and she grinned. "The new Lockheed has ample room."

"No, it doesn't," he disagreed.

"The training versions do. I know for a fact, they had two of them at this very base," Lennon said.

"How does an airport mechanic from Three Points have this level of information?"

"I may have kept an eye on the field. I was bored. And I missed the force, and the Dark Teams." Lennon hated admitting anything to Rutger, but her obsession might pay off.

"What are you two talking about?" Winnie asked.

"This fighter jet has room for us, and vertical takeoff. We won't be landing in the rainforest otherwise, and I don't want to eject unless necessary."

Winnie's eyes bugged out. "You mean like jumping from the jet and using a parachute?"

"Precisely."

"Maybe I should stay..."

"You'll be fine."

They neared the city with no resistance as they drove to the military base. The gates were wide open, and half of the vehicles were missing. One truck was hung up on a concrete block, and a crate of M4s sat open, exposed to the elements.

"Let's go shopping." Rutger slowed, and Lennon exited, tossing a couple of weapons and spare ammunition in the back of the 4X4.

"Do I get one?" Winnie asked, rubbing her palms together.

Rutger didn't mince words. "No."

Lennon had a few explosives, as well as the Stalker's pulse rifle they'd retrieved from their boat, but she still felt like they were rushing into this battle naked.

"How many of us are left?" Lennon took the tablet and checked, hoping it might give her the answer. But Booth must have locked it down, because the operatives' network showed a loading icon.

"Not enough," Rutger whispered.

They encountered another fenced yard right next to the coastline, and Rutger slowed, coming to a stop. They glanced around the base, trying to see if guards lingered. But from what they could tell, it was empty.

Even if they went to the Signal, pulled Atlas out of trouble, and killed every last Stalker, they were in considerable danger. According to Booth, a second *Interloper* might be approaching, not to mention countless infected people around the world. How far had their influence spread? Lennon and Rutger didn't have that information.

"It'll be okay," Rutger said, as if reading Lennon's mind.

"Was I that obvious?"

"No. You never are. I just understand you."

"Are you two married?" Winnie asked, interrupting their conversation.

"Us? No." Lennon laughed. People like them didn't tie the knot. They were married to their work.

"Booth will know what to do. He always does," Rutger said, ignoring the girl behind them.

Lennon nodded instead of relaying her doubts. The Association loved to think they had all the answers, but she doubted they were prepared for this. Maybe if it had just been the Stalkers, but not the Crawlers. They'd changed the game. As Lennon stared forward at the rows of jets, she recalled something from the *Interloper*. "Where are the other ones?"

"What other ones?" Winnie spoke loudly.

"The four-legged freaks," Lennon said, picturing the monstrosities as they'd simultaneously walked on the floors and ceilings of the *Interloper*'s corridors.

"The Stalkers have four legs," the girl mumbled.

Rutger clenched his jaw. "You're right. We've been so busy with the Stalkers... there was no evidence they brought that species with them on the escape pods."

"Then they crashed into the ocean with the *Interloper*."

"Maybe they're dead," Rutger offered.

Lennon shook her head. "We assumed that with the Crawlers, and look how wrong we were. Damn it!"

"We can deal with them later. For now, we have to get to Atlas." Rutger stepped on the pedal. "Hang on." He raced through the parking lot, bashing into a chain-link fence. The gate sprang wide and recoiled, slamming together as they flew past.

Rutger stopped a short distance from the two jets. They were clean, standing in the sunlight like beacons of hope.

Lennon went first, climbing up to the cockpit. "It's a little tight." Even the enlarged training model was compact.

"That's okay. There's two of them." Rutger gave her a smile she didn't expect to ever see on his face again.

Lennon motioned her up. "Winnie, get in."

Five minutes later, Lennon tested the comms, feeling the thrum of the powerful jet under her. This was where she belonged. This was living.

She spoke into the mic. "Dark One, you set?"

"Roger that," he said.

Lennon fired the thrusters on, hovering the jet over the tarmac. "Race you."

Rutger took the bait, and she shot south, smirking at the gasps coming from the seat behind hers.

***

Atlas

The Grazer Ship, Remote Amazon Rainforest

Atlas' arms were fatigued, his muscles protesting his efforts to excavate the vessel. From the looks of it, the Grazer craft was five times the size of the one he'd located in Vietnam. He hadn't been expecting that. James worked tirelessly, sweat pouring off the slightly older operative.

"Do you think it worked?" Atlas asked, probably for the third time.

"The beacon?"

Atlas nodded.

"It better have," James grunted as he dug.

They had half of the length cleared, and Atlas grew excited as he began uncovering what appeared to be an entrance. With a final bout of energy, they dug the earth from the rocky hull, panting and resting on their haunches when they were done.

"I hear something," James whispered.

Atlas strained his ears, but didn't notice anything out of the ordinary. From here, the Amazon River roared nearby, and the sound of singing birds occasionally drifted through the air. But maybe James was right. The jungle seemed quieter, which was an indicator of travelers. The wildlife would be watching any incoming visitors with interest.

"Try the key," James suggested, and Atlas grabbed his pack, pulling the artifacts free. They remained connected while he stared at the three dots, then at the tattoo James had given him earlier in the day. His fingers touched the indentations; then he rotated the disc, spinning it until it clicked and locked in position.

Nothing happened.

"Try again," James ordered.

Atlas did, but with the same heart-wrenching result. "Why isn't it working?"

"Damn it." James grabbed a gun, looking north. "Someone's here."

Atlas clutched the alien weapon with shaky arms and aimed it.

The three bodies were covered in black, and Atlas almost drew the trigger, until he realized they were much shorter than Stalkers. These soldiers had greasy green paint on their cheeks, and prowled into the clearing with authority.

"Dark Seven," the lead man said, setting the stock of his rifle to the ground. He surveyed the area, and the other soldiers stayed focused behind them, their automatic weapons at the ready.

"Dark Eleven." The two operatives clasped wrists. "You made it."

The guy was big, a hulking beast of a soldier. All three wore armor, and their visors glowed softly around the edges. Atlas had seen the same technology in the basement of Booth's facility.

"We had a few close calls. Lost Dark Forty-Six."

"I'm sorry," James said.

"All part of the job." Dark Eleven regarded the half-covered alien ship with wide eyes, as if he'd only just noticed it. "I see you've been busy."

"He did the heavy lifting," James said, nodding toward Atlas.

"Is that so?" the soldier asked. "Nicely done." Atlas noticed his gaze linger on the tattoo. "You're one of us now."

"Do you have contact with Booth?" Atlas asked.

Dark Eleven glanced at James. "Booth?"

"Dark Leader."

"Sure." He passed a Holo to James.

"I'll inform him that we have the Signal, but that the key doesn't work," James said. "Where were you located?"

"Panama." Dark Eleven slapped a meaty paw on his shoulder, killing a mosquito. "Never been a fan of the jungle."

"You and me both," Atlas muttered. "Do we have the other team's coordinates?" There would be safety in numbers, and he doubted their chances with just five of them holding off a horde of enemies.

They waited for a response from Booth, and with the help of the other soldiers, continued digging.

Atlas heard a Stalker shriek from a distance. "I'll check it out."

James hesitated. "I'll go with you."

Atlas nodded, and they clambered to the riverbank, hiding behind a tree trunk. Atlas' heart leaped into his throat when he spotted them through the scope.

"We have a problem," he whispered to James. Across the river were fifty Stalkers, and another hundred or so infected.

"Stay out of sight," James replied.

The Stalkers walked forward, destined for the nearest village. He thought about the kid running around with the Stalkers' weapon, and what they'd think if they encountered some of their own technology in the town.

"We have to help," Atlas said.

"No. We stay here. Protect the Signal. There's nothing we can do for them." James' words weren't intended to be callous, but they stung regardless. Maybe Atlas wasn't made for this after all.

When the entire group had passed their position by about a mile, James returned to the task at hand.

"I'll keep watch," Atlas said, and James nodded his agreement.

Atlas' gaze was glued to the opposite riverbank, keeping an eye out for Stalkers. A few minutes later, there was an explosion in the direction of the village. He smelled smoke, followed by billowing flames licking into the sky above the jungle.

He glanced up, hoping to see more incoming Dark Teams arriving to aid their mission, but he wasn't so lucky. A half hour passed, and Atlas spied the first Stalker on the opposite bank.

"We have company," Atlas told James.

Dark Seven arrived, checking the scope. "What are they doing?"

"They can't cross," Atlas said. "They don't have a boat."

Dark Eleven startled him, sneaking up silently. "This could be trouble. We saw them using technology in Panama. Some form of freezing ray."

"Freezing ray?" Atlas watched as two Stalkers arrived, holding a massive cannon. The barrel glowed orange, and they aimed it at the river.

"They can't be seriously planning on..." James was interrupted when the cannon fired. Crackling auburn blasts spat out, striking the water. As predicted, it froze the surface in heavy chunks. The operators repeated the process, freezing an entire section of the river.

"This is impossible," James said.

Atlas backed up, almost tripping over a pile of dirt from their excavation. "They're on the way."

"Ready up," Dark Eleven said. "Time to make our stand."

Atlas raised his gun as the first of the Stalkers stepped onto the ice bridge.

THIRTY-TWO

Carter

USS John F. Kennedy

Carter marveled at the giant rock sitting in the carrier's hangar. "What is this?"

"Ask your friend." Booth pointed to Chris with his free hand. His other clutched a dangerous-looking rifle to his chest. The make and model were unfamiliar, but it reminded Carter vaguely of the weapons he'd seen the Stalkers using. "We're too far from the Amazon to arrive in time with conventional aircraft," Booth explained. "But this baby is our ace in the hole."

The Grazer hummed softly. Patterns in the vibrations clicked into place in Carter's brain, and he translated almost without thinking. "He asks who else is coming."

"The four of us," Booth said, and jerked his chin to Dark Sixty-Two, who was armored up and carrying a rifle identical to Booth's.

"Will we fit?" Carter wondered aloud.

Chris mumbled and ran a hand along the dark hull; then his fingertips dipped into depressions in the rough surface and he gave a twist. It opened, and Chris clambered inside.

Booth hurried after him, with Carter two steps behind. Dark Sixty-Two was the last one in, and both he and Carter had to crowd into the back.

"It's a tight squeeze," Carter muttered, feeling claustrophobic.

The door slid shut, sealing them in.

"Tell him to hold on," Booth said. "We have to move to the flight deck."

But unlike them, the Grazer needed no translation. He understood them perfectly. His attention was locked on the vessel's strange control systems. Two curving handles protruded from the dash, and a vast array of holographic buttons and displays flickered to life. The front end of the vessel shimmered, becoming transparent, giving them a view into the hangar.

Booth spoke urgently into his Holo. "Get us in the air now!" he snapped to whoever was on the other end. "Then get the proper clearances! We're taking off with or without them."

Machinery groaned to life, and something *thunked* beneath them before they swiftly rose from the hangar. The alien vessel was already sitting on an aircraft elevator. An expanding swath of sunlight appeared ahead of them as the flight deck opened.

Before the elevator had even reached the top, Chris grabbed the control handles, and the alien ship rocketed up. The carrier dwindled swiftly below them, and then Carter slammed into Dark Sixty-Two. The pair were pressed to the rear wall as Chris sent them blurring across the rippled surface of the ocean. After a moment, Chris nosed up, roaring into the clouds.

Carter's vision grew hazy and dark. The operative beneath him spoke, but he missed it.

His mind blanked along with his vision—

When he came to, they were streaking through space and following the glowing white curve of the atmosphere to Earth's southern hemisphere.

"Do you mind?" Dark Sixty-Two groaned beside Carter's ear. "Your elbow is grinding into my..."

"Sorry," Carter managed, and shifted his position. Acceleration still had him pinned, but he felt it lessening now. He noticed that Booth had avoided joining their human pancake by occupying the seat behind the Grazer's.

"Ask him how long before we reach the target," Booth said.

Chris replied, and Carter translated. "Fifteen minutes."

"Is he sure? Does he understand what a minute is?" Booth asked.

More humming filled the cramped space.

"He says he's not stupid. How do you think he knows what you're saying? He's had ten years to learn about us. He wants to hear what your excuse is."

"Wise ass," Booth muttered.

THIRTY-THREE

Atlas

The Grazer Ship, Remote Amazon Rainforest

"What do we do?" Atlas asked James, but his attention was elsewhere.

"Check in with the others." James tossed the tablet at Dark Eleven. "I hear—"

Five operatives materialized, sweat clinging to any visible skin. The leader slowed, flipping his visor up. "Dark Seven, you're here."

"Your timing couldn't have been better," James told him.

Atlas still didn't favor their odds, but this changed things ever so slightly. No introductions were made, and Atlas used the scope, finding half the opposing force busy crossing the icy passage. Water flowed over the bridge, threatening to pull some of them under, and a human slipped, splashing into the river. No one went to help them, and they floated by, arms flailing.

James stood near the Grazer's vessel. "We can't let them acquire the Signal."

"Where is it?" Dark Eleven asked.

"In there."

The soldier knocked on it, the sound a dull thud. "Tough nut to crack. What if we try to blow it open? Get this device and bail?"

James shook his head emphatically. "We're not to harm the ship."

But Atlas thought the operative had a good suggestion. "A destroyed Signal is better than no Signal. I mean, what's the difference if we're not using it?"

James seemed to consider the matter. "There's no time."

He was right. The first Stalker reached the bank, only a hundred yards from their position.

"We have to fight," James told the Dark Teams.

"Been kicking their asses for almost a week now. I'd gladly take a chance to—" A distant eruption shook the ground, and Atlas saw the blinking light rolling near his feet. He kicked the sphere, sending it back in the enemy's direction, and it exploded in the Stalker's face, killing him instantly.

Atlas stood in shock for a moment, and the battle began. An operative handed him a modified Stalker gun, and he shoved the pistol into his waistband.

"If you're using ammunition, hit them in the hips or the eyes," Dark Eleven yelled. "You got the alien tech, blast away!"

Atlas hefted the Stalker weapon, targeting a giant alien. The pulse narrowly missed his target. Instead, it obliterated an infected human. His stomach flipped, but he continued, knowing it was either them or him. And Atlas hadn't come all this way to fail.

The Dark Team spread out, but James stayed close to Atlas, which he appreciated. The other soldiers wore armor, unlike James and Atlas, and it was obvious they were attempting to protect the pair.

Everywhere Atlas looked, Stalkers shrieked orders to the infected. Not all of the humans appeared to have Crawlers embedded in their necks, which was unsettling. But with the streaks of pulses, and the rattle of ammunition spouting from their weapons, he had no time to discuss it.

Atlas hollered in anger while he climbed onto the rock-shaped ship, firing over the soldiers' heads. The blast made contact, charring a Stalker's carapace. The alien stopped, glanced at the hole in his chest, and fell, dropping an additional sphere. It blinked a few times, then detonated, killing a nearby Stalker.

"They have explosives. Aim for them!" Atlas called, and Dark Eleven abandoned the heavy pulse gun and switched to a Glock, pulling the trigger three times. Another bomb erupted, and for a second Atlas thought they might have turned the tide.

But the Stalkers weren't staying hidden in the jungle. He peered over his shoulder to find more coming. "They have us surrounded," he muttered to James.

"Then we'd better hope for a miracle." James took two humans down, and an errant bullet slammed into his shoulder. He spun, almost releasing his gun.

Atlas found the perpetrator, a middle-aged local. He realized it was the guy who'd sold them the boat. His dull gaze locked with Atlas', and he lifted the rifle. Atlas fired first. The alien weapon hummed and recoiled, shooting a stream of shining plasma balls at the guy. Half his body disintegrated from the impacts.

He felt bad knowing it was the Crawlers' fault, not that of the people they faced, but there would be time for repentance in the hours after the battle. If he survived.

The Stalkers came closer, steadily firing as they walked. Atlas sensed the end coming when two of the Dark soldiers were killed in the front lines. Atlas slid off the Grazer ship, wishing he could access the Signal.

He kicked at the entrance, and even tried the key again. But it was futile.

James grabbed Atlas, tugging on his collar. "We're done."

"We can't be," Atlas whispered.

James shared a look with Dark Eleven, and the big man nodded once. Atlas searched the area, finding a dozen of the Stalkers had been killed. But now he saw more than he'd originally anticipated. Others funneled in from the outskirts, drawn to the noises of the jungle skirmish.

He wouldn't go down without a fight.

A helicopter's rotors sounded above the canopy, and Atlas felt a surge of optimism. The two Stalkers dragged the ice cannon into the field, kneeling beside it.

He knew what they were trying. "Shoot them!" he exclaimed, and his gun whined as it depleted its charge. The orange beam shot up, and the rotors froze, the commotion vanishing from the air.

"Look out!" Eleven shouted, and the helicopter crashed into the trees, landing twenty yards from the alien vessel. Atlas dove behind it, hauling James with him as the explosion shot flames in all directions.

Dark Eleven was on fire, his skin red and angry, but it didn't stop him. He screamed like a primal beast as he rushed the Stalkers. He fired his handgun, plinking the first shot off his target's armored face. The second bullet hit its mark, and the Stalker died. The huge soldier went berserk, killing a Stalker before they ended him.

"What do we do?" Atlas glanced around, realizing there were only four defenders left standing, including himself.

"We fight until we can't," James replied. Blood seeped through his dirty white linen shirt at the shoulder, and he took one step toward the incoming group.

The helicopter continued to blaze, the scent of burning flesh and fuel filling Atlas' nostrils, along with the repulsive notes of rotting fish.

Atlas figured he'd go down in a blaze of glory, like Dark Eleven had only moments ago, when a white-hot stream of plasma raked across the Stalkers' ranks. The ground was torn apart in a neat line, separating their group from the Signal, and another volley hit, vaporizing a group of infected humans.

James smiled. "The cavalry's here."

Atlas caught a glimpse of the small rocky hull, and almost laughed when he realized it was the other Grazer craft coming to the rescue.

***

Carter

"Yeah, baby!" Carter cried. "Take that!"

Chris hovered above the jungle, raining shining torrents of deadly fire across the Stalkers and infected humans. The high-powered energy weapons carved deep rifts in the ground, vaporizing enemy soldiers and sending the Stalkers flying.

The remaining groups fled into deeper cover, scattering and regrouping. The odd potshot came from the trees as they returned fire. The hull shuddered with each impact, and Chris began twisting and jerking the controls to make them a moving target.

"How much of this can we take?" Booth asked.

The air shivered as Chris replied.

"Not much," Carter translated. "We have to land somewhere."

The Grazer was already taking them lower. Branches scraped and broke, splintering as they lowered to the forest floor.

"Are we going to make it without air support?" Dark Sixty-Two wondered aloud. "It looks like they have us outnumbered."

"We'll do what we can," Booth replied, slapping his rifle. Silence swelled through the cockpit as they settled to the ground and the engines died.

A whistling roar shattered that brief stillness, and Carter spied something else in the air. Two fighter jets, hovering low. A solitary burst of plasma shot between them.

Then the fighters' Gatling cannons roared to life, breaking trees and digging up clods of dirt. Plasma fire streaked after the two fighters, but they flew in low circles above the trees, expertly weaving out of sight and ripping through enemy ranks. Muffled screams sounded, and Carter caught a glimpse of people fleeing for their lives, only to be cut in half by the shimmering golden waves of high-caliber tracer rounds.

Booth had his Holo to his ear, and he was shaking his head. "They can't access the Signal's ship! Tell your Grazer friend—"

The alien hummed loudly, cutting Booth off.

"He knows," Carter explained. Chris abandoned his seat as the vessel's door slid open. "He'll do it for us."

Dark Sixty-Two exited first, laying down cover fire. "Go go go!" he cried.

Carter went next, only to misjudge the landing and fall on his face. Booth jerked him to his feet. "Try to keep up!" he snapped.

All three of them chased the Grazer to a big, smooth black boulder protruding from the jungle floor.

THIRTY-FOUR

Carter

The Grazer Ship, Remote Amazon Rainforest

Carter peeked over Booth's shoulder as they sheltered behind the half-buried craft. He recognized the alien scanner in Dark Leader's hands—the *overseer.* Green-shaded Stalker silhouettes and infected yellow humans were retreating steadily, scattering in the jungle.

"Dark One and Three have bought us some time," Booth said, squinting through the thick canopy to glimpse the hovering fighters.

"But how much?" Dark Sixty-Two asked. The giant man shot Carter a grim expression. "Tell your friend to hurry."

"He's working on it!" Carter replied.

A group of familiar-looking soldiers in matching black camo-patterned armor abandoned their positions around the buried ship.

"Sir!" One of the men stood at attention and saluted, swaying on his feet. His simple linen shirt made him resemble a civilian, but Carter knew better than to make any assumptions. The man's clothes were drenched with blood from a wound in his shoulder, yet somehow, he was still standing, and carrying an energy rifle like Booth's.

"Get into cover," Booth snapped at him.

The man dropped to his haunches beside them.

"Report, Seven," Booth ordered.

"We're down to four, but we've been unable to crack the objective open. The Signal is presumed to be inside."

Another man dashed beside the first and sheltered against the hull of the alien craft, breathing hard. Carter recognized him as the treasure hunter he'd briefly met in Long Island. Atlas Donovan. He looked like he'd been through hell and back, his sweat-matted hair in disarray, clothes and face smeared with dirt and his exposed skin red with angry welts and bites.

"We're on it," Dark Sixty-Two said, jerking his chin to Chris. "Take a beat. Get that shoulder fixed."

"Medic!" Booth cried.

"He's dead, sir," Dark Seven replied weakly, his eyes on the Grazer.

"I'll sort it," Sixty-Two said. "Hold still."

Carter watched him work, keeping half an eye on Chris, who was feeling around blindly on the outer hull of the buried ship, as if not quite certain what he was searching for.

The other Dark operatives acted mildly surprised to find the alien working with them, Atlas especially. But Chris was different enough from the Stalkers that nobody accidentally shot him.

"Who is he?" Atlas asked.

"A friend," Booth replied. "Can he do the task or not?" he demanded of Carter.

Chris hummed a reply.

"The controls are hidden, caked with dirt," Carter explained. "He's searching for—"

Suddenly Chris stopped searching, and began working frantically to clear dirt from the panel. His fingertips sank in, and he twisted his wrist. A rectangular section of the hull slid away. Dim green lights turned on in a room with familiar, porous black walls.

"It still has power?" Carter wondered.

"Let's go!" Booth said, not questioning their good fortune as Chris dropped inside.

"We'll guard the exit," Dark Sixty-Two suggested as he made a compression wrap around Dark Seven's shoulder.

Carter raced after Booth and plunged in next to him. Chris already had the inner hatch wide, and he slid down a sloping, rocky corridor. Carter and Booth dove in, landing hard on the next bulkhead. The ship appeared to have crashed nose first. The corridors hadn't collapsed, but in several places they had deformed and buckled, with strange, crumbling fissures. Chris led them through the vessel, and seemed to know exactly where he was going.

When they arrived in the crumpled remains of the ship's bridge, they found the light fixtures flickering ominously, and tree roots dangling like vines from ruptures in the hull. The Grazer cast about frantically, digging and kicking the debris in search of the Signal.

"What does it look like?" Carter asked.

"Like a rock," Booth muttered, studying the wreckage at his feet. "What else?"

Chris squealed triumphantly as he produced a smooth black stone. He touched a three-holed pattern on the top, and it began glowing from within, emanating a bright green light.

Booth's rifle snapped to his shoulder.

"Wait!" Carter cried.

"He's activating it!"

Chris thrummed a reply and withdrew his fingertips from the alien device. It turned opaque and black once more.

"He didn't send a message. He was just checking to see if it still works. If not, he says we wouldn't have to worry about the Stalkers recovering it."

"But it does work," Booth said.

Chris said something else.

"He says we should destroy it," Carter translated.

"After coming all this way?" Booth demanded. "No, that's a last resort. With this, we have a bargaining chip. And bait."

"Sounds like an unnecessary risk to me," Carter replied.

"They already have us by the throat!" Booth growled. "President Carver is infected. The Chiefs of Staff. Entire cities, islands... we're at their mercy. At least now we have something that they want. We must get it out of here." Booth stamped over to Chris and snatched the Signal away, stowing it in his combat vest.

The Grazer made no attempt to stop him.

Carter felt the blood draining from his face as he processed what Booth had said. The three of them began to climb out. They moved as quickly as they could, but it was much tougher with gravity working against them. A minute later, they emerged from the alien craft.

"Did you find it, sir?" Dark Sixty-Two asked.

"We did," Booth confirmed.

Atlas looked grim. "What's our escape plan? Can we use this ship?"

Booth glanced at the half-buried alien vessel and regarded the Grazer with one eyebrow raised.

Chris spoke in a cracking voice. "*No.*"

"It speaks?" Booth asked.

"*Yes, I can,*" Chris said, then hummed.

"He says our language makes his throat hurt."

"Tell him to embrace the suck!" Booth shouted. He withdrew the alien scanner from his vest and spent a moment studying it. "They're coming back. Must've smelled it."

The sound of fighter jets roaring and Gatling cannons screaming to life filled the air.

"We need to leave now," Dark Sixty-Two said, jerking a thumb to the Grazer ship they'd flown in on.

Atlas' eyes turned glassy and round as he studied the alien vessel. "Will we all fit?"

Carter could almost feel the man's despair.

"No, we won't," Booth replied.

The air left Atlas' lungs in a rush. "Understood."

"You're coming with us, Donovan. Sixty-Two will take your place on the ground."

"What about James?" Atlas asked, looking angry. "He's wounded."

"Dark Seven knows what he signed up for."

"Copy that," the injured man replied, lurching to his feet. He grabbed the treasure hunter's shoulder with his good hand. "This is where we part ways."

Atlas appeared to hesitate. Carter frowned. This was taking too long. "We need to—"

A burst of plasma dazzled his eyes, exploding in front of his face. Chris became a blur of churning arms and legs, scooping Carter up and sprinting for his ship.

Booth cursed and ran after them. "On me, Donovan!"

Bright flashes tore up the ground, pelting them with dirt and rocks and scalding flashes of heat. Moments later, Carter was catapulted into the air—

—only to crash into the alien ship. A fishy smell breezed in behind him, and Carter groaned as he pushed off the deck to see Chris falling into the pilot's seat. Booth dropped into the seat behind that one, and Atlas squeezed into the empty space on the floor with Carter. The door slammed shut in their wake, and Carter tried to grab hold of something. "We'd better brace ourselves before—"

Chris took off, plastering them to the deck, making it impossible to move. The jungle became a hazy green blur that quickly turned to a carpet as they emerged from the canopy.

Those two fighter jets were still dancing above the trees, laying down covering fire. Plasma bolts streaked back in return, missing consistently.

One of those shots *crunched* into their hull, hissing loudly as it burned through their armor.

"I must link to them... There. Got it." Booth spoke urgently into his Holo. "Keep us covered! We have the Signal."

"*Copy that, Dark Leader,*" a woman replied. Carter felt certain that he recognized that voice. He placed it a moment later. Lennon Baxter. She was alive! And flying one of those fighters.

"Take us to the carrier, Chris!" Booth ordered.

The nose of the craft tipped up, and then a gut-sucking roar erupted behind them. Both Carter and Atlas were thrown into a tangle of limbs.

Carter registered the muddy sole of a boot pressing into his forehead before he blacked out again.

THIRTY-FIVE

Lennon

Near the Grazer Ship, Remote Amazon Rainforest

The alien ship departed, and Lennon flew along with it, staying a short distance behind until it took off, the black hull a blur. It vanished from her radar a moment later.

She let out a small cheer, aware Dark Leader had been on that vessel. It meant they had the Signal, and they'd actually won this damned battle. With the destruction of the Arecibo Observatory and the retrieval of the Signal, things had slightly improved. But there were still Stalkers on the loose, countless infected humans, and somewhere, the hideous beasts with legs for arms remained.

The war wasn't finished, but this sure as hell turned the tides in their favor.

As Lennon raced through the air, she felt alive again. Her fighter sped above the canopy, giving chase to the fleeing Stalkers.

"Dark One, you see them?" she asked over the comms.

"Negative. I'm just glad they have no aircraft to intercept us," Rutger said.

"How are you doing, Winnie?" Lennon couldn't see the girl, but she was in the rear seat.

"I think I'm going to hurl!" Winnie exclaimed.

"Wait another few minutes. We have to give our soldiers air support," Lennon told her. With the sheer volume of adversaries in the region, she was extremely grateful Rutger had his own jet to pilot. This would have been much tougher as a solo act.

253

"There they are," Rutger said, his comm crackling slightly. *"Bring them to me, Dark Three."*

"Roger that." Lennon glanced at the HUD and brushed her finger on the pickle switch. She waited for the opportune moment and pressed it. The laser-guided bomb hissed from its ordnance bay, propelling through an opening in the trees. The explosion was incredible. It struck the riverbank, cracking what appeared to be a bridge of ice. Ten or so humans plunged into the water, floating away with the current, and she was gone, switching to her trigger. She tapped it, holding for a few seconds, preferring not to deplete her rounds on a single pass.

It did what she'd expected. The Stalkers fled in the other direction, heading north. Right into Rutger's trap.

The next explosion was followed by a subsequent one, and she chased in, using the trigger again.

"Who are you guys!?" Winnie cried. "This is awesome!"

Lennon had to agree. The feeling was—

"Someone's targeting you from below," Rutger warned.

Lennon hauled back on the throttle and saw what he meant. Two Stalkers aimed a giant cannon, orange lights flashing.

Lennon sped away, circling back for a strafing run. She nosed down and blinked through a crimson haze as the blood rushed to her head. She hit the pickle switch, but it failed. With a scan of the HUD, it showed the munition was still locked and loaded. She touched it again, with the same result.

The orange pulse flew at her, and she didn't think releasing a flare would do anything to redirect the incoming blast. It struck her cockpit, and ice formed over the glass. "Rutger, we have a problem!"

The engines were off, the HUD flickering before vanishing from the glass and her helmet-mounted cueing system. "Dammit!" Lennon tried to stay composed, but the controls were dead.

"I don't want to die!" Winnie shrieked, but Lennon tuned out her sobbing.

The ejection handle was within reach, and she touched the yellow and black button. "Do exactly what I say, Winnie."

"What? No. You can't be serious."

The tops of the trees approached quickly.

"When I release us, you hold onto me. Okay? Do not let go!"

"I can't do it!" Winnie shouted.

"You don't have a choice." Lennon lifted the release, and the cockpit's canopy remained where it was. Lennon was unstrapped, and she shoved her hands up, ice cracking as the glass frame broke free. Wind buffeted them, and Lennon clutched the panicked girl, heaving her from the seat.

Lennon recalled every jump she'd ever done, and almost laughed at the irony. She was going to die with a parachute on her back, as she'd predicted.

She leapt from the jet as they neared the trees. Their momentum carried them sideways, and Lennon held Winnie close, as if she was her own flesh and blood. The parachute opened, but they were far too low. It snagged on a tree limb, snapping the tether. Winnie slipped from her grip, and Lennon rolled end over end, only noticing the water a second before impact.

The Amazon River greeted her with a rush of water, and she felt the tug as she was dragged deeper. Lennon stayed calm, knowing that struggling would cause more harm than good. Eventually, when the pressure eased, she kicked her legs, swimming toward the light. She glanced around, wondering where Winnie was, but couldn't spot her.

Lennon dove under, pulling a knife from her leg. She saw the remnants of the parachute floating farther down the river, and swam after it, riding the current.

She caught sight of Winnie's leg and pushed herself faster. Lennon managed to grab the chute, and she cut the strap, seeing it was twisted on Winnie's ankle. The girl wasn't moving, just bobbing along with the water.

Diving below, it took three aggressive saws with her blade, and Lennon had the teenager free. She was out of air. Kicking higher, she breached the murky water and gasped. Something large lingered near her, blocking the light, but she couldn't dwell on it now.

She ducked back under, keeping pace with Winnie, and swam with all her might. A moment later, she had hold of an arm, and she heaved the girl toward the shore. Her hand slipped on the damp riverbank, sliding on the mud. Lennon spotted a root from a nearby tree jutting through, and she timed it, wrapping her wrist around it. She bashed into the bank, almost losing Winnie, but she held fast.

The shadow came closer, the boat stopping. Lennon expected Stalkers to swarm the coast and kill them, but she met the gaze of a big operative, wearing black.

"Let me help you." His expression was grim, his left eye obscured by a glowing monocle. Dark Four. The man was almost as much a mystery as herself, retired a couple of years into her service. It seemed that Dark Leader had managed to recruit everyone into the field.

"Turn around!" she called, spitting water from her mouth.

"We don't have time—" He glanced to the north, where a series of gunfire rang out.

"Just do it."

He did, yanking the back of his uniform down. "We're clean."

"Okay." She allowed Dark Four to take Winnie, and a second later, she was on the borrowed riverboat's deck, staring at the sky. Everything hurt, and she winced while sitting up. A rib was broken, and it ached to breathe.

One of the operatives was doing CPR on Winnie, and Lennon wanted to ask her to be careful. Winnie's head tilted to the deck, and she coughed up at least a liter of water, then rolled over, staring at Lennon.

"Remind me to fly commercial next time," Winnie groaned.

The scent of smoke stung Lennon's nostrils; the sounds of battle raged in the distance, and her ribs ached, but she laughed until tears fell from her eyes.

"Dark Three, get it together." Dark Four hauled her up, and she steadied herself on the rail.

She noticed the scar under the lens, where the man's eye had been gouged on a mission no one spoke about. "I'm fine." Lennon patted her uniform. She was soaked, but more importantly, she was unarmed. Even the knife was lost after her efforts to save Winnie. "I need a..."

A woman passed her one of the high-tech weapons. She barely had the strength to carry it, but accepted the gun with a grim smile and checked that the charge was full. "And a..."

Dark Four reached into his holster, unclipping his personal handgun. It was matte black, with gold etchings along the edges. "Don't lose it," he said.

"I'll treat it like my own," she said, also accepting an earpiece. "Where's Rutger?"

Dark Four touched his earpiece, nodding. "He's landed. Out of ammunition. He's drawing them to this DZ." His beard was speckled with gray, his hair even lighter. "Everyone hustle up!"

Ten Dark Team members hurried from the deck, landing on the ground next to the docked boat.

"Winnie, stay here," Lennon said.

The girl's color had returned, and her clothing clung to her like a second skin. She shook her head, eyes darting between the soldiers. "No way. They'll kill me."

Lennon couldn't do what was necessary while babysitting this kid at the same time, but there wasn't much of a choice. "Stay behind me. And do—"

"Exactly as I say," Winnie finished for her.

Lennon narrowed her eyes at the girl.

Winnie's bravado faded the moment she heard the first Stalker erupt in a shuddering screech. "Whatever happens, don't forget, we're doing what we have to," Lennon said. "The humans here are just like the ones in Puerto Rico. They are not on our side."

Winnie nodded, her eyes welling with tears.

Lennon inhaled through her teeth, felt the bite of her broken rib, and shoved all the pain aside. This battle would only take a few minutes. Then it would be over, one way or another.

The important thing was that Dark Leader had the Signal. She reminded herself of that as their small force crossed an opening in the dense jungle. The alien ship remained half buried in the earth, and Lennon's gaze drifted to the jet parked beside it. Rutger hopped from the cockpit, landing on the ground, his weapon in hand.

"Dark Seven?" She spotted James Wan in civilian clothing a short distance ahead. There were a couple of others with him. This was one hell of a reunion.

"Lennon, it's good to see you." He didn't make eye contact as he gawked at the incoming force.

"What's the count?" Dark Four asked.

"These guys did a great job of splitting them up. Best guess, we have thirty infected humans and a dozen Stalkers."

Dark Four cracked his neck from side to side and lifted his gun. "Those are odds I can handle. Let's end this."

Lennon let him take charge. She motioned to the ship, holding Winnie's wrist. "Hide behind that. When this is over, I'll get you."

The woman that had done the CPR on Winnie came and shoved a pistol into her hand. "Be careful. Only use it if you have to."

Lennon walked up to Rutger and smiled, despite the constant shooting pain in her chest. "You okay?"

"Me?" Rutger laughed. "You're the one that bailed seconds before turning into a fireball."

"Don't you remember? I'm invincible."

"I believe it. Come on, let's finish—" Rutger's words caught in his throat when a familiar orange pulse carried from the trees to the north. The blast struck one of Dark Four's soldiers, and the man turned into a frozen ice block. It was followed by the rattling of a machine gun, and he broke apart, shattering into a hundred pieces. It took a moment for Lennon's brain to process what she'd just witnessed.

"They're here!" she called, moving for cover.

This was it: the final showdown. Lennon pictured the *Interloper*, then the horde of Crawlers at Arecibo. Their world had been invaded, infected. It was up to the Dark soldiers to rid the planet of these extraterrestrial intruders.

Lennon saw a Stalker in her periphery and spun, shooting it with the alien weapon. She struck its gun arm, and the weapon and the alien flesh fused together. Instead of draining the charge with another shot, she rushed over and tapped the handgun's trigger twice. The second bullet hit its eye, ending the threat.

She moved farther into the jungle, sweeping at a Stalker. He stood still, as if awaiting instructions. Lennon took aim, hitting his primary legs with the pulse. He was easy to finish off.

Lennon moved like a jungle cat, silently hunting her next prey. A human woman seemed startled to find her there, and she lifted her hands. "I'm not with them. I—"

Lennon gritted her teeth, seeing the festering wounds on the woman's neck even from this angle. "I'm sorry," she whispered, shooting her in the chest. Dark Leader would be working on a cure, but for now, the only way forward was to kill them.

She was already haunted. Blood on her hands wasn't new.

Lennon watched as Dark Four fought a Stalker near the river. The ice bridge was torn apart in the center. Their riverboat was docked a half mile down, and Lennon saw the pair running in that direction. That might be their only escape route, and Lennon wasn't about to lose their means of evacuation.

She glanced at Dark Four, seeing his weapon splashing into the river. He grappled with a Stalker, jumping to plant his feet on the thing's knobby front knees. The retired operative clutched the Stalker's temples, and he shouted in fury, spinning the bald armored head. A loud crack sounded, and the Stalker dropped. Dark Four looked around, prepared to fight. He met her gaze, and she nodded once in acknowledgement of the impossible feat.

Lennon continued tracking the Stalkers. She tapped her earpiece, hearing a bit of conversation. "How many?" she asked.

"*This area is clear*," someone said.

"Not quite. Two tangos heading for the boat," she replied, and ran. Lennon slowed, seeing they still had that damned ice cannon, and were dragging it to the riverbank.

Lennon was the only operative here. She checked the charge, unclipping the energy cell, and slammed it back in. Two bars. Enough for one more pulse. She had to time this right.

The Stalkers placed their cannon down, aiming it for the boat. They chittered and grunted. The device started to glow orange, and Lennon stepped closer. "I don't think so, mother—"

The trigger stuck.

Lennon watched in slow motion as the Stalkers turned their attention on her. They stood their full nine feet, eyes blinking open and closed, nostrils flaring. The hideous beasts seemed to find the sight of her amusing. Before she could drop the jammed gun, they fired.

Lennon saw the beginning of the orange pulse forming, and she ducked.

Rutger dove in from the side, shielding her from the blast. Lennon landed in a heap, her fingertips cold, her eyelashes stuck together. A shattering sound confused her, and she stumbled back.

Rutger lay in pieces, his frozen body broken from impact.

Lennon screamed in rage. "No. No. No. Nooooooo!" She pictured Rutger when she'd met him. The way his brow lifted when she questioned his methods. Their first drink together. That one hot night in each other's arms, trying to forget the horrors of their mission.

Lennon barely knew what she was doing. She wiped the ice off her face and stretched her hands, feeling the lingering cold. The Stalkers attempted to use the cannon again, but apparently it also had a charge delay. She lifted her gun and shot from twenty feet. It hit the target. Lennon shifted her weight to the right, missing the second. The Stalker dove, attempting to recover his sidearm. Lennon kept walking, straight into danger. Because nothing mattered anymore. Only revenge.

Her earpiece was full of shouting soldiers, but she ignored them all.

The Stalker rose, standing over three feet above her. Lennon kicked out as it swung the gun at her. The weapon clattered to the dirt, and she shot the alien in the foot with her handgun. The bullet didn't bounce off. It shrieked, tilting its head back. She shot the throat and slammed her heel into its left knee. The Stalker buckled, staggering to the ground.

"I'll see you in hell." Lennon pressed the barrel into its eye socket and fired.

Soldiers arrived, tugging on her and dragging her from the carnage. The jungle was in flames, the air thick and acrid with sweat, blood, and smoke.

Her ears rang, and her legs were like lead as the survivors walked to the waiting boat. Winnie stared at Lennon, her hands shaking. She looked away, expecting the girl to be terrified of her. Instead, she felt arms wrapping her in an embrace.

They lingered in silence, and eventually boarded. The riverboat's engine sputtered to life, and they departed.

Rutger was dead. His voice began whispering in her ear, and she swatted a hand through the air, as if shooing a fly. "Not this time."

His voice drifted into the wind. He'd saved her life, and she would remember him for it until her last breath.

EPILOGUE

David

USS John F. Kennedy

David stood with Kate and Rachel, watching anxiously through an observation window as Dr. Marcus and her support staff worked on Mark. He was heavily sedated in the carrier's operating room, hooked up to all manner of wires and tubes.

Reversing the infection was supposedly a simple matter of exposing infected subjects to radioactive gas or a liquid injection. But there were risks with either procedure, since it was basically the same as radiation therapy for cancer.

At Kate's insistence, Dr. Marcus had suggested an alternative treatment. The alien parasites had apparently also shown susceptibility to focused ultrasound applied at specific frequencies targeted on the brain of the infected host. It was already an accepted treatment for Parkinson's disease, and enabled them to focus on specific regions without damaging surrounding tissues. But it was a delicate procedure, and not without its own risks.

"What if it doesn't work?" Kate asked. "What if it paralyzes him or—"

David squeezed her hand. "Shhh. Think positive thoughts. Mark is going to be fine." He nodded to himself. "He'll be fine," he whispered again, this time to convince himself.

An hour later, their feet ached from being in one spot for so long, but they couldn't bring themselves to leave. Even Rachel was still standing patiently, up on tiptoes to peek through the observation window.

Dr. Marcus removed her gloves and stepped from the operating table, shaking her head.

Kate gripped David so tightly he thought his hand might break. A stifled sob tore out of her, and she buried her face against his chest.

The door to the operating room swung wide, and Dr. Marcus froze in the opening. Her brow furrowed and she tugged her mask off, looking confused. "The procedure was a complete success... Mark should be waking up any minute now."

"What?" Kate exploded. "But you seemed disappointed—I thought—"

"I was just grateful it worked, Mrs. Bryce."

Another doctor emerged from the operating room. "He's asking for his parents."

Kate dashed by them, pushing both doctors aside. David and Rachel hurried in behind her.

Mark sat up with another doctor's help. "Mom?" he blinked sleepily at them. "Dad? Where..." He glanced around.

Kate pulled him into a crushing hug, sobbing and laughing. "You're fine, baby. You're okay. I've got you."

Mark looked bewildered. "What happened? The last thing I remember was playing with that crab at the lake."

David's blood ran cold with that admission. Ever since the Crawler had latched onto Mark's neck, they'd been dealing with an alien entity, not their son. Until now, David had thought the infection might have had a slow progression, but in reality it had been instant.

David gripped his son's shoulder, fighting to speak through the knot in his throat. "It's good to have you back, son."

"Where did you go?" Rachel asked.

"What?" Mark replied.

"When the aliens were inside your head," Rachel explained. "Where did you go?"

"I don't..." Mark blanched. "I had *aliens* in my head?"

Kate shot Rachel a sharp glare.

Someone cleared their throat, and David turned to see a familiar group lingering in the open doorway of the operating room. Alan Booth, flanked by Carter and the Grazer. The doctors glanced nervously from one to another as the alien entered the room, and Mark stiffened. "What is that?!" he cried.

"Relax, buddy, he's on our team," David whispered.

Booth smiled and clasped his hands in front of him. "I apologize for interrupting this happy reunion, but we have another infected subject to treat, and Commander Bryce is needed urgently elsewhere."

David hesitated, feeling torn between a duty to humanity and his duty to his family.

"It's all right," Kate said. "Go. I'll see you later."

"I'm afraid it's not that simple, Mrs. Bryce," Booth explained. "He's requested on the mainland, and I cannot guarantee when you will see him again."

"For what, exactly?" David demanded. Anger burned in his chest at the idea of leaving his family for another extended mission. "I thought it was over. You got the Signal, and we're already figuring out how to reverse the infection. What does any of that have to do with me?"

"As you already know, a second Stalker vessel is on its way, and we have to ensure that it doesn't arrive."

"ORB doesn't have any more rockets that we can use," David said. "Does it?" he asked, suddenly doubting himself.

"Not ORB," Booth replied. "I have something to show you. Say your goodbyes and meet us on the flight deck. We're wheels up in ten."

David gaped, watching as Booth turned and strode from the room, but Carter and the Grazer stayed.

"Sorry, mate. We'd do it without you, but we need a pilot."

David stared at his family, feeling lost and angry. "I'm not going," he decided. "They can find someone else."

A muscle twitched in Kate's jaw, and a smile flickered to her lips. "*Is there* someone else?"

He hesitated. "I... there has to be!"

Kate shook her head sadly. "If there were, they would have asked them. You're their first choice for a reason. I get it. You were mine, too."

David's chest exploded with a sigh. "I was?"

"Are. Still are," Kate clarified, and leaned across the operating table for a kiss.

"Ewww," Rachel groaned.

"Get a room," Mark muttered.

David smirked and tousled his hair. "Look after your sister and your mom, okay, buddy?"

Mark nodded slowly. "You're leaving?"

"Again?" Rachel whined. She latched onto his legs. "I don't want you to go!"

David pried her away and dropped to his haunches. She was crying already. "Last time you left I missed you so, so much."

David's heart cracked just a little. "I know, sweetie, but you have to be brave. A lot of people's lives depend on it. And if Daddy can help them, don't you think he should?"

Rachel's expression flickered uncertainly. "But what about us?" she sniffled.

"They'll stay here," Dr. Marcus supplied, breezing back into the room.

Mark had his arms crossed over his chest. David pulled him into a quick hug and kissed the top of his head.

"Bye," Mark said.

"Love you, too, kiddo—" He caught Kate's eye and then Rachel's. "All of you."

***

Atlas

USS John F. Kennedy

His work was done. Atlas strolled the deck, enjoying the cool night air. The sky was a black canvas of starlight, the moon a small sliver, and it all reminded him there was far more out there than Earth.

"Atlas, right?"

The voice startled him, and he almost fumbled for a gun that wasn't there. He sensed the trauma he'd experienced over this adventure would cling to him for years to come.

"That's me. And you're... Lennon?"

She nodded, limping over to his position at the edge of the carrier's top deck. Lennon peered at the water, her hands clutching the railing tightly. "I had a really shitty week."

"Me too."

"Want a drink?"

"I sure do." Atlas went with her, noticing the wincing breaths. "Did you see a doctor?"

"They were occupied," she told him. "Bryce's kid."

"That's right. Hope it went well."

"I overheard on the way up. He's fine." Lennon descended the metal stairs, leading him through the carrier to a mess hall. She knew her way around far better than he did. In the late hour, the place was deserted. The operatives had returned an hour ago, and since then, it had gone quiet.

Atlas had been thrilled to see that James Wan had survived, though he looked like a dead man walking. Lennon didn't seem to have fared much better, but he could tell she wanted someone to lend an ear.

"Let me," he said, heading to the fridge. An assortment of beers was available, making him wonder who stocked this thing. He took out two green bottles and cracked the tops.

Lennon didn't move when he set the beer on the table. Her face was red, with patches of severe burns. Her hair fell into her eyes, and she didn't swipe it away. "He's dead."

Atlas almost asked who, but it clicked. Rutger. "I'm sorry."

"It's not like we were..." She took a long pull from the bottle. "But then he came back, alive and well, after all that time thinking I'd lost him. When I was really the one kicked to the curb by Dark Leader."

"You don't have to stay," Atlas said.

She glanced over. "What do you mean?"

"This." He wagged a finger around. "You can leave."

"What's left for a broken soldier out there? Half the world is infected. I have no one, Atlas."

"Maybe that's not true." Atlas glanced at the doorway, where a girl stood watching them from the shadows.

"Winnie?" Lennon frowned. "What are you doing? You should be in bed."

"I wanted to check on you."

Lennon gestured between them with the neck of her beer. "Winnie. Atlas. Atlas. Winnie."

"Nice to meet you," he said.

"Same."

"Can I have one of those?" Winnie asked.

Lennon didn't answer her question. "Have you reached your family?"

Winnie sat, elbows on the table. "No."

Lennon nodded at the fridge. "Atlas, do you mind?"

"She's a kid," he said.

"A kid who just witnessed..."

"Fine." Atlas brought another bottle.

Winnie tasted it, made a face, and slid it away. "Yuck. People actually drink this stuff?"

"It grows on you," Atlas replied.

"What about you?" Lennon asked, nodding to him. "Are you being sent off on another mission for our illustrious leader?"

"Not that I know of." He'd been in touch with Hayden, who was extremely grateful for the heads-up. His family was still safe and sound in Vermont. Atlas expected he'd go hide out with them until the dust settled and things went back to normal. Assuming that ever happened.

They stayed for a while, and eventually, Dr. Marcus arrived. "We can finally assess you. Are you drinking?"

Four empties sat between them.

"If I was *drinking*, it would be whiskey," Lennon said, pushing off from the table. "Winnie, go to bed. Atlas... I'll see you later."

She walked away with the doctor, and Atlas sighed, finishing his drink. "Come on, kid. Time to hit the hay."

Atlas strolled the carrier deck, unable to shake the feeling that his job here wasn't quite finished. He glanced at his arm and lifted the sleeve, seeing the tattoo. He was one of them now.

***

David

Area 96, Texas

It was a long flight over the Gulf, and then a tense ride in an Army transport truck across a remote, dusty field somewhere in Southern Texas.

After passing through multiple razor-wire fences with biometric locks and dire warnings about trespassing in a place called *Area 96*, Booth finally braked in front of a giant warehouse with rusty corrugated metal sides and roof. "This is *it*?" Carter asked. He didn't sound impressed.

"Never judge a book by its cover. It's what's inside that counts." Booth jumped out.

Carter and David traded looks, and the Grazer hummed something that Carter didn't bother to translate.

They crossed the cracked tarmac to the hangar. Booth was already dragging a door open, and David noticed another truck was parked close by.

"Come on," Booth beckoned to them.

David stepped from the sunlit tarmac into the shadows of the moldering edifice and sucked in a sharp breath.

"You like it?" Booth asked, grinning broadly.

"What are we looking at?" Carter asked, frowning.

Sleek and silver, with thick metal struts rather than wheels. It was much bigger than a fighter jet, but just as aerodynamic, with a hint of wings, and no sign of a cockpit canopy. It had neither the porous, spiked black hull of the alien vessels, nor the simple cylindrical fuselage of a conventional rocket. This was something else entirely.

"This is the FTLS-9. Code-named the *Peregrine*," Booth said.

"How..." Carter trailed off. "You only found the alien ships recently."

"But then how did I reverse-engineer their weapons?" Booth countered, raising an eyebrow at him.

Neither of them had an answer ready for that, and a momentary silence fell.

David caught a glimmer of movement in the shadows at the far end of the hangar. At first he thought it might be a wild animal, but then the sheer size of it became clear. He picked out four skinny legs and two, long loping arms.

Four glinting eyes appeared.

The air began to sing as Chris uttered an urgent warning.

"Stalker!" Carter cried, pointing to it.

"Relax!" Booth said as the alien emerged into the light next to the *Peregrine.* "Einstein is on our side. Not every Stalker wants to see their people devour the galaxy one star system at a time."

"Einstein?" Carter muttered.

Chris cringed, humming and muttering to himself, retreating steadily. The Stalker shrieked at him, and the Grazer bolted through the exit to the tarmac.

"What did they say?" David demanded.

Carter looked confused. "The Stalker? No idea. But Chris said they can't be trusted."

"Get him back here," Booth growled.

Carter nodded and darted after the Grazer, seeming eager to leave the hangar.

"And for the record," Booth said, "if we couldn't trust Einstein, he never would have helped us to reverse engineer his people's tech. He's been working closely with us for almost as long as Chris has been, and he's been considerably more cooperative about it."

"FTLS-9," David said, working some moisture into his mouth. "Does that mean this thing can fly faster than light?"

"Of course."

"You've tested it?" David pressed.

"Successfully," Booth confirmed.

"Then why didn't we use this instead of the *Beyond III?*" David demanded.

"Because the *Interloper* appeared to be derelict. I wasn't sure if it would be necessary, so I didn't want to play all of my cards. That, and knowledge of the *Peregrine*'s existence is confined to a very select group of people. A group that doesn't include any of the governments who sent your mission. But now that those governments are compromised and the Stalkers have another ship coming, we have no choice but to show our hand."

"What exactly are we supposed to do?" David asked.

"Intercept the enemy ship and, this time, destroy it before it reaches Earth."

Einstein interrupted with a muttered question. *"Are they coming, or not?"*

"It speaks our language?" Carter erupted. They turned to see him standing in the open doorway with Chris. He was holding the Grazer by the arm. Chris' knees were shaking, the vertical slit of his mouth opening and closing restlessly, and a visible sheen had broken out all over the alien's body.

"They can all *speak* it," Booth explained. "They're exceptional mimics. But only our Grazer friend and Einstein have been exposed to us long enough to interpret what the words mean. We'd better go inside so Einstein can show you how it works before he loses his patience." Booth led them across the polished concrete floors to the *Peregrine* and the supposedly friendly Stalker.

"What happens when he loses his patience?" Carter asked, following Booth at a wary distance.

"You don't want to know," Booth replied.

David sucked in a deep breath to steady his nerves. He studied the alien-engineered vessel as they passed beneath its gleaming hull, wondering quietly to himself about the one issue that Booth had yet to address. What were they supposed to do when they reached the second Stalker ship? They were a small crew and two aliens going up against an entire warship on high alert. David had a bad feeling that this wouldn't be anything close to as easy as sneaking aboard the derelict *Interloper.* And they almost hadn't survived that encounter.

Armed with alien tech or not, David couldn't help feeling like this was yet another Hail Mary in what was fast becoming a string of them.

Carter glanced his way as they stopped in front of the nine-foot-tall alien at the bottom of the *Peregrine*'s boarding ramp. "At least this time we know what we're up against," he said.

David frowned, regarding the alien warily. "Does that help?" he asked as it hissed at them, and slowly turned to lead them up the ramp.

Carter shrugged. "Not really."

***

Lennon

One Day Later
USS John F. Kennedy

"Son, you have to tell us again," Dark Leader said.

The young boy acted petrified.

"You're scaring him," Lennon muttered. Commander Bryce's son was a spitting image of his father. In a few years, his narrow shoulders would fill out, and his rugged good looks would start to turn the heads of his classmates. But that would only happen if they stopped the Stalkers from destroying everything first. Lennon took a deep breath and faced Mark.

"This will be a lot faster if you just tell Dark... Alan what he needs to hear," she said. Dark Leader was an imposing figure, capable of terrifying grown soldiers. She couldn't imagine what it was like for a child to stare into the man's scarred visage while he glowered at you.

"I only remember it in bits and pieces like a dream," Mark said, fidgeting with his hands.

"And they're underground?" Dark Leader repeated.

Mark nodded.

"What else can you recall?" Lennon kept her voice light, smiling even though it hurt to do so.

"There were different ones. With round bodies. They walked on the ceiling, and..."

Booth's brows shot up, and Lennon's stomach clenched. "And the floor?"

Mark pursed his lips, then licked them. "I think so."

271

"Where was this?" Booth's voice stayed low.

"I'm not sure."

Lennon took the boy's hand, and he seemed shocked by the contact. "You have to tell us. People's lives are at stake."

"It's cold."

"In here, or..." Lennon stopped when he shook his head.

"No. There. It's cold. They burrow underground to stay warm," Mark said.

Booth powered the scanner on. Lights glowed from the screen, and Lennon wracked her brain. "We crashed near Boston. They must have swum to shore. If they'd followed the others, we should have seen them." Lennon's eye twitched. She was still exhausted, and now that she'd seen the new ship Bryce was taking to intercept the second Stalker vessel, she wanted to go with them. This didn't seem as important. "Mark said somewhere cold, right?"

"Canada?" Booth suggested.

"The southern areas are closest, and too populous. Try Greenland," she said.

"Greenland? That's too far. How could they possibly..." Booth trailed off as he moved the target on the display to the Nordic island. His jaw slackened. There was a single green marker near the southern coast. And it vanished.

"They're hidden from the sensors below the surface," Lennon suggested.

"If you're right, there could be thousands of Crawlers, hundreds of Stalkers, and God knows how many of those other things."

"And this is why I can't join Bryce and Robinson?" Lennon waited for his acknowledgment.

"You can go, son," Dark Leader told Mark, and the kid scurried from the room, rushing through the door and into his mother's arms.

"We're working on the gas bombs. A prototype will be ready to test in a few days. If it works in Puerto Rico, we can use the technology to counter the infection. Everyone will regain control of their bodies, without the memories of whatever the Stalkers made them do. We can salvage our planet, Lennon. But this... if they're hiding out, we have to deal with them.

Your expertise is required one last time. Help me ensure that every alien entity is eradicated from our world."

Lennon stared at him, then cracked her knuckles. "The mission always comes first."

GET THE SEQUEL FOR FREE

The story continues with...

FROM BEYOND: SURVIVAL
Get it From Amazon

OR

Get a FREE e-copy if you post an honest review of this book on Amazon and send it to us here:

https://files.jaspertscott.com/fb3free.htm

Thank you in advance for your feedback!

MORE FROM NATHAN HYSTAD

Keep up to date with his new releases by signing up for his Newsletter at

www.nathanhystad.com

The River Saga
The Survivors Series
The Bridge Sequence
Baldwin's Legacy
Final Days
Space Race
The Resistance
Rise

MORE FROM JASPER T. SCOTT

Keep up to date with his new releases by signing up for his Newsletter at

www.jaspertscott.com

Dark Space Series
New Frontiers
Broken Worlds
Rogue Star
Scott Standalones
Final Days
Ascension Wars
The Cade Korbin Chronicles
The Kyron Invasion
Architects of the Apocalypse

ABOUT THE AUTHORS

Nathan Hystad is the best-selling author of The Event. He writes about alien invasion, first contact, colonization, and everything else he devoured growing up. He's had hundreds of thousands of copies sold and read, and loves the fact he's been able to reach so many amazing readers with his stories. Nathan's written over twenty novels, including The Survivors, Baldwin's Legacy, and The Resistance.

Jasper Scott is a USA Today best-selling author of more than 30 sci-fi novels. With over a million books sold, Jasper's work has been translated into various languages and published around the world. Jasper writes fast-paced books with unexpected twists and flawed characters. He was born and raised in Canada by South African parents, with a British heritage on his mother's side and German on his father's. He now lives in an exotic locale with his wife, their two kids, and two Chihuahuas.